Praise for

New York Times and *USA Today* Bestselling Author

Diane Capri

"Full of thrills and tension, but smart and human, too. Kim Otto is a great, great character. I love her."
Lee Child, *#1 World Wide Bestselling Author of Jack Reacher Thrillers*

"[A] welcome surprise… [W]orks from the first page to 'The End'."
Larry King

"Swift pacing and ongoing suspense are always present… [L]ikable protagonist who uses her political connections for a good cause…Readers should eagerly anticipate the next [book]."
Top Pick, Romantic Times

"…offers tense legal drama with courtroom overtones, twisty plot, and loads of Florida atmosphere. Recommended."
Library Journal

"[A] fast-paced legal thriller…energetic prose…an appealing heroine…clever and capable supporting cast…[that will] keep readers waiting for the next [book]."
Publishers Weekly

"Expertise shines on every page."
Margaret Maron, Edgar, Anthony, Agatha and Macavity Award-Winning MWA Grand Master

TRACKING
JACK

by DIANE CAPRI

Published by: AugustBooks
http://www.AugustBooks.com

ISBN: 978-1-962769-47-1

Original cover design by: Cory Clubb

Published in the United States of America.

Visit the author website:
http://www.DianeCapri.com

ALSO BY DIANE CAPRI

The Hunt for Jack Reacher Series

(in publication order with Lee Child source books in parentheses)

Don't Know Jack • (The Killing Floor)
Jack in a Box (*novella*)
Jack and Kill (*novella*)
Get Back Jack • (Bad Luck & Trouble)
Jack in the Green (*novella*)
Jack and Joe • (The Enemy)
Deep Cover Jack • (Persuader)
Jack the Reaper • (The Hard Way)
Black Jack • (Running Blind/The Visitor)
Ten Two Jack • (The Midnight Line)
Jack of Spades • (Past Tense)
Prepper Jack • (Die Trying)
Full Metal Jack • (The Affair)
Jack Frost • (61 Hours)
Jack of Hearts • (Worth Dying For)
Straight Jack • (A Wanted Man)
Jack Knife • (Never Go Back)
Lone Star Jack • (Echo Burning)
Bulletproof Jack • (Make Me)
Bet On Jack • (Nothing to Lose)
Jack on a Wire • (Tripwire)
Tracking Jack • (Gone Tomorrow)
Jack Rabbit • (Night School)

The Michael Flint Series:

Blood Trails
Trace Evidence
Ground Truth
Hard Money
Dead Lock

CAST OF CHARACTERS

Kim Otto
Carlos Gaspar
Charles Cooper
Reggie Smithers
Lamont Finlay

Ed Docherty
Daisy Hawkins
Melissa Black
Marcus Molina
Theresa Lee
Zoe Seltzer
Eugene Cannon
John Sansom

and
Jack Reacher

Perpetually, for Lee Child, with unrelenting gratitude.

TRACKING JACK

GONE TOMORROW
By Lee Child

"Word on the street is it's all about a file on a USB," Theresa Lee said.

"Close enough," Reacher replied.

"Do you know where it is?"

"Close enough."

"Where is it?"

"You'll figure it out."

"Do you really know? Docherty figures you don't. He figures you're trying to bluff your way out of trouble."

"Docherty is clearly a very cynical man."

"Cynical or right?"

"I know where it is," Reacher said again.

"So go get it," Lee challenged.

CHAPTER 1

Friday, June 17
Atlanta

SWAYING WITH THE TRAM'S movement while feeling the familiar hum beneath his feet, Ed Docherty rode the crowded Plane Train through Atlanta's Hartsfield-Jackson Airport. He scanned the faces around him, ever vigilant. Habit of a lifetime.

The car was crowded with travelers. Singles and small groups. Business passengers headed home. Families, couples, adventurers, all paying little attention to their surroundings. Living in their own heads or focused on electronic devices, probably.

He noticed a couple arguing quietly. A mother soothing her baby. A man in a suit tapping on his phone. In short, nothing obviously remarkable or noteworthy.

Docherty adjusted his stance as the tram slowed. His body moved with the rhythm, instinctively, naturally.

He leaned against a pole, arms crossed. A young kid tugged at his father's sleeve, pointing at the passing lights outside. The father nodded absently, eyes glazed with fatigue.

Docherty shifted his gaze to the electronic sign crawling in lights above the doors. It flashed the name of the next stop. He checked his watch. Time moved differently in transit between places.

A pleasant human voice spoke over the intercom announcing the next terminal, which was not his stop. He was headed toward the end of the line to catch his connecting flight to Tampa. He stood aside to allow passengers to exit.

After a few moments, the doors slid closed. The tram jolted slightly and resumed its course. He felt the pull, the gentle sway. He steadied himself while watching the passing lights, concrete, and people milling around.

A family of four got on at the next stop. Kids chattering excitedly, parents looking harried but happy. Docherty smiled to himself, remembering days like that when his kids were small. Simpler times. Before the divorce. Before his daughter moved away. Before his son died in the war.

He focused on the rhythm of the journey. The tram, the people, the steady movement forward. It was a brief respite, a pause in the rush of life.

His phone buzzed in his pocket. He ignored it, preferring the quiet, the momentary peace. There would be time for calls later.

Docherty spotted her as the tram lurched around a bend. A woman. Petite. Dark hair, dark eyes. Wearing a heavy coat despite the stifling summer heat. She looked anxious. Restless.

He studied her reflection in the window. Watched her fidget with her sleeves. Check her watch compulsively. Sweat beaded on her forehead and dripped down her temple.

A memory flashed through his mind. The subway. New York. Years ago. A case he'd worked when he was NYPD. Before he retired.

A suspected suicide bomber.

Similar woman wearing a different coat, but the nervous energy was the same.

He was not in the subway car, but he'd watched the CCTV so many times the memory had embedded in his brain.

Jack Reacher had saved lives that night. He'd recognized the threat and took action.

The wrong action.

Gut wrenching horror had followed.

Docherty's stomach clenched. A cold tingle crept up his spine.

Like before, something about this woman was off. He felt it instinctively.

But was he feeling intuition or paranoia?

He tried to shake the uneasy déjà vu. Told himself he was jumping to conclusions. Overreacting based on a vague similarity and traumatic memories.

The fear was ridiculous, surely.

But he couldn't quite convince himself. Couldn't ignore the dread knotting his gut. The nagging certainty that something wasn't right.

The tram swayed. The woman swayed with it. Muttered something.

Docherty strained to hear over the rattle and hum of the tram and the noise of the other passengers. His hearing wasn't the best. He couldn't make out her words.

"Look away, Ed," he muttered silently. "Mind your own business. There could be a hundred explanations. None of them dangerous."

His hand settled near his concealed sidearm anyway. An unconscious reflex. He could feel the ghost of the long-ago subway killer's coat skimming his fingertips.

Instinct warred with logic. Observation with bias. Memory with the present moment.

A woman in the wrong coat on a summer day.

Maybe that's all she was.

But after decades with NYPD and his private security work since, his very experienced gut told him otherwise.

Insisted something was wrong.

Very wrong.

Screamed danger.

Just like that other time.

The tram slowed again. His stop was coming up.

He had a choice to make.

And not much time to make it.

Docherty kept his eyes on the woman, watching her without appearing to watch. He was good at that. He noticed everything, filing it away in his mental catalog of suspicious activity.

If you see something, do something. The mantra of every New Yorker after 9/11.

She couldn't keep still. Hands clenching and unclenching. Fingers drumming a frantic beat against her thigh.

Her gaze flickered around the tram car, alighting on every passenger, every exit, every window. Assessing. Planning.

She gripped her bag tightly to her chest like a shield. Or precious cargo. White knuckled. The fabric strained.

Docherty's own grip tightened on the pole. Tension coiled in his muscles, ready to spring into action. But he needed something concrete. To be sure.

The tram jostled as it slowed for the next stop. Passengers swayed.

The woman stood and stumbled. Caught herself. Her coat gaped open for a split second.

That's when he saw them. Wires. Colorful. Tangled. Snaking out from beneath her coat. Disappearing into her bag.

His blood ran cold as his heart hammered against his ribs.

No doubt now. She was wired.

What was in the bag?

Adrenaline surged through him. The world narrowed to this moment, this threat. Everything else fell away.

He was moving before he realized it. Shouldering through the oblivious crowd. Laser focused.

Passengers moved aside as he made his way through. Panic rippled through the car when they noticed his determined march.

But Docherty only saw her.

It all crystalized in his mind with terrifying clarity.

The bomb.

The trigger.

The lives at stake.

He had to stop her. Had to end this.

Before it was too late.

Before she turned the tram into a screaming metal coffin.

There was no time for backup. For negotiation. For anything but action. Decisive. Immediate.

Lives hung in the balance. Innocent lives.

Docherty was the only thing standing between them and oblivion.

And he would not fail them. Not this time. Not ever again.

He was four feet away when she looked up. Met his gaze. Saw his intent.

Her eyes widened. Her right hand plunged into her bag.

He lunged forward, crashed into her, and his momentum carried her to the ground.

He grappled with her, trying to gain control.

She fought back, thrashing and clawing at his face with one hand while the other remained firmly in the bag. Was she holding a detonator?

"Stop resisting!" he grunted, struggled for a better grip.

For a tiny woman, she was surprisingly strong and fierce.

She snarled something in a language he couldn't understand and lashed out with her elbow catching him in the jaw.

Docherty's head snapped back, but he didn't let go.

Chaos erupted around them. Passengers screamed and scrambled away from the struggling pair, tripping over each other in their haste. A few brave souls tried to intervene, but Docherty waved them off.

"Stay back!" he shouted.

Passengers froze in shock, eyes wide and mouths agape. A few fumbled for their phones, recording the scene with shaking hands. Children cried out as parents tried to soothe their fears.

The tram slowed as it approached the next stop. The recorded voice announced the arrival, and the doors slid open.

Docherty ignored it all, focusing only on the woman in his grasp.

He shifted his weight, using his bigger, heavier body to his advantage.

With one practiced move, he pinned her to the ground, wrenching her free arm behind her back. She bucked and twisted, but he held fast, his knee pressed firmly into her spine. If she held a detonator in her hand, he knew these might be his last moments on earth.

"Everyone stay calm!" he yelled over the commotion. "The situation is under control. Police are on the way. Just give us space!"

A moment later, a team of airport security officers swarmed the tram, weapons drawn, assessing the threat.

"Over here!" Docherty called, jerking his chin toward the woman.

The officers surrounded them, forming a tight perimeter. One of them, a burly man with a salt-and-pepper beard, knelt down to cuff the woman's free hand while Docherty kept her pinned.

"I think she's got a bomb. Found wires under her coat," Docherty said quietly through labored breaths. When the officer eyed him suspiciously, he added, "Former NYPD. Retired."

"Thanks," the officer said, giving Docherty a nod of respect. "We'll take it from here."

"If she does have a device, it could be rigged to blow." Docherty hauled the woman to her feet, keeping a firm grip on her arm until the officer had her secured.

Every law enforcement agency and airport security team in the country had protocols for such situations. The security team wasted no time implementing them.

Docherty stood aside as they searched the woman thoroughly, emptying her pockets and patting her down with practiced efficiency. Wires, a detonator, and packets of suspicious substances tumbled out of her coat and the bag.

She wasn't holding the detonator, but it was within easy reach.

"Jesus," one of the younger officers breathed.

They practically carried her away, still kicking and screaming in defiance. Docherty sagged against the wall as his muscles trembled with spent adrenaline.

That had been close. Too damned close.

He shuddered to think of the carnage that could have unfolded. The lives that would have been lost.

But they'd stopped it. He'd stopped it. That's what mattered.

He only had a moment to draw breath before the second wave of armed responders flooded the area.

CHAPTER 2

Saturday, June 18
Atlanta

A SWARM OF LAW enforcement poured in, which meant the bomb scare had rocketed up the priority chain. They zeroed in on Docherty like bloodhounds on a scent. They led him to a quiet corner and began rapid fire questions faster than he could keep them straight.

"What's your name?"

"Ed Docherty."

"ID?"

He pulled out his wallet to show his driver's license and his old NYPD credentials. The officer took both and handed them to a second officer, who scurried off to verify.

"What happened here?" the first officer asked. "How did you spot the suspect and what made you believe she carried an explosive device?"

Docherty walked them through it all, step by step. The woman's suspicious behavior. The telltale bulges and wires peeking from her coat. The reflexive lurch in his gut that had screamed danger.

"I've seen this kind of thing before." He shook his head. "The nervous energy. The clothing. The way she was fidgeting with something in her bag. All the signs were there."

He could have said more. Could have told them about the twelve-point list the Israelis developed years ago used to identify suicide bombers.

Eleven points if the suspect was a woman.

But they probably already knew. Every law enforcement officer on the planet should have known. The less said now the better, if he wanted to get out of here tonight.

The third officer, a woman with sharp eyes and a no-nonsense bearing, scribbled furiously in her notepad.

"You said you've seen this before," she pressed. "What exactly did you mean by that?"

Docherty hesitated, painful memories threatening to resurface. Screams and smoke and blood. The choking taste of departmental failures. He pushed them back down, clenching his jaw.

"Yeah," he said finally. "You could say that. Twenty years with NYPD working one of the top terror targets in the world. There are reasons I trusted my instincts on this one."

The officers exchanged loaded looks, a whole conversation passing between them in the span of a glance.

"Alright, Mr. Docherty," the first officer said. "We'll need to take a full statement from you. Sorry for the inconvenience."

Docherty swiped a weary hand down his face. He could already feel the weight settling into his bones. The questions, the implications, the breadcrumb trail of clues that always led to more trouble.

"Yeah, sure. I know the drill." Resigned to missing his flight to Tampa, he followed the female officer to a quiet room where he went through it all again, on video this time.

Hours later, well past midnight, Docherty finally walked out of the airport police station. Statement signed, contact information left, duty done. For now.

Cases like this tended to go on for years. He'd be an old man before it was all over. Good Samaritans had no idea how the system could chew them up and spit them out. Docherty knew exactly what to expect.

He collapsed into the driver's seat of the rental car and let his head fall back against the headrest with a sigh. All he'd wanted was a smooth flight and a quiet night before his meetings tomorrow. Instead he'd landed smack in the middle of a nightmare.

His phone chirped. He fumbled it out of his pocket and squinted at the screen. Theresa Lee, his former partner. He'd planned to meet her for dinner, but he was beyond late now. He hit the call back button.

"Theresa, it's me. I'm sorry, I—"

"Where are you?" She cut him off, her voice sharp with worry. "I've been blowing up your phone for hours. The news is showing something about a guy tackling a terrorist at the airport. Please tell me that wasn't you."

"Yeah, you can take the cop out of the NYPD, but…" Docherty pinched the bridge of his nose. "I'm fine, but it's a long story. I'm on my way to the hotel now. I was planning to fly to Tampa after dinner, but I missed my connection. I'll be here overnight. Let's have breakfast in the morning. I'll fill you in when I see you."

There was a long pause. "Why do you always have to play the hero, Ed? You're going to get yourself killed one of these days."

He chuckled wearily.

Theresa hung up and Docherty tossed his phone onto the passenger seat. He took a deep breath to calm the whirlwind in his head.

He started the car and pulled out of the parking lot. It was late. Traffic was light. He was distracted, reviewing the events at the airport again in his head.

At first, the drive was easy. Uneventful.

Until it wasn't.

As his rental approached the businessman's hotel a few miles from the airport, Docherty's world exploded.

At the exact moment Docherty's sedan sailed into the intersection on the green light, an oncoming driver accelerated to beat the red light.

Docherty never saw it coming.

The double decker private coach slammed into the side of his electric sedan at full speed, crumpling the metal like tissue paper.

Glass shattered, steel screamed, and Docherty's sedan flipped over in a dizzying spiral of chaos.

Silence. Stillness.

Nothingness.

Docherty awakened slowly. His head was a ringing muddle of confusion and pain. He blinked once, twice, trying to clear the haze. Trying to remember.

After a few moments he realized he was slumped over the steering wheel in the mangled vehicle. His vision was blurred and his hearing muffled like he was underwater.

He could taste blood in his mouth, feel it trickling from his nose and ears.

Everything hurt.

With great effort, he turned his head, searching, for his phone. He needed his phone. But it was gone, lost somewhere in the twisted wreckage.

He heard sirens in the distance, drawing closer.

Help was coming. He just needed to hold on.

His eyes fell on the shattered remnants of his phone lying just out of reach, the screen somehow still glowing faintly.

The world began to fade at the edges, darkness creeping in.

Docherty tried to move, to reach for the phone, but his body wouldn't cooperate. Everything felt heavy, distant, disconnected.

As his eyes fluttered shut and the numbness spread, a thought flitted through his mind.

One last realization before the void claimed him.

A warning.

Docherty breathed a final, shuddering breath as the sirens reached a crescendo. First responders jumped from their vehicles with emergency equipment and dashed toward his mangled car. They worked feverishly to save him without success.

CHAPTER 3

Eleven Days Later
Tuesday, June 28
Washington, DC

THE LONG FOURTH OF July holiday weekend loomed ahead as FBI Special Agent Kim Otto leaned against the back wall and scanned the room.

The one-day national law enforcement and security conference in DC buzzed with activity. Hundreds of additional officers and agents were gathered in advance of the anticipated celebratory crowds.

She rarely attended events like this. Her FBI training was comprehensive and constant, which was more than she typically needed. These presentations had been first rate, though.

FBI Special Agent Reggie Smithers, Kim's chosen new partner, had just wrapped up his workshop on advanced interrogation techniques. He stood at the front of the room responding to private questions from members of the audience. Looked like he'd be tied up for a while yet.

When Smithers finished, they'd hit the road on the hunt for Jack Reacher.

For now, she slipped out of the lecture hall to the break room and grabbed a coffee. She moved aside and found another wall to lean against while she watched the entrances. An ingrained habit she didn't intend to break.

Kim noticed a woman moving toward her. Small and slim. Dark hair tied back and a small oval face. No jewelry. Not even a wedding band.

Mid-forties, maybe. Attractive, relaxed, friendly. She carried herself like a cop. Probably ex-military, too. A lot of law enforcement officers and agents were well trained by another of Uncle Sam's branches before they became cops of one kind or another.

"Agent Otto?" The woman's voice was steady, determined, confident.

Kim nodded, wary. Her badge wasn't visible. How did this woman know her name? "Yes, that's right."

"I'm Theresa Lee, private security." She pronounced Theresa like *the* or *them*. Th-reesa. Maybe the surname Lee came from an old marriage or was an Ellis Island version of Leigh, or some other longer and more complicated name. Or maybe she was descended from Robert E.

"I understand you've been assigned to fill in the blanks on Jack Reacher's old personnel files to bring them up to date," Lee said without preamble.

Kim felt a flicker of suspicion in her gut. "I have a lot of cases."

"I'd like to help you with this one." Lee's eyes didn't waver. "I need to find Reacher. It's about my former partner, Ed Docherty. He was murdered."

Everything the woman said raised Kim's internal threat level into the red zone and held the needle there.

How did she know who Kim was?

How did she know about her top-secret assignment?

How the hell did she know anything about Jack Reacher?

Kim said none of that. No way was she discussing Jack Reacher. Nor would she affirm whatever intel Theresa Lee claimed to have somehow acquired.

Instead, she offered platitudes. "I'm very sorry about your partner. I'd like to help. But my work is classified. I can't disclose details or add unauthorized members to my team."

"I'm not asking you to talk. I'm asking you to listen." Lee leaned in slightly, lowering her voice. "Docherty's death was called an accident, and the case was closed barely a minute after he died. No one is investigating his murder. I owe him that much. Give me a couple of hours and I can get whatever authorization you need to let me join you."

Kim said nothing. She revealed her cover story only on a need-to-know basis and never revealed her actual objective. Her assignment was not only classified, it was off-the-books and so deep under the radar no outsider could possibly have discovered it.

Only a handful of people knew Kim was hunting Reacher. Maybe a dozen more had heard her official cover story.

Yet, Lee seemed to know.

Which meant Lee was connected to one of those people in a way that made Kim nervous. She needed to know who was leaking the highly classified intel to this woman.

Not that she intended to grant Lee's request for access. Not for a hot New York minute.

Kim's boss, Charles Cooper, would never authorize Theresa Lee to participate in hunting Reacher. Not for any reason.

Hell, Cooper wouldn't even tell Kim why he wanted to find Reacher and what he intended to do with Reacher after she found him.

She wouldn't even ask. She already knew what his answer would be. Not only no, but hell, no.

Lee handed Kim a folder. "My partner, Ed Docherty, was hit by a bus. How often does that happen accidentally to a man who just took down a suicide bomber and survived? I'll tell you. Never. Not one single time in the history of the world. Until now."

Kim opened the folder, flipped quickly through the gruesome photos of Docherty's fatal crash. She handed the folder back to Lee. "Why do you believe any of this relates to Reacher?"

"A while back, when Docherty and I were still NYPD detectives, Reacher stopped a suspected suicide bomber on the subway. He hunted down those responsible and dealt with them," Lee explained. "I worked with him. Got to know him fairly well. Which means I know Reacher can do the job I need done. He did it once. He can do it again. When I find him."

"You believe the two incidents are related? Docherty's death and the New York subway case?" Kim asked, raising her eyebrows in surprise. She hadn't heard about the old subway case, but if Reacher had been involved, she needed to know everything.

Lee shrugged. "Doesn't matter whether the two are connected. They're two sides of the same coin."

"How's that?"

"Terrorists. They don't deserve to breathe the same air we breathe. Reacher understands that."

"Plenty of law enforcement and military resources are devoted to defending against terrorism," Kim pointed out reasonably in an effort to get Lee to back off.

"You think I haven't already knocked on those doors? They've decided Docherty's death was just bad luck," Lee said. "They're wrong. I don't believe it. Not for a minute."

"Say you're right. And say we do find Reacher. And then say he agrees to do this thing you're asking." Kim gave her a slow nod, responding seriously. "You're inviting a nightmare into your life. Reacher gets started, he won't quit until he's the last man standing. That's a lot of weight for you to carry."

"You don't need to protect me. I know what he's capable of," Lee said sternly. "I've seen it firsthand."

"Okay. Reacher can do the job," Kim replied. "Why do you think he will help you?"

"He owes me," Lee said simply as her eyes hardened with conviction. "And I owe Docherty. His death has been officially closed. Nobody is following up. Nobody cares."

"That's hard to believe," Kim replied.

"Believe it. If I had another option, I'd have used it." Lee was adamant. "We need Reacher. He's one of a kind."

Don't I know it. Kim had been hunting Reacher for months. So far, she'd had several close encounters, but each time, he'd slipped out of her reach.

At the moment, she had no leads at all, and she needed to find him. Soon.

Cooper was getting impatient. He had some sort of deadline and time was running out. Kim had vowed to find Reacher. She wouldn't quit, no matter what. But was Lee's quest a distraction or an actual lead?

Kim had to admit that Theresa Lee might have better luck finding Reacher. At the very least, she could fill in the blanks on Reacher's background check, which could lead Kim to finding him.

Hell, Reacher had probably slept with Lee.

Every woman Kim had met so far who had a personal relationship with Reacher had been his lover. All of them had been oddly protective of Reacher. Kim had interviewed several of his women by now and they had certain characteristics.

All were strong females who could take care of themselves. Several worked in law enforcement in local cop shops or three-letter federal agencies.

Theresa Lee seemed to fit the mold.

Maybe she *did* know something useful.

Maybe Reacher would show up for her. He'd turned up before when his friends and lovers were in trouble.

At the moment, Kim had nothing to lose here. Why not give Lee a chance?

Lee was asking for a favor. Which meant Kim could quit anytime if things went too far south.

She couldn't run the idea past Cooper first. He'd manipulate the situation to his advantage. No, this was strictly a don't ask and don't tell situation. At least, for now.

"I'll be right there with you all the way," Lee said as if Kim had objected and needed more persuasion. "Ed Docherty was my partner. He was a good man. If we get Reacher on this, whoever killed Docherty will be located, exposed, and *handled*. In the most final way possible."

Kim continued to hesitate, thinking it through, examining all the ways any cooperation with Theresa Lee could go wrong and produce disastrous consequences.

"Don't overthink it. You've been searching for Reacher alone. You've failed. I'm offering you a lifeline here." Lee handed Kim a classy, embossed business card. It was black with gold letters. *Theresa Lee, Security.* "Senator John Sansom's private security team. Check me out. You'll find I have access to intel you don't have and can't get. Intel you will find useful, I promise you. I'll even agree up front to answer whatever questions you have about Reacher. I've heard you've had trouble getting first-hand reports."

Kim slipped the card into her pocket. Docherty's death, a staged bus accident, the woman with the bomb. All pointed to terrorism, which wasn't her area of expertise. Not even close.

Reacher wasn't likely to be in bed with terrorists of any kind, either literally or figuratively. What she'd learned so far about the man and his background said he was as patriotic as they came. Even if his definition of patriotism might be a little off plumb.

But Kim didn't know everything, as she was all too aware. What she didn't know could easily kill her. Ignorance of facts on the ground was a disaster waiting to happen. Always.

Still, Theresa Lee should be vetted before Kim agreed to anything. The woman could be a total nutcase. There were plenty of those walking around.

"Here's the short version," Lee said when Kim still didn't consent. "I can work with you to find Reacher and give you more intel than you'll ever get any other way. Or I can follow you around and find him anyway."

Kim smirked as she replied, "When you put it that way, it makes more sense for us to work together, doesn't it."

"Exactly," Lee said, satisfied finally. "I'll gather what we know about the Atlanta incident and Docherty's death. We can go from there."

CHAPTER 4

Saturday, June 29
Washington, DC

SEVERAL HOURS LATER, KIM'S phone buzzed on the nightstand, pulling her out of a light sleep after only ten minutes in bed. She squinted at the screen, recognizing the number immediately. Special Assistant to the President, Lamont Finlay, PhD.

She sat on the edge of the bed and turned on the light before she cleared her throat and accepted the call. "Otto."

"We need to talk," Finlay said in his deep, rich baritone. She'd often thought he should be soothing sleepless women on late night radio with that voice.

Kim's pulse quickened. Finlay only called for a good reason. Which meant she hadn't spoken to him in a while.

"Where?"

"The Waldorf. The Townhouse Suite."

"I'll be there in twenty," she replied, ending the call and hurrying to get dressed.

After splashing her face with cold water, she slipped into jeans, boots, and a black T-shirt. A black leather blazer concealed her shoulder holster. Her badge wallet slid into an interior pocket along with her personal phone and one clean burner. She slipped her hair into a ponytail and wrapped it into a chignon at the base of her neck.

Total elapsed time? Eight minutes. Giving her twelve minutes to get there. Plenty of time.

The Townhouse Suite at the Waldorf was the most expensive suite in DC. Exactly the sort of place Finlay would choose. It was a cab ride and about two thousand dollars a night away from her hotel.

When the cab stopped at the curb, Kim paid the driver and walked briskly to the suite's outside entrance. She rang the bell and waited.

Finlay's unexpected call and its urgency had her on edge. What did he want?

Travis Russell, Finlay's Secret Service detail, opened the door. Russell was a good man. He knew about her black-ops Reacher assignment, and he'd helped her out of a tough spot a few weeks back.

She owed him and they both knew it.

Which was okay.

Kim always paid her debts.

"Agent Otto. Good to see you again," Russell said, stepping aside.

"You, too," she replied as she entered the suite, noting the luxury appointments.

Expensive furniture, fabrics, rugs. The pricey digs didn't intimidate her, although she realized she was seriously underdressed.

Russell led the way through the living room past the sixteen-seat dining room. They ascended to the upper level where a second, quieter and more private living room awaited.

Russell offered coffee and gestured toward an armchair. "He'll be with you as soon as he can."

"That's fine."

Kim's relationship with Finlay was more than complicated. Finlay was no fan of Kim's boss, Charles Cooper, and the feeling was mutual.

Both men seemed satisfied with their détente while keeping fingers poised above the detonator of some imaginary weapon that provided mutually assured destruction.

Gaspar didn't trust either of them, but Kim trusted Gaspar implicitly in all things. With good reason.

But so far, Finlay had come through for her every time, no questions asked.

She couldn't say the same for Cooper.

Did Finlay have ulterior motives? Probably. Who didn't?

"It's good to see you, Agent Otto. How have you been?" Finlay said, interrupting her thoughts as he entered the room, smooth as river rock and twice as hard.

"Busy," she replied, managing a small smile. "But good enough."

His expression softened. "Still haven't found Reacher, though."

"Not yet," Kim replied. "But I will."

"Possibly."

"Definitely. You can take that to the bank."

Finlay nodded with a smile and then his expression grew more serious. "I've been following your situation. Just to clear this up at the outset, Theresa Lee's approach was not authorized."

Kim blinked, taken aback. Although she shouldn't have been. Finlay always seemed to know everything, long before she had a chance to decide whether to tell him.

"No one sent her to you. She's not acting on orders from me or Cooper or anyone else." Finlay recapped quickly. "Lee offered to help to find Reacher for her own reasons. Not mine."

Kim absorbed both his words and the implications. "I can't be sidetracked chasing her agenda."

"Your concerns are valid. But you should reconsider." Finlay leaned forward. "Reacher is your top priority. Lee's personal stake and personal knowledge will give you an edge. If you could find Reacher on your own, you'd have already done it. Why not accept help when it's offered?"

Kim frowned, trying to read between the lines. "You're suggesting we cooperate with her? Join forces to find Reacher?"

"Exactly. Theresa Lee was a top detective for NYPD." Finlay settled more comfortably in his chair. "Now she's working for John Sansom, a US Senator chairing the powerful Armed Services Committee. And Reacher has a way of joining in when he's needed, doesn't he? This situation could be one of those times."

Kim wasn't shocked by the suggestion. Reacher had shown up for her several times already, seemingly out of the blue.

She had her theories about Reacher's uncanny timing, but no hard evidence to prove them. Mostly because neither Cooper nor Finlay had ever been straight with her.

All three were tight lipped. They shared other similarities as well.

"Why do you think Reacher will show up for Theresa Lee?"

"Reacher knew Docherty, too. If he were already in the area, he'd be all over this thing. Especially if Lee asked him to help," Finlay said.

"Because they were lovers?" Kim challenged.

Finlay smiled again but he didn't confirm. "Because Reacher likes Lee. He also likes a good fight. And he always wins."

Kim nodded slowly. She respected Finlay's judgment. He'd never led her astray before. But she wasn't persuaded. "I'll talk to Smithers. See what he thinks."

"Of course," Finlay agreed. "But trust me on this, Agent Otto. Aligning with Theresa Lee could turn out to be the best move you make in this situation."

"Why?"

"She's got intel and experience with Reacher. She's met the guy. Worked with him. She knows how he ticks," Finlay paused for emphasis. "And you're not likely to get another volunteer with such a pure motive."

Kim cocked her head. "What kind of intel and experience?"

"You'd have a trustworthy operative on your team who knows things you don't. Which is always a good thing. Think about it. Make your own decision. Maybe you've got better options that I'm unaware of." Finlay stood and smiled, making it clear his time was up. On his way out, he said, "Russell will call a car. Keep in touch."

"What kind of intel and experience does Lee have that would be helpful to me?" Kim asked again, more forcefully this time.

Finlay said nothing more as he left the room.

A few moments later, Kim gulped the last of her coffee and followed Russell to the exit where, as Finlay had promised, a car and driver waited.

Back at her hotel, Kim found Smithers in the lobby, sipping coffee and reading the paper. He looked up as she approached, noting the determined expression on her face.

"Where've you been?"

"Meeting with Lamont Finlay," she said, sitting down across from him. "Remember I told you that I was approached by Theresa Lee?"

He nodded.

"Finlay thinks we should cooperate with her. Join forces to find Reacher."

Smithers raised an eyebrow. "That's a twist. Why's a guy like Finlay sticking his nose into our business?"

Kim shrugged and avoided the question. Smithers had been her partner for two weeks. There were many things he didn't know. Things Kim might not want to share with him. She'd yet to make those decisions.

"We need a different approach. Lee claims to have intel and connections," Kim said. "She knows Reacher. She might even know where to find him. Or at least, how to find him."

Smithers leaned back, considering. Then he shrugged as if he'd made some sort of decision. "Nothing ventured, nothing gained."

Kim nodded seriously. "Let's get some sleep. Theresa Lee is coming by in the morning. We'll hear her out and then decide."

CHAPTER 5

Sunday, June 30
North Carolina

MARCUS MOLINA STOOD RAMROD straight at the floor-to-ceiling windows of his mountain retreat. A vast expanse of North Carolina land stretched before him. The predawn light began to illuminate the freehold where his family had thrived for generations.

From here, he could see the fields and streams where he and his brother had played and fished and lived what Molina now viewed as the good life. Simpler times, to be sure. Long before adulthood and his brother's death had separated them.

Molina was an imposing man. Honed by years of military service and continued rigorous training, he stood tall and straight. Dark hair, blue eyes, and a neatly trimmed beard gave him a chiseled appearance.

But for the scowl on his face, he resembled Captain America. Which was exactly how he thought of himself. A warrior fighting for the American way of life.

The room hummed with electronic activity. Banks of computer screens lined one wall, flickering with data streams and surveillance feeds, punctuated by soft keyboard clicks and the occasional beep of incoming messages.

"The good news is that Docherty's dead," Molina said, his voice low and controlled, barely masking his simmering fury.

He turned from the window and settled his steely gaze on Eugene Cannon, his right-hand man. "Otherwise, the Atlanta operation was a total disaster."

"It's a setback. Definitely." Cannon nodded from his position at the high-tech command center. He met Molina's steady gaze without flinching. "Daisy didn't even make it to the gate before Docherty stopped her. Once she was in custody, we had to clean up. Terminated the threat as quickly as possible. All's well that ends well. Only problem is that we're down one asset."

Molina's jaw clenched, causing the muscle to twitch beneath his skin.

The botched airport bombing was more than a setback. It was a catastrophic failure of resolve, a glaring weakness that he couldn't tolerate.

Daisy had been a test, carefully chosen and meticulously prepared. She was tasked to prove her commitment to the cause, to demonstrate the strength to carry out their mission and encourage others to do the same.

She had failed spectacularly.

And she'd paid for her mistakes with her life.

Which wasn't the message he'd been trying to send to the others or to the world.

"We sent her to Atlanta," Molina growled as he paced the length of the room. "We risked exposure, used valuable resources, all to avoid drawing attention here. And for what? She never delivered the message. Not even a footnote on the evening news. Total waste of time and resources."

"We're drawing too much of the wrong kind of attention as it is," Cannon warned as he swiveled in his chair, gesturing to the screens before him.

News reports from several Atlanta stations flashed across the monitors speculating about the failed airport attack and its perpetrators. But the incident had failed to get wider attention.

The damned law enforcement agency must have squelched the story, which was infuriating, too. The threat, they claimed, was successfully thwarted.

Losing Daisy was bad enough. Now, all of Atlanta was reassured instead of bloodied and terrified. The airport continued to expand as a blight on what had once been some of the richest farmland in the country. When would it stop?

Molina crossed the room to a large map of the United States dominating one wall. Red pins dotted the landscape, each identifying a target. His fingers traced the contours of the map, lingering over the pins.

Molina turned to face Cannon, his eyes blazing with conviction. "We can't lose sight of our mission, no matter how many setbacks we face."

Cannon nodded, understanding the weight of Molina's words. "The members are getting restless. Our backers, too. They want more action, more impact. Daisy's failure has destroyed their confidence."

Molina's fist clenched at his side. He understood the sentiment well. He too felt the burning need to do more and strike harder.

Molina strode to a dark wood cabinet and pulled out a bottle of bourbon and two glasses. The amber liquid caught the weak sunlight as he poured, glowing like liquid fire. "We've been too cautious. Too precise. It's time to show the world what we mean."

"Works for me." Cannon accepted the offered glass. "What are you thinking?"

Molina took a long sip, savoring the burn as it slid down his throat. When he spoke, his voice was cold and determined, each word carefully measured. "We're going to hit them where it hurts. Not just one target. Not just one operation."

He returned to the map, bourbon in hand. With a sweep of his arm, he indicated the entire collection of red pins. "We'll take them all out. Simultaneously."

Cannon's eyes widened and the glass froze halfway to his lips. "All of them? But that would require—"

"Resources. Manpower. Coordination." Molina's smirk played at the corners of his mouth. "We have it all. We've been building to this moment for years. Every recruit, every dollar, every scrap of intel. It's all been leading up to this."

He turned his hard expression to Cannon. "It's time to show the world that we're not just talk. We're a promise. A reckoning."

Cannon nodded slowly, a smile spreading across his face as he grasped the magnitude of Molina's plans. "When do we start?"

Molina drained his glass and set it down with a hard thump to punctuate his orders. The sound echoed for a moment in the room. "Now. Get everyone in place. Time is of the essence."

Cannon spun to the command center and set his fingers flying across the keyboard. Coded messages raced out across secure channels, setting the grand plan in motion.

The room seemed to fill with a new energy, a sense of excitement that had been missing since Daisy's complete debacle.

Molina returned to the window, staring out at the lightening sky. Anticipation built in his chest, a heady mixture of excitement and righteous anger.

They would change the world. Very soon. Not decades or centuries in the future, but now.

The thought brought a cold, satisfied smile to his lips.

But a flicker of movement in the trees caught his eye. He leaned closer to the glass, squinting into the morning light.

There it was again. A shadow where no shadow should be, moving steadily through the underbrush.

Molina's satisfied smile was replaced by a look of intense concentration.

He reached for the secure phone on the desk and punched a code with swift, sure movements.

"Perimeter breached," he said quietly into the receiver, his voice tight with controlled urgency. "We have an intruder."

He didn't give the intruder another thought. Cannon would deal with him, as he always did. Problem solved.

CHAPTER 6

Washington, DC

AGAIN AND AGAIN, THERESA Lee's fist connected with the heavy bag with a satisfying thud. The impact reverberated through her arm. Sweat glistened on her skin as she continued her assault. Each punch landed with precision and power.

The private gym was quiet at this early hour. Only the rhythmic pounding of her blows and her controlled breathing broke the silence.

Nestled in the basement of a nondescript building in downtown DC, the gym was a haven for those who valued privacy as much as fitness. Its sparse decor and state-of-the-art equipment ranked function over luxury. The air was heavy with the familiar and comfortable scent of leather and sweat.

Senator John Sansom held the bag steady. His muscular body barely moved with each of Lee's strikes.

"You destroy the bag and it'll take a while to replace it," he commented in a low, calm voice.

Lee paused and steadied the bag with one gloved hand. She took a moment to catch her breath while her chest heaved with exertion. "Couldn't sleep. Too much on my mind."

Sansom nodded, understanding. "Docherty?"

Lee's jaw tightened almost imperceptibly. "Among other things."

She stepped back and started to unwrap her hands. The tape came away damp with sweat. "I made contact with Agent Otto yesterday."

Sansom raised his eyebrows, and a flicker of interest crossed his face. "Oh?"

Lee took a long swig from her water bottle before answering. The cool liquid relieved her parched throat. "She's cautious. Didn't commit to anything, but she didn't shut me down either."

"Good." Sansom moved to sit on a nearby bench, The metal creaked slightly under his weight.

Lee joined him, her face set in serious lines. The bench was cool against her skin, displacing the heat radiating from her body.

"The timing in Atlanta bothers me," she said. "Docherty takes down the bomber, turns her over to Federal agents. They question and release him. He dies less than half an hour later. It's all way too convenient."

"Agreed." Sansom nodded slowly, interlacing his fingers as he leaned forward to stretch. "Who has the resources to coordinate something like that? And why? What's going on with all of this? Makes no sense."

"I don't know," Lee admitted. Frustration edged her voice, and her hands clenched into fists on her thighs. "But I'm damned sure Docherty's death was no accident."

"No question." A steel edge crept into his tone. "But we need proof. And we need to know why. Where's the motive?"

Lee leaned back against the cool wall. She considered the possibilities, each scenario more troubling than the last. "It could be related to one of his cases. I'd lost touch with him these past couple of years. Was he working on anything big enough to kill for?"

Sansom's face remained impassive, but Lee caught a flicker of something in his gaze. Concern? Recognition? She couldn't be sure.

Years of military service engaged in covert operations, followed by more years of political maneuvering, had taught him to mask his emotions.

"Reacher worked with me and Docherty on that subway case in New York. He's smart and clever and he'll do what it takes to get justice for Docherty." Lee watched Sansom carefully for any subtle reaction. "All I have to do is find him."

Sansom's expression didn't change, but Lee noticed his shoulders tense slightly. It was a minute tell, one she might have missed if she hadn't been looking for it.

"Reacher's a ghost," he said evenly. "Even if he's willing to do what we want, we need to find him first."

Lee offered a humorless expression that didn't reach her eyes. "As you said before, that's where Otto comes in. Finding Reacher is her job."

Sansom nodded thoughtfully. His fingers drummed a quiet rhythm on his knee. "Just be careful. Whoever is behind the bomber and Docherty's murder, if that's what it was, has some heavy talent and equipment to deploy. That much is obvious."

"I'm always careful. Remember me? Twenty years at NYPD, I've seen just about everything there is to see," Lee assured him as she stood and stretched her muscles as they began to cool. "I'm not backing down. I owe it to Docherty to find out what happened and deal with the perpetrators. That's my plan."

"Simple as that, huh?" Sansom gave her a good-natured grin.

"No. But just because the mission can be simply stated doesn't make it impossible, either," Lee replied gravely before she headed toward the shower.

She'd been working for Sansom a while now. He knew more than he was letting on. But she trusted him, and she understood the position he was in.

Whatever he wasn't telling her, she was sure he had good reason. His clearance level was significantly higher than hers anyway. But he was worried about what had happened in Atlanta. She was sure of it.

The gym's locker room was as austere as the main floor. None of the frills and services that drove up fees and encouraged dilettantes. Which was another thing that made the place her first choice.

Lee showered and changed quickly. Her routine was familiar after years of early morning workouts. As she zipped up her jacket, she caught sight of her reflection in the mirror.

The woman staring back at her looked tired, the weight of recent events evident in the set of her shoulders and the tightness around her eyes. She shrugged. No rest in her future until she found Docherty's killer.

"Suck it up, Lee," she murmured as she headed toward the door.

Sansom was waiting for her by the exit, gym bag slung over his shoulder. In his tailored suit, he looked every inch the powerful senator that he was.

"Keep me updated on Otto and Reacher, too," Sansom said as they stepped out into the predawn chill. "And Lee? Watch your back."

"Always." She nodded, her jaw set with determination.

The street was quiet while the city was not yet fully awake. Streetlights cast pools of yellow light on the sidewalk, creating a patchwork of light and shadow.

She walked toward her car, parked a short distance away. The cool air was refreshing against her skin, helping to clear her mind.

As she reached for her car door, a man stepped out of the shadows between two parked cars. He was tall and broad-shouldered, but his features were obscured by the brim of a baseball cap.

There was something familiar about his stance, the way he carried himself. When he came closer, she recognized him. One of Sansom's personal bodyguards.

"Ms. Lee?" His voice was low, gravelly. "We need to talk."

"So talk. I'm listening."

"Daisy Hawkins is dead," he said flatly.

Lee's breath caught in her chest. "How?"

"Suicide. Hanged herself in her cell."

"They didn't have her under suicide watch?" Lee asked incredulously.

"Sure they did. Standard procedure in cases like this."

"But they failed? Or are you suggesting she was helped along by someone inside?" Lee demanded.

He shrugged. "There will be a full investigation, of course. It's likely to conclude that she was more resourceful than anticipated."

"If Hawkins was dead, I'd have heard about it already," Lee said.

"Only if we wanted you to hear about it. Which now, we do," he replied just as a truck sped past along the road, backfired, radio blasting hard rock from every pore.

When Lee turned her gaze back to the man, he was gone. He'd slipped into the shadows again. She didn't bother to chase him. No point. She could find him easily enough if she needed to.

CHAPTER 7

Washington, DC

THE HOTEL RESTAURANT BUZZED with the low hum of early morning conversations and the clink of cutlery against plates. Kim sat across from Smithers at a corner table, both nursing cups of strong black coffee as they waited for their breakfast to arrive.

"I asked Gaspar to run down intel on Theresa Lee, Ed Docherty, and John Sansom. He should have something for us by noon," Kim said. "I also asked him to find out what happened with that subway incident back in New York."

"Okay. We need to know what we're getting into." Smithers frowned as he set down his cup. "Something you should know. I was working in the city when the subway thing happened."

Kim raised both eyebrows, surprised. "You were?"

Smithers shrugged. A rueful smile lifted the corners of his mouth. "I was new to the bureau at the time. Very junior, barely two months on the job. I wasn't read into most of what was going on."

"What do you remember about it?" Kim asked.

"Chaos, mostly. I was one of six hundred law enforcement agents from various agencies searching for those terrorists that night." Smithers leaned back slightly as he recalled the events. "They had me doing low-level grunt work, barely any intel to go on. My team was running on adrenaline and vending machine coffee, combing through the subway tunnels, questioning anyone who looked even slightly suspicious."

Kim nodded, encouraging him to continue.

"The thing is," Smithers went on, "Reacher's name was never mentioned, at least not to any of us on the ground. But Lee and Docherty? They could have been two of the NYPD detectives involved. The incident occurred in the 14th Precinct. Midtown South on 35th Street."

Kim leaned forward. "Did you ever see the official report?"

"I was too low on the totem pole for that," Smithers shook his head. "I remember the buzz. The higher-ups were tight-lipped, but you could tell something major had gone down. There were whispers about a lone wolf, some ex-military guy who'd cracked the case wide open and took down the perpetrators."

"Reacher," Kim said, more a statement than a question. "Got his fingerprints all over it."

"Probably, although I'd never heard of Reacher back then," Smithers agreed. "His name never made it into the official channels or any official reports. At least not the ones I was privy to."

Kim sat back. "So, what do you think about Lee's proposal now?"

"It's still risky. We don't know her full agenda or how much she really knows about Reacher." Smithers took a moment to consider while drumming his fingers lightly on the table. "But if she was involved as one of the detectives in that case, she has first-hand knowledge and probably some intel we can't get otherwise."

Kim nodded. "Assuming she's telling the truth."

Conversation paused when the waiter arrived with the food. Spinach and feta omelet for Kim. Smithers opted for bacon and eggs.

"Speak of the devil," Smithers muttered under his breath after the first couple of bites.

Kim looked up to see Theresa Lee approaching their table, posture straight and confident. She wore a charcoal gray blazer over a crisp white shirt and a neutral expression. But there was an intensity in her dark eyes bordering on zeal.

"Agent Otto, Agent Smithers," Lee said by way of greeting. "Mind if I join you?"

Kim exchanged a quick glance with Smithers before gesturing to an empty chair. "Please. We were just discussing your proposal."

"And?" Lee sat down and waved the waiter away. Her gaze flicked between Kim and Smithers, assessing.

Kim noticed Lee's hands were steady and calloused in a way that suggested many hours at the shooting range and the gym. "Your connection to Docherty complicates things."

Lee's gaze hardened as a flash of emotion broke through her composed exterior. "Reacher worked with us on the subway case in New York. He's connected to Docherty, too. That's the whole point."

Smithers leaned forward to speak for their ears alone. "What makes you think Docherty's death wasn't an accident?"

"Instinct," Lee replied without hesitation. There was a certainty in her voice, as if she had actual knowledge. Which she probably didn't. "And timing. Docherty takes down a suicide bomber. Six hours later, he's dead."

Kim and Smithers exchanged glances.

"Tell us more about Docherty," Kim said as she took another bite of her rapidly cooling omelet. "What kind of cop was he?"

Lee's expression softened slightly. "He was old school. Tough, but fair. Had a nose for trouble like you wouldn't believe. He could smell a lie from a mile away."

"And the old subway case? The one in New York?" Smithers's tone was carefully neutral. "You mentioned Reacher."

"Not much I can say about the case. All of it was classified at the time and buried since then. No need to alarm the public when the threat was successfully thwarted." Lee's gaze darted between them. A flicker of suspicion. "But Reacher was involved and so was Docherty. And now Docherty's dead."

"And you think Reacher might be next?" Smithers leaned back in his chair.

"They might try, I guess. Or maybe Reacher knows about Docherty already and he's going after them. He's a dangerous enemy." Lee shrugged, but her shoulders were tense. "Regardless of his killer's motives, I need to find Reacher. You need to find him for other reasons. No point in all of us running around like fools, doubling our workload."

"If we agree, no holding back intel from us. You volunteer what you think we need to know. Beyond that, we ask, you tell." Kim felt the weight of unknown facts hanging between them. "Otherwise, we go our separate ways right now and forget about your proposal."

"Agreed," Lee said without hesitation, her gaze steady. "But that rule cuts both ways. I need to know everything you know about Reacher's whereabouts, his patterns, his contacts."

"Sorry. That's a nonstarter." Kim shook her head. "You know we've been asked to complete Reacher's background check. That's as much as we're authorized to say. We won't say more."

Lee cocked her head and leveled a flat stare at Kim for a while. Then she nodded almost imperceptibly.

"First question," Kim said. "When did you last see Reacher in person?"

"At the end of the case back then," Lee replied without hesitation.

"You've not had any contact with him since?" Kim asked.

Lee shook her head. "No reason to. On either side, I guess, since he hasn't contacted me."

"Which means all of your knowledge about Reacher is several years old," Otto replied.

"Yeah, I guess. But my contact period with him was intense. And it was personal. Which is more than you or Smithers can say, isn't it?"

Kim said nothing because her answer was obvious. If she'd had any contact with Reacher, personal and intense or otherwise, she wouldn't need Lee at all.

Lee reached into her bag and pulled out a thick folder. She placed it on the table with a soft thud, resting her hand on top. The folder looked as if it had been thumbed many times.

"This is my private file on the Atlanta airport bombing," Lee said. "And everything I've learned so far about Docherty's death and the woman with the bomb."

Lee opened the folder, spreading out photos and reports.

Kim felt a familiar surge of adrenaline. Was this the break in her search for Reacher she'd been hoping for? Or was she making a wrong turn here?

Her gut said to move forward until she had a reason to stop.

Lee thumbed through photos of the Atlanta airport tram, diagrams of the bomb and its components, intel on the suspect, witness statements, and more.

Otto shuddered. If that bomb had detonated as planned, hundreds of victims would have been scattered across the airport. Docherty had done the right thing.

"The bomber," Kim said, studying a grainy security camera image. "Do we have an ID?"

Lee pulled out another document. "Daisy Hawkins, age twenty-one. No prior record, no known terrorist connections. Lived a quiet life in Georgia, by all accounts."

Smithers frowned, examining the bomb diagram. "This is sophisticated work for an amateur. Who trained her?"

"That's the million-dollar question," Lee replied, voice tight. "And why target the airport tram? Not as high-profile as other potential targets and a tight security surrounding her on all sides. Seems like an ambitious target for an amateur."

Kim replied thoughtfully, "Unless the tram wasn't the real target. Maybe it was about who would be at the gate when the tram stopped."

Lee's eyes widened slightly. "Or who would stop her from completing her mission. Docherty was supposed to be on a flight out that day. He wasn't meant to be on that tram."

"Which could mean he wasn't a target," Smithers said slowly.

Kim shook her head. "Then why kill him? What turned him from a good Samaritan into a murder victim?"

"That's not the sort of thing I'm comfortable discussing in a hotel dining room," Lee replied.

"Good point. Let's go upstairs," Smithers said while signing the check.

Kim led the way to her room.

CHAPTER 8

Washington, DC

THE FLUORESCENT LIGHTS BUZZED softly overhead as Kim stepped into the small conference area of her room. Smithers and Lee followed.

The maid hadn't cleaned yet and the lingering scent of stale coffee had settled over the room like a cloud.

They found chairs around the worn conference table. Kim noticed the fatigue etched on Theresa Lee's face. She'd been working nonstop since Docherty died, and it showed.

Lee took her seat, placing her laptop and the thick file on the table with a soft thud. The screen's glow illuminated her face, casting sharp shadows across her features. Kim and Smithers leaned forward.

"I've completed the social media analysis on the bomber, Daisy Hawkins," Lee began, cutting through the silence. Her fingers danced across the laptop's surface, bringing up a series of images and text. "The results are interesting, to say the least."

Kim fixed her gaze on the screen. "Give us the highlights. What are we looking at here?"

"Over the past six months, there's been a dramatic shift in Hawkins's online presence." Lee paused as if organizing her thoughts. "She went from posting about everyday life such as meals, friends, work complaints, to obsessing over environmental issues, particularly those affecting rural areas."

Smithers frowned. "Radicalization?"

"It certainly looks that way," Lee confirmed, swiping to a new set of images. "She connected with numerous new accounts tied to extreme environmental groups. Started sharing articles from fringe websites about corporate environmental crimes. The change was rapid and intense."

Kim leaned back in her chair, which creaked under her weight. "Any specific groups mentioned?"

"Yes, and this is where it gets interesting." Lee's finger hovered over the keyboard for a moment before selecting a particular post. "I found multiple references to several eco-groups in comment threads and private messages. Nothing specific. No names. But the groups seemed to be at the center of Daisy Hawkins's new obsession."

The room fell silent as Kim and Smithers exchanged meaningful glances. Eco-terrorism was a threat they understood. Hours of FBI training had prepared them.

"There's more," Lee's tone cut through the tension. "Hawkins used hashtags like 'EcoWarrior' and 'SaveTheHeartland' frequently. But the most telling thing is her interactions with an account called 'EcoWarrior.' Based on the frequency and nature of the exchanges, I suspect it's the movement's main profile."

Smithers leaned forward to rest his elbows on the table. "What about location data? Any clues about where this EcoWarrior might be operating from?"

Lee nodded. "That's where things get really interesting. Daisy's last posts included photos from what she called a 'camping trip.' They were geotagged in a remote area of North Carolina. The captions were cryptic, hinting at 'big changes' and 'fighting for what's right.'"

Kim stood to pace the length of the small room. Her footsteps were muffled by the carpet.

"So we have a possible connection to eco-terrorism groups, a possible base of operations in North Carolina, and a young woman who was radicalized in a matter of months." Kim paused and turned to face them. "What about Daisy's finances? These eco-groups always need money and there are usually radical people willing to fund them. Did you find anything there?"

"I did, and it corroborates what we've seen in her social media activity." Lee tapped her keyboard once more to bring up a new set of data. "There's a clear pattern of small but regular donations to various environmental charities over the past few months. Nothing too suspicious on its own, but it aligns with her increased online activity."

Smithers leaned in for a better view. "Anything more concrete?"

"Not really. But two things stand out," Lee continued. "First, she took a large cash withdrawal a few days before the attempted bombing. It's significantly larger than any of Daisy's usual transactions."

"Could have been for supplies," Smithers mused, already considering possible scenarios.

Lee nodded in agreement. "The second red flag is a purchase of camping gear, followed by a bus ticket to North Carolina. The timing lines up perfectly with the 'camping trip' photos we saw on her social media."

Kim resumed her pacing as she thought things through. "So we have financial evidence tying Daisy to North Carolina before the attempted bombing. It's not definitive, but it's another piece of the puzzle."

"There's one more thing," Lee added gravely. "I found a transaction labeled 'Initiation Fee.' The money was sent through an online payment system to an account with a username that matches EcoWarrior."

Smithers offered a low, sharp whistle. "That's about as smoking gun as it gets."

Kim agreed. "We need to identify the North Carolina group, if there is one, and EcoWarrior, and get financial records. If we can follow the money, we might be able to trace it back to their leadership."

As if in response to her comment, Kim's phone vibrated against the table. The buzz seemed amplified in the tense silence. She reached for the phone and scrolled through the message.

"Interesting," she murmured.

Smithers looked up from the notes he'd been scribbling. "What is it?"

Kim noted Lee's attentive posture and Smithers's anticipation.

"Army CID has been quietly vetting recently discharged veterans with explosives training," Kim said, reading through the text quickly. "Trying to identify disgruntled vets who could be volatile and would have the knowledge to do something about it."

Lee straightened in her chair. "And?"

"I've asked about Daisy's contacts," Kim said as she finished the text, shut off the screen, and placed the phone on the table. "I also have a list of potential suspects with photos. The vets identified so far were disgruntled and dangerous. Several were former Explosive Ordnance Disposal Specialists. Served in Afghanistan. All were honorably discharged several years ago."

"Last known addresses?" Smithers's set his pen on the table.

"I asked for those. Nothing yet." Kim nodded decisively.

Kim's chair scraped against the floor as she stood. "We need more intel on all of these names and the North Carolina camping site. Property records, financials, associates.

Smithers, contact Gaspar. He can dig without leaving his fingerprints all over everything."

Smithers reached for his secure phone. "What about the North Carolina property? We can't just waltz in there unless we know what we're dealing with, what kind of opposition we'd face."

Kim's fingers drummed on the table's edge. "We need eyes on the property and intel about what's going on out there. Quietly."

A hint of a smile tugged at Smithers's mouth. "I know a guy. Ex-military. Does freelance surveillance. He's discreet and owes me a favor."

Kim replied, "Set it up. Observe and gather intel only. We don't want to spook them if this really is a base of domestic terrorism operations."

"One more thing." Lee cleared her throat. "Daisy Hawkins committed suicide in custody not long after she was arrested."

Smithers shook his head. "Do we believe she killed herself?"

"You mean, was she murdered? That would be my guess," Lee replied. "I've got no facts to support the idea, though. Not yet."

Kim paced to the window. The city sprawled below in a maze of lights and shadows. Her reflection stared back at her, superimposed over the urban landscape.

"Daisy, what were you thinking?" she murmured.

CHAPTER 3

North Carolina

MELISSA BLACK STOOD AT the table, white-knuckled hands clenched on its edge. The map spread before her showed the rolling hills of North Carolina. She stared unseeing while her mind churned with frustration and anger.

Thirteen days had passed since Daisy's failure, and she carried the heavy weight of that disaster every minute. She wasn't sleeping. Could barely eat. The rage consumed her in ways she hadn't anticipated.

But then, she had expected Daisy to succeed. They'd practiced until Melissa could recite every step of the plan in her sleep. How could Daisy have failed so spectacularly? Melissa shook her head again in angry disbelief.

The door creaked open. Marcus Molina's heavy footsteps crossed the old floorboards. He moved to stand behind her and wrapped his arms around her waist.

"Still at it?" he asked while nibbling on her neck.

Melissa didn't look up. "Someone has to be."

"We've been over this. Daisy's failure wasn't yours, Mel."

"Wasn't it?" Melissa straightened and turned to meet his gaze. "I trained her. I pushed for her to take the mission. Her weakness in execution was my weakness in training and preparation. No other way to look at this."

Marcus shook his head. "You're being too hard on yourself. Daisy made her own choices."

"And now she's dead," Melissa said bitterly.

"Cannon handled it," Molina confirmed. "Now we're sure she won't talk."

"Small comfort. She should never have been in a position to talk in the first place." Melissa snorted and slammed her palm on the table. "We need to move now. Show our members and our critics that we aren't crippled by one setback."

"At this point, they know nothing about us. Daisy died before she had a chance to enlighten anyone." Molina's voice took on a sharp edge. "I won't risk everything with a rash action now. No. We stick to the plan."

"The plan?" Melissa scoffed. "While they keep destroying our world? Every day we wait is another forest cleared, another river polluted, another species pushed to extinction. We can't afford any more patience."

Molina stepped closer, his voice low and intense. "Listen to me. I understand your frustration. I feel it too. But we can't let emotion cloud our judgment. One misstep now could undo years of work."

Melissa glared at him. "So what do you propose? We do nothing?"

A slow smile spread across Molina's face. "Oh, we're going to do something. Something they'll never see coming."

Despite her anger, Melissa felt a flicker of curiosity. "What are you talking about?"

Molina released his hold and moved to pull out a larger map from a nearby drawer. He spread it across the table, covering the North Carolina map she'd been studying.

Several locations were marked across the country. Melissa leaned in, her gaze darting from point to point.

"On July 4," Molina said, as his finger traced a path across the map, "our teams deploy. Simultaneously. We hit every target we've planned for, all at once. A nationwide wave of environmental justice."

Melissa's mouth dried up. She blinked hard, forcing herself to focus on each mark. "All of them?"

"Bold? Risky?" Molina nodded. "And absolutely devastating to our enemies."

Melissa studied the targets. Power plants, factories, corporate headquarters, politicians' homes. The scope was overwhelming.

"How long have you been planning this?" she demanded.

"Months. Years. Forever," Molina admitted. "Daisy's failure just confirmed we need to go big. No more single strikes they can dismiss or cover up while they pick us off one by one."

Melissa nodded slowly, then faster. "Yes. This could work. They won't be able to ignore us after this."

"Exactly." Molina grinned like a toddler at Disney World. "It's what we've worked for, Mel. Everything we've sacrificed. In three days, we change the world."

Melissa stood straight, anger transformed into fierce determination by the sheer audacity of the plan. "We'd better get to work. Coordinating so many hits in such a short time won't be easy."

Molina nodded. "I've already started reaching out. But I need you to handle the final preparations for the eastern seaboard targets."

"Consider it done," Melissa said. She paused, frowning. "What about our moles inside the agencies? Should we warn them to lay low?"

Molina shook his head. "We need them in place, feeding us information until the last possible moment. They might be discovered, I guess. But it's worth the risk."

Melissa's frown deepened. "If you're sure. I'd hate to lose those assets."

"Sometimes sacrifices are necessary for the greater good," Molina said. "You taught me that, remember?"

Melissa's expression softened slightly. "I remember. We've come so far. Lost so much. I can't bear to think about failing now."

"We won't fail," Marcus said firmly.

Melissa pushed aside her doubts. "You're right. We've planned too long, worked too hard. Nothing can stop us now."

She turned back to the second map. "We'll need to coordinate safe houses for the teams to lay low after the attacks. And escape routes."

Molina joined her at the table. "Already in progress. Cannon's working on it."

"Good," Melissa said. "What about supplies? Some of these targets will require specialized equipment."

"Cannon's handling that too," Marcus replied. "He's got connections we don't want to know about."

Melissa's lips thinned. "I still don't trust him completely."

Marcus shrugged. "We don't have to trust him. We just need him to do his job."

"And if he doesn't?" Melissa asked.

Molina's eyes hardened. "Then we'll deal with it. Like we always do."

Melissa nodded, satisfied. She didn't adore Eugene Cannon like Molina did. But if Cannon incurred Molina's wrath, it would be the last thing he ever did. Cannon had a strong preservation instinct. She expected him to rely on it.

Melissa focused on the map again, tracing the route between targets. "We'll need to synchronize the attacks carefully. Even a few minutes' delay could give them time to react, to protect other targets."

"I've also got Cannon working on a secure communication system," Molina said. "Each team will receive the go signal simultaneously."

Melissa raised an eyebrow. "And if the signal fails?"

"Then they proceed at the designated time," Molina said. "Every member of each team knows failure is not an option."

Melissa grimaced. "We can't afford another Daisy."

Molina caressed her arm. "Don't let that eat at you. We learned from it. We're stronger now."

Melissa took a deep breath. "You're right. And after this they'll have no choice but to take us seriously."

"They'll do more than take us seriously," Molina said harshly. "They'll fear us. And that fear will force change."

Melissa met his gaze, seeing the same fire that burned within her. Kindred souls.

"For the Earth," she said softly.

"For the future," Molina replied.

They turned back to the map, immersing themselves in their preparations. They plotted the downfall of those who would destroy the planet.

On July 4 the world would see fury unleashed.

CHAPTER 10

Washington, DC

KIM PACED THE LENGTH of the hotel room. Her footsteps were muffled by the worn carpet. Smithers leaned against the wall, arms crossed, while Lee sat perched on the edge of her seat.

"We're missing something," Kim said, stopping to face them. "Daisy Hawkins didn't just wake up one day as a fully formed suicide bomber. How did she reach that point? Something must have triggered her. What was it?"

Smithers nodded. "Hawkins was a pawn. What we need to know is who was playing her? Why did she agree to do this?"

Lee replied, "What about Marcus Molina? His name was on your list of disgruntled Afghanistan veterans with expertise in explosives. We've been focused on Hawkins, and we've barely scratched the surface with him."

"Good point," Kim said, turning back to the room. "What do we know about Molina?"

Smithers pushed off from the wall. "Army vet. Explosive Ordnance Disposal specialist. Served in Afghanistan. Honorably discharged a few years back. Last rank was major."

"That's the official story," Kim agreed. "But there's got to be more. You said rural North Carolina, right?"

Lee replied, "Yeah, some property he inherited after his father and brother died. Isolated area, lots of land."

Kim cocked her head. "Perfect for a training camp. Or a base of operations."

"You think eco-terrorists are operating out of there?" Smithers asked.

"It's worth checking out as a hypothesis," Kim replied. "Can you ask Gaspar to dig deeper into Molina's military background. Focus on his time in Afghanistan. Look for any incidents, connections, anything that might have pushed him toward extremism."

Smithers pulled out his phone to make the call. When he finished and rejoined the conversation, he reported, "Gaspar's on it. He said he'd prioritize Molina's Afghanistan tours and any incidents that might have occurred there."

Kim turned to Lee. "You've been through Hawkins's background. Was there any indication she'd been to North Carolina more recently?"

Lee frowned as if she had total recall of all she'd discovered thus far. "There was a gap in her activity about a month before the airport incident. During that two-week period, we saw no digital footprint or financial transactions. It's like she dropped off the grid and then resurfaced."

Kim nodded slowly. "That could have been her window. She might have been with the group behind the attack during that time. Can we confirm?"

"How?" Lee asked. "We can't exactly knock on doors and ask if anyone is running a terrorist training camp."

"No," Kim agreed. "But we might be able to place Daisy in the area. Check transportation records, car rentals, anything that might show she traveled to North Carolina during that time."

Lee stood, stretching. "I can check to see if there has been any chatter about environmental protection groups setting up shop in rural areas of North Carolina. Might give us a lead on potential training locations."

Almost before Lee finished her sentence, Kim's phone buzzed. She glanced at the screen and frowned as she read the message.

"Everything okay?" Smithers asked, pausing at the door.

"Just some bureaucratic nonsense. I'll handle it."

After they left, Kim stared at her phone, rereading the message from Finlay: "Urgent. Car outside in ten minutes."

She moved to the window, scanning the street below. A black SUV with tinted windows idled at the curb.

What could be so urgent that Finlay would risk a face-to-face meeting?

The one thing he'd been adamant about from the outset was that his fingerprints could never be found on anything related to the hunt for Jack Reacher. Whatever he wanted now must be something important to justify breaking his own first commandment.

She grabbed her jacket and headed for the elevator, instinctively checking to confirm that her weapon was where it should be. She paused to survey the lobby before stepping outside.

The air was cool against her face as Kim approached the SUV. Her senses were on high alert, scanning for any signs of trouble. The street was quiet, but she couldn't shake the feeling of being watched.

The rear door opened as she neared the SUV. Kim hesitated for a split second, then climbed inside and closed the door behind her.

Finlay sat in the back, his face grave even in the dim interior light.

The driver pulled the SUV away from the curb as soon as she was inside, merging into the flow of traffic. A sense of unease settled in her gut.

"What's this about?" she asked, facing Finlay directly.

He handed her a file. "Two hours ago, we intercepted this communication. It's encrypted and we're still working on it, but our analysts managed to pull out a few key phrases so far."

Kim opened the file and scanned the contents. Words she'd learned in the past few hours jumped out at her:

"ecoterrorists," "nationwide," "simultaneous strikes." But there was more. Phrases like "strategic targets," "maximum impact," and "environmental retribution" peppered the partially decrypted text.

She looked up at Finlay, her voice tense. "How credible is this?"

"Credible enough that I'm sitting here," he replied. "Whatever Daisy Hawkins was involved in, it was deadly serious and it's happening soon. We need to get ahead of it."

"What do you need from me?" she asked.

"You've uncovered a connection between Hawkins and an ecoterrorism group. One we hadn't picked up ourselves," Finlay said. "We've got hundreds of agents working on this now."

"So you just wanted to get the little bit of intel I've managed to gather? I'd have sent it to you if you asked. No need for the cloak and dagger," Kim replied.

"It's more than that," Finlay said. "We think they might be planning multiple attacks. The scale of what they're hinting at is unprecedented for any kind of domestic terrorism."

As the SUV wound through the city streets, Kim began to brief Finlay, revealing all she knew at this point. Which, admittedly, was nowhere near enough.

"What about potential targets?" Kim asked when she'd finished. "Any leads on where they might strike?"

Finlay shook his head. "Nothing concrete. But based on the rhetoric, we're looking at places symbolic of environmental destruction. Power plants, oil refineries, maybe even corporate headquarters of companies with poor environmental records."

"Why are you telling me all of this?" she asked.

"You're in the middle of a hornet's nest here. Real trouble is brewing, and you don't want to be caught in the crossfire," Finlay said. "Just know that Reacher won't stand down because he's a stubborn sonofabitch."

Kim nodded thoughtfully. "So what you're saying is that my chances of finding Reacher now are high if I stay the course on this."

"You and Reacher are more alike than you know." Finlay chuckled and shook his head before he expanded his warning. "If Reacher is involved, then yes. You could find him. But it might not work out the way you think it will. There will be a bright spotlight of publicity and lots of blowback if things don't go well. Count on it."

"Reacher didn't get spotlighted during the New York subway bombing investigation," Kim replied reasonably. "Why should this be different?"

"I can't cover this up for you if it goes south. Or even if it resolves successfully," Finlay warned. "You should report to Cooper. His ability to deep six inconvenient truths is well known."

Kim was already shaking her head with her lips pursed before he finished his thought.

"Let Cooper run interference. He's got means, motive, and opportunity." Finlay ignored her stubborn refusal. "He doesn't want you or Reacher spotlighted. For once, let him have his way."

"I'll consider it," Kim replied, knowing she would do no such thing. "That's as far as I'm willing to go right now."

The SUV turned onto a quiet side street, and Finlay leaned forward. "One more thing. Speculation about a connection between Daisy Hawkins's bombing attempt and domestic ecoterrorism stays between us. We can't have a mass public panic on our hands along with the rest of it."

He didn't need to insist. Kim understood the weight of the situation.

Whatever Hawkins had been doing, Kim's gut said it would make the airport incident look like a warmup. Which it probably was.

The SUV had pulled up in front of her hotel again. Kim reached for the door handle to get out.

Before she had the chance, Finlay said, "Have you seen any trace of Reacher yet?"

She gave him a solid stare. "No. Have you?"

An impatient driver blasted his horn behind the SUV. A few other vehicles joined in. The noise was overwhelming.

"We're attracting the wrong kind of attention," Finlay said by way of dismissal. "Keep in touch."

Kim stepped out of the SUV and closed the door. She watched Finlay disappear into traffic.

She was once again racing against a clock she couldn't see, working with imperfect intel and untested alliances.

Hawkins's group was out there, planning mass attacks, and she was still fumbling in the dark.

"If you're watching, Reacher, now would be a good time to give us a hand," she said aloud to no one.

CHAPTER 11

North Carolina

MARCUS MOLINA WATCHED THE bank of monitors on the wall. Beside him, Eugene Cannon stood relaxed and at ease, as if he found the situation a curiosity and nothing more. Melissa Black's fingers flew across the keyboard completing the surveillance setup.

"Audio's coming in clear," Black reported. "Visual feeds are stable on both Gary and Leslie."

Molina nodded, watching the scene unfold through the body cams worn by both patriots. The date, time, and location had been carefully selected for their final challenge.

If Gary and Leslie performed well, they'd be assigned a bigger target for the upcoming grand finale. If not, a different decision would be required.

The night-vision feed Black had set up showed the deserted strip mall near Raleigh clearly.

Gary's voice came clearly through the speakers. "This is it."

His body camera panned up to show the "Bella's Beauty" sign above the boutique cosmetics store. Bella was a chemist who had developed her own line of beauty products. Unfortunately, the research was done in a country where laws protecting animals from unethical research were nonexistent.

Formal complaints lodged with the appropriate governmental agencies and industry groups had gone unheeded by Bella and the authorities. Molina's patience was exhausted.

A while ago, Cannon had approached Bella with a simple request to cease and desist selling her cosmetics due to the animal cruelty. She had flatly refused. Her products were approved by the foreign government, she'd said. She wasn't required to do more.

Cannon had simply nodded and said, "We understand your position."

Soon, Bella would understand Molina's position, too.

"Remember the objective," Leslie's voice crackled forth from her body cam through the speaker at headquarters. "Total destruction. No mercy for animal-torturers."

Molina winced when Gary's camera jerked, accompanied by the sound of splintering wood. The feed stabilized as the two entered the back door.

"Showtime," Black whispered, her gaze glued to the monitors as she remotely disconnected alarms and wireless signals. Afterward, the shop was literally wide open for maximum destruction.

Through split screens, they watched Gary and Leslie tear through the shop. Shelves toppled. Glass shattered. Colorful liquids splattered across floors and walls.

"For the animals," Gary's voice growled as he sprayed graffiti on the flat surfaces.

Molina frowned when he checked the timer. "Tell them to hurry. They're taking too long."

Black leaned into her mic. "Wind it up. Clock's ticking."

On screen, Leslie paused. "Roger that."

Suddenly, red and blue lights flashed through the shop's windows and across the camera feeds.

"Abort!" Molina barked. "Get out now!"

The cameras swung wildly as Gary and Leslie ran for the back exit. But as they reached the door, a voice boomed from outside.

"This is the police! Come out with your hands up!"

"Dammit," Black hissed. "Where did these guys come from?"

The cameras showed Gary and Leslie spinning in circles near the back exit, trapped.

"Options?" Leslie's panicked voice came through.

"There's no way out," Cannon said as he ran a hand through his hair. "They're blown. We can't have them in custody."

On screen, Gary and Leslie raised their hands as the police stormed in, weapons drawn. The last image Molina saw was a close-up of an officer's face before Black cut both feeds to avoid detection.

She slumped back in her chair. "What now?"

Cannon's response was flat, hard, and unyielding. "Damage control."

Molina paced the small command center, sweat beading on his forehead despite the air conditioning. The humid summer heat seemed to seep through the walls.

"Scrub them from our systems," Molina said, turning to Black. "How much time do we have before the police identify them?"

"Not long. Assuming they stay strong and don't give themselves away, it could take a couple of hours. Neither one has ever been arrested, so there should be no fingerprint or DNA match," Black replied, focused on the keyboard. "I'm wiping digital footprints now. But the physical evidence at the scene can't be avoided or neutralized. We don't have any backup down there."

"We were so close." Molina slammed his fist on the desk. "They failed. We can't let that failure compromise the big operation."

"Using amateurs comes with risks. We all knew that going in," Cannon said calmly.

Black finished the cleanup and glanced at him fiercely. "If Gary or Leslie break under interrogation, we're well and totally screwed."

"You think I don't know that?" Molina snapped.

But fear gnawed at him.

He stared at the static-filled screens watching the police swarm around Gary and Leslie on the monitors.

He glanced at Cannon, who nodded. The three agreed.

Molina turned to Black, his voice ice-cold. "Initiate the Protocol."

Black nodded, repeating her complete agreement. "Sending the signal now."

On the screens, Gary and Leslie suddenly convulsed, both body cams shaking violently.

Leslie collapsed to the ground and stopped breathing as confused shouts and chaos erupted from the police.

Gary went down next.

"Poison capsules," Cannon murmured with satisfaction. "Implanted before they set out. They don't know. The capsules are untraceable and fast-acting."

"Perfect," Molina said, nodding approval.

After several minutes of fruitless effort, Police stopped CPR and called time of death on both bodies.

Black said, "It's done. They're gone."

Cannon nodded. "Confirm you've removed everything. Gary and Leslie were never connected to us in any way. They must be totally eliminated from all of our systems immediately."

For the next hour, they worked in tense silence. Black scrubbed databases, erased records, and planted false leads. Cannon checked her work as Molina made calls, his voice low and threatening as he ensured that all loose ends would be tied up permanently.

Much later, Black leaned back in her chair. "It's done. Gary and Leslie never existed."

Cannon stood by the window, watching the sky lighten. "And we live to fight another day."

"We're short staffed now. We were counting on Gary and Leslie to round out the star patriots. It's too late to replace them or abort the selected target." Molina turned to them both, his eyes glinting with a dangerous light. "The operation continues as planned."

Black matched his fierce grin. "It'll be a blaze of glory no one will ever forget."

"Exactly," Molina nodded.

"Let's not get ahead of ourselves," Cannon warned. "For now, we adapt. We evolve."

Molina added, "And soon we remind this country what true patriots are willing to do."

The day's setback was already forgotten, not even a footnote in the grand plan. Very soon, Molina would have his reckoning, and all of America would feel his fury.

CHAPTER 12

Washington, DC

THERESA LEE SAT ACROSS from Senator John Sansom in his Georgetown home study. In the past few minutes, a fierce summer storm had rolled in, complete with thunder, lightning, and driving rain.

The antique clock on the mantle ticked softly. Heavy curtains shrouded the windows as an imperfect shield against surveillance.

They'd chosen to meet here, away from Sansom's office on Capitol Hill, to avoid unwanted attention. The less anyone knew about this conversation, the better.

"Otto has agreed to work with me on the Docherty case," Lee reported. "In return, I'm helping her with their search for Reacher."

"Has my name come up in these discussions?" Sansom asked.

"Only insofar as I told them I'm working for you. They don't know that you were involved in the old subway bombing case or that you know Reacher."

"Keep it that way." Sansom nodded, his expression neutral. "What have you uncovered?"

"Not as much as I'd hoped," she replied. "We've established a fragile connection between Daisy Hawkins and a man named Marcus Molina."

Sansom's eyes narrowed. "Molina? Any relation to Peter Molina from the New York case?"

Lee leaned forward. "Unconfirmed. But I believe they were half-brothers. Same father, different mothers."

"Peter Molina," Sansom mused, his fingers drumming on the polished mahogany desk. "His mother was the suicide bomber in that subway incident. The one involving Reacher."

"Exactly," Lee confirmed. "Peter's body was found after she died, but we thought at the time that his death was the motivator for the mother's actions. Marcus being Peter's half-brother could explain a lot about his motives, too."

Sansom stood, moving to a cabinet against the wall. He poured two glasses of scotch, handed one to Lee. "What else do we know about Marcus Molina?"

"Still working up the profile," Lee took a sip before answering. "We know he's an Army vet. EOD specialist. Served in Afghanistan. Now he owns property in rural North Carolina. It's been in his mother's family for generations."

"An Army vet? I can run down his experience and military record without drawing attention to the case," Samson said.

"He'll have had extensive training in munitions as well as experience with suicide bombers."

"Yes. Which means we're dealing with a guy who is much more sophisticated than Daisy Hawkins," Lee replied.

"Definitely," Sansom agreed. "As for the rural property, it sounds like an ideal location for an eco-terrorism base of operations."

Lee replied, "Otto thinks so too. We're investigating further."

Sansom returned to his desk, glass in hand. "And Daisy Hawkins?"

"There's a two-week gap in her digital footprint about a month before the airport incident. We're trying to pinpoint her location during that time."

"You suspect she was with Molina?"

"It's a possibility we're exploring."

Sansom's expression turned grave. "Any progress on finding Docherty's killer?"

Lee shook her head. "Not yet, but I'm working on it. I believe this North Carolina connection might lead us there."

Sansom's personal cell phone buzzed. He glanced at it and frowned. "Interesting. I put some quiet feelers out. One's come through. Looks like Reacher was spotted in Virginia two days ago."

Lee straightened. "How reliable is the information?"

"Usually quite dependable. The sighting was in a small town just across the state line."

"That's close," Lee said thoughtfully. "Could Reacher be aware of Molina and the potential connection to Docherty's murder? The Atlanta airport situation was covered on national news. Reacher might have seen it. I'm not sure how he'd have made a connection to Molina, though."

Sansom shrugged. "With Reacher, it's hard to say. He's clever. Knows things most people don't. He's got Army contacts, too. So he could have made the connection. Either way, it's worth following up."

Lee nodded, already formulating a plan. "I'll head to Virginia tomorrow morning. See if I can pick up his trail."

Sansom warned, "Approaching Reacher could be challenging."

"I can handle myself, Senator. I wouldn't have this job if I couldn't." Lee's lips curved into a sour grin. "Reacher and I have history. He might be willing to talk to me."

Sansom nodded but his concern seemed to linger. "Ecoterrorism poses a significant domestic threat. Potential targets could include major infrastructure, corporate entities known for environmental violations, even government facilities. We can't afford any missteps."

"Understood," Lee replied. She finished her scotch. "I should go. Long day today and another one tomorrow."

As she reached the door, Sansom said, "Theresa?"

She turned back. "Yes?"

"Be cautious with Otto. Her allegiances are complex."

Lee nodded, acknowledging the warning. "I'll keep that in mind."

"One more thing," Sansom added. "If Molina's using the skills we trained him to master, we could be looking at a whole new level of ecoterrorism."

Lee paused, hand on the doorknob. "What are you thinking?"

Sansom stood, pacing behind his desk. "EOD specialists don't just know how to defuse bombs. They know how to make them. And if Molina's got a grudge against Reacher, he'll be doubly dangerous."

"You're worried that he might be planning something to draw Reacher out," Lee finished. "You're worried that he blames Reacher for his brother's murder."

"Exactly," Sansom nodded. "And with that property in North Carolina, he's got the space and privacy to plan whatever he wants."

Lee turned back to face Sansom fully. "Otto is working on getting satellite imagery of the property. But given the urgency, do you have faster channels?"

Sansom raised an eyebrow. "I might be able to expedite things. I'll see what I can do without raising any flags."

"Time isn't on our side here," Lee said.

Sansom nodded. "Do what you need to do. But remember, this goes beyond just finding Docherty's killer now."

"I know," Lee said.

"Keep my name out of this. Stay under the radar. Lots of people know you work for me and if you're targeted, I'm targeted," Sansom said.

"Got it."

"And Theresa? Watch your back," Sansom warned. "If Molina is half as dangerous as we think he is, this could get very ugly very fast."

"I'll find Reacher and we'll go from there. Whatever it takes," she said flatly on her way out.

CHAPTER 13

Monday, July 1
Mill River, Virginia

"I'M HEADED TO MILL River, Virginia," Lee said into her phone when the call from Smithers came through. "Good intel says Reacher was spotted there two days ago."

Smithers's voice crackled through the speaker. "Hold on. Does Otto know about this?"

Lee hesitated. "Not yet. I wanted to check it out first. Could be a wild goose chase. I didn't want to waste her time."

"You know that's not how this works," Smithers's tone was conciliatory but firm. "We agreed you wouldn't chase leads alone, regardless of how good the intel is. In fact, if you have good intel, you need to tell us first, not after you've vetted the tips."

"I'm not trying to step on toes here, Smithers. But we need to move fast on this. Reacher could be long gone by the time I do all of that," Lee replied, keeping her gaze on the road.

Smithers sighed. "Otto won't see it that way. She'll want to be there and handle this herself."

"Then let's give her something solid to work with. I'll do a quick recon and report back. If it's promising, Otto can take point from there."

A pause on the line. "She won't like it. But you're halfway there. If you actually spot Reacher, do not engage. Call it in immediately and we'll catch up. Clear?"

"Crystal clear," Lee replied before she ended the call.

Three hours later, Lee approached the small town of Mill River, Virginia. The town stretched along a single main street. Brick buildings from the early 1900s lined both sides. American flags hung from lamp posts. A few locals strolled the sidewalks. They nodded to each other as they passed.

She parked her car in front of Dot's Diner. The building's white paint peeled at the edges. Weathered wood showed beneath. Its neon sign flickered. The "D" occasionally went dark.

A bell jingled as she entered. Coffee and grease scented the air. Formica tables lined the windows. Locals hunched over plates of eggs and toast. They looked up briefly from their breakfasts, then returned to their plates.

Lee approached the counter. A middle-aged waitress wiped the surface with a rag. Her name tag said she was Dot, the diner's namesake.

"Coffee, please," Lee said. "And some information, if you're willing."

Dot poured a cup and slid it across the counter. "Information's free. Coffee's a buck fifty."

Lee placed a five-dollar bill on the counter. "I'm looking for someone who passed through here recently. Big guy, over six feet tall, probably wearing jeans and a plain T-shirt."

Dot's eyes narrowed. "You a cop?"

"No," Lee replied. "Just looking for an old friend."

"Uh-huh." She was unconvinced. "Lot of people come through here. Can't say I remember anyone specific like that."

"He might have asked about local history or landmarks. He's interested in that sort of thing." She pulled out her phone and showed the waitress a photo. "This is him. Have you seen this man?"

Dot leaned in, squinting at the screen. Her eyes widened with recognition. "There was a fella few days ago who looked something like that. Asked about the old Civil War sites around here."

"Did he say where he was headed next?"

"Nope. But he was interested in the battle of Grand Cedar. Took place about an hour from here."

Lee nodded and sipped her coffee. "Anything else you remember about him?"

Dot seemed to think about the question for a moment. "Yeah, actually. He paid with an old two-dollar bill. Said it was for good luck."

Lee took note of this detail. "Thanks, that's helpful. Any other strangers been through town lately?"

Dot shrugged. "Some environmental researchers were asking about abandoned properties in the area recently. Said they were doing a study on land use."

"Environmental researchers?"

"Yeah. Talking about saving the planet and all that."

Lee gulped the rest of her coffee and left a five-dollar bill on the counter. "One last thing. Any motels around here where my friend might have stayed?"

"Just the Pinewood Inn on the edge of town. Can't miss it."

Lee stood and placed another five on the counter between them. "Thanks for your help."

Outside, Lee pulled her phone from her pocket and pressed the redial. Smithers answered on the first ring.

"I've got a lead. Reacher was here, asked about Civil War sites. I'm heading to check out the local motel."

"Good work," Smithers replied. "Did you learn anything about ecoterrorism groups in the area?"

"Maybe. Some environmental researchers were asking about abandoned properties. Could be nothing, but worth looking into."

"Agreed. Keep me posted."

Lee disconnected, used her phone to search for directions to the Pinewood Inn. She followed the navigation and arrived ten minutes later. The place was small, with peeling paint and a flickering vacancy sign. Just the sort of place where she imagined Reacher would stay, given his spending and travel habits.

She parked in the lot and walked around the potholes to the front entrance.

Inside, the office smelled of pine scented disinfectant attempting to cover stale food and body odors. A slovenly clerk sat behind the desk.

"I need to know if this man stayed here recently," Lee said. She showed the man her photo of Reacher.

He barely glanced at it. "Can't give out information on guests."

Lee placed a fifty-dollar bill on the desk. "It's important."

The clerk pocketed the money and looked at the photo again. "Yeah, he was here. Checked out."

"When?"

He shrugged.

"Did he leave anything behind?"

"Didn't have nothing with him to leave. Walked in here with just the clothes on his back and whatever he had in his pockets," the clerk replied.

"Say where he was going?"

"He did ask about buying an old truck. Told him about the place down the street. Sells used wrecks for cheap, which was what he said he wanted." The clerk pointed with his thumb.

Lee nodded. "Thanks."

Back in her car, Lee called Smithers again.

"Reacher was here, but he's gone. He might have access to an old truck now. I'm going to see if I can get any information about that. We might be able to trace the vehicle."

"Keep in touch," Smithers said. "We've got a possible lead on suspect activity near Richmond to check out. We'll regroup later today."

"On my way," Lee replied as she started the car and pulled out of the motel parking lot.

Reacher had been here, asked about Civil War sites, and acquired a vehicle. But why? And did any of this connect to Docherty's murder?

Questions without answers were piling up faster than she could count them.

CHAPTER 14

North Carolina

MARCUS MOLINA DESCENDED THE narrow staircase into the underground bunker beneath the main compound. The reinforced steel door hissed shut behind him, sealing out the world above. Here, twenty feet below the earth, was where the real planning happened.

Melissa Black stood at the far end of the room. A large digital map of the United States dominated the center screen, red dots pulsing at key locations.

The underground bunker hummed with the low drone of air filtration systems and computer servers. Cool, recycled air carried a faint metallic tang. LED lighting cast harsh shadows across the room's steel and concrete surfaces, giving everything a clinical, almost alien appearance.

Molina's boots echoed on the polished concrete floor as he crossed to join Black. The main screen's glow painted their faces in an eerie blue light, highlighting the exhaustion etched there. Empty coffee mugs and energy bar wrappers littered a nearby desk after their marathon planning session.

"Status report," Molina said, crossing the room to join her.

Black's taut expression carried to her words. "We're on schedule, but there's a hiccup at the Liberty Fuel Pipeline."

Molina's eyes narrowed. "What kind of hiccup?"

"They've upgraded their security protocols. Our insider at the control center says we'll need to adjust our timing."

Molina leaned in, studying the pipeline's route on the screen. "Show me."

Black pulled up a detailed schematic of the pipeline to display on the big screen.

"We were planning to hit these three points simultaneously," she said, indicating blinking markers. "But with the new system, we'll have a shorter window at the northern station."

"How much shorter?"

"Four minutes, maybe five."

Molina exhaled slowly. "That's cutting it close. What about our other targets?"

Black swiped the screen to bring up a list. "Ten locations, as planned. The teams are moving into place, waiting for the signal."

Molina nodded, his eyes scanning the list. A coal plant in West Virginia. A chemical facility in Texas. A controversial dam project in Oregon. Each target carefully chosen for maximum impact.

"And our operatives?"

"Sixty-eight, spread across all locations. We're stretched thin, but it's doable."

As they discussed the operatives, Molina paced the length of the room, his movements sharp and agitated. He paused at a wall covered in photos and maps, each representing a piece of their grand plan. His fingers traced the outline of the Liberty Fuel Pipeline, feeling the weight of what they were about to unleash.

Black remained at the computer station, her posture rigid as she pulled up file after file. The clicking of rapid-fire keys punctuated the conversation with a staccato rhythm emphasizing the tension.

Molina rubbed his eyes, fatigue settling in. They'd been working nonstop since he'd declared the countdown, fine-tuning every aspect of the plan.

"What about our key players? The patriots who won't be coming back?"

Black straightened, a hint of pride in her voice. "Ten suicide operatives, one for each target. All have passed final evaluations. I've personally vetted each one. They're as ready as we can make them."

Molina nodded. Black's ability to read people, to find those willing to make the ultimate sacrifice, was unparalleled. It was her forte, the reason she was invaluable.

They scrolled through the profiles. Among them were: a former soldier, eyes hardened by tours in Afghanistan; a young college dropout, her face alight with fervent belief;

an older man with terminal cancer, determined to give his death meaning. Each of the ten heroes were perfect for the mission.

"Garcia concerns me," Molina said, pausing on one file. "His psych evaluation showed some hesitation."

Black nodded. "I've been monitoring him closely. His commitment to the cause is absolute, but he'll leave a sister behind. It's weighing on him."

"Is he reliable?"

"Yes," Black said firmly. "When the time comes, he'll do what needs to be done. I'm one hundred percent certain."

Molina studied her for a moment. "Like you were with Daisy Hawkins?"

Black's jaw tightened, but she didn't flinch. "Hawkins was an anomaly. A mistake I won't repeat. These ten? They're solid. I'd bet my life on it."

Molina held her gaze for a moment longer, then nodded. "Good. Because we'll be betting a lot more than that."

"Yes," Black said firmly. "As I said, when the time comes, Garcia will do what needs to be done. And so will the others."

Molina studied the faces on the screen. A diverse group, each chosen for their unique skills and unwavering dedication. The culmination of years of planning and preparation.

"We've come so far," he murmured. "There's no turning back now."

Molina's comment about Daisy Hawkins hung in the air like a physical presence. Black's fingers stilled on the keyboard, her knuckles white with tension. For a moment, the only sound was the soft whir of cooling fans and the distant drip of a leaky pipe somewhere in the bunker's infrastructure.

Then Black stood and squared her shoulders. She moved to a large tactical board on the opposite wall, covered in timelines and contingency plans. "I've triple-checked every variable. We've planned for every conceivable outcome."

Molina joined her at the board, shoulders nearly touching as they surveyed the intricate web of plans. "And the inconceivable ones?"

Black's lips quirked in a humorless smile. "That's where faith comes in. Faith in the cause. Faith in our people."

Molina nodded slowly. He scanned the images of their chosen martyrs one last time. Each one a true believer, ready to die for the planet. For a future they would never see.

The moment was broken by the sudden flashing of the red alert light. The harsh, intermittent red glow turned the bunker into a scene from a nightmare, shadows leaping and retreating with each pulse.

Suddenly, a red light also began flashing silently above the bunker's entrance. Molina and Black exchanged alarmed glances.

"Unauthorized entry alert," Black said, moving swiftly to the control panel near the door.

Molina nodded, his hand instinctively moving to the weapon at his hip. "Identify," he commanded.

Black's fingers flew over the keypad. A small screen flickered to life, showing a young man in camouflage fatigues standing in the antechamber above, his face pale and drawn.

"It's Ramirez," Black said, recognition in her voice. "From the Montana camp."

Molina's eyes narrowed. "Let him in."

The heavy door slid open with a pneumatic hiss. Ramirez stumbled in, breathing hard as if he'd run the whole way.

"Sir," he gasped. "We've got a problem."

Molina straightened. "What is it?"

"The Montana training camp. It's been raided. Local law enforcement. They've arrested at least a dozen of our people."

Black's eyes widened. "How? That location was secure."

Ramirez shook his head. "We don't know, but... there's evidence it wasn't random. Someone tipped them off."

Molina felt the blood drain from his face. A mole. A traitor in their midst.

He locked eyes with Black, seeing his own shock and anger reflected there. Everything they'd worked for was suddenly balanced on a knife's edge.

"Lock down all communications," Molina ordered. "No one goes in or out of any facility without my direct authorization. Find the leak and find it now."

As Black and Ramirez rushed to comply with Molina's orders, the bunker erupted into controlled chaos. Screens flashed with incoming data, printers spat out updated reports, and the air filled with the urgent chatter of secure communications being established with their remote cells.

Molina stood at the center of it all, a pillar of calm in the storm. He turned back to the main screen, where the map of their targets still glowed. Each pulsing red dot represented years of planning, countless sacrifices, and the future of the planet itself.

Soon, the world would be changed forever. The only question was whether his team would be the ones to change it, or if an unseen enemy would bring it all crashing down around them.

CHAPTER 15

Mill River, Virginia

LEE PULLED INTO THE parking lot of Mill River Car Rentals. The small office sat in a converted gas station. The faded logo was still visible beneath a fresh coat of paint. She walked across the potholes in the parking lot toward the entrance. The air smelled of hot asphalt and car exhaust.

She entered the office. A blast of cold air hit her as the door swung shut. A young man in a polo shirt looked up from his computer, his fingers paused mid-type.

"Can I help you?" he asked.

Lee approached the counter, spying his name tag. "Mike, I need some information about a customer who might have been looking for a vehicle here recently."

Mike looked up from the screen, indicating she'd captured his attention.

She showed him Reacher's photo on her phone. "He would have been here in the last few days."

Mike's eyes narrowed. He leaned back in his chair, crossing his arms. "We don't give out customer information. Company policy."

"That's a good policy," Lee nodded. "But this is important. I'm not asking for anything confidential. Just confirmation that he was here and what kind of vehicle you hooked him up with."

Mike cocked his head and aimed an inquisitive stare her way. "Are you with the police?"

"No," Lee admitted. "I'm a private investigator. This man is a person of interest in a case I'm working on."

Mike frowned. "I could lose my job."

Lee leaned in slightly. "Look, I'm not asking you to do anything illegal. I'm just trying to find this man. He's not in trouble, but his family is worried about him. They haven't heard from him in a while."

She pulled out a generic white business card with her name, phone number, and the words Private Investigator under it. She placed the card on the counter. "I'm just asking for a little help to ease his family's mind."

Mike glanced at the card, then back at Lee. He sighed. "What exactly do you want to know?"

"Thank you, Mike. You're doing a good thing here." Lee's tone patted his head as she smiled. "Can you tell me what kind of vehicle he bought?"

Mike's expression had softened slightly, although he was still wary. He glanced at Reacher's photo again. "Hard to forget a guy that size. It was a crappy old SUV."

"What kind of SUV?" Lee pressed.

Mike hesitated, then said, "He said he wanted something cheap. Took a ten-year-old Chevy. Black."

"Did he use a credit card?" Lee asked.

"Paid cash, which was unusual. Most folks use a card these days."

"What about the title work? Insurance? Plates?" Lee asked.

Mike shook his head. "Brought his own license plates with him and said he'd deal with the insurance later. He wasn't interested in waiting for a new title. Said he'd get it later."

Lee nodded encouragingly. "Did he say where he was going?"

"Nah, he didn't mention."

"Can I get a copy of the sales agreement?" Lee was pushing her luck, but now that the kid was cooperating, it seemed like a good time to press him.

He shook his head. "Nope. Sorry. That's a breach of policy for sure. I need this job."

"Okay, just give me the license plate number," Lee said, backing off a bit. "It could make all the difference."

Mike ran a hand through his hair, conflict clear on his face. After a long moment, he turned to his computer and punched a few keys with his index fingers.

"Okay," he said, scribbling on a piece of paper. He slid it across the counter. "But you didn't get this from me."

Lee pocketed the paper without looking at it. "Thank you. One more thing. There was a protest in town recently. Do you know anything about that?"

"Yeah, it was happening when your guy bought the car." Mike's eyebrows arched over his brown eyes as if he were surprised by the question. "Bunch of college kids with signs outside Mill River Research Park. Some cosmetic company there does animal testing and they're dumping chemicals in the water, or something."

"Any violence? Property damage?"

He shook his head. "Nah, nothing like that. Just a lot of yelling and sign-waving. Didn't last long. No idea how it ended up."

Lee nodded. "Thanks for your help, Mike. You've done a good thing today."

As she turned to leave, Mike called out, "Hey, is Reacher in some kind of trouble?"

Lee paused at the door, her hand on the handle as a frisson of electricity raced up her spine. Mike knew Reacher's name. Which meant Reacher had actually been here. Up until that moment, she hadn't been certain.

"I hope not. But if he comes back or if anyone asks about him, give me a call." She handed him her card.

Outside, the heat hit her like a wall. Lee leaned against her car, the metal hot enough to burn against her back. She pulled out her phone and dialed Smithers with the good news. When he didn't pick up, she left a message simply saying she'd call back.

Lee drove through Mill River, following directions to the Mill River Research Park where the protest was held. The "park" turned out to be a single-story building surrounded by a chain-link fence. A sign near the entrance read "Radiant Beauty Labs: Innovative Cosmetics Research."

She parked across the street and approached the security guard at the gate.

"Excuse me," she said. "I'm looking for a friend who might have been here recently." She showed the guard Reacher's photo. "I heard there was a protest here. I'm wondering if he might have been involved."

The guard, a middle-aged man with a weathered face, studied the photo. "Don't recognize him. But there were a lot of people here that day. Bunch of kids with signs, mostly. Someone from the local TV station. That's about it."

"What were they protesting?" Lee asked, feigning ignorance.

"Animal testing," the guard said. "But they kept going on about bigger issues too. Climate change, corporate greed. You know the type."

Lee nodded. "My friend's always been interested in causes like that. Did you notice anyone who seemed to be organizing things? Maybe someone older than the students?"

He thought for a moment. "There was one woman. Bit older than the rest. Kept talking to them, seemed to be giving directions."

"What did she look like?"

"Very short dark hair. Athletic," he said, as if he were trying to recall her image. "She had a weird tattoo on her left arm."

"Tattoos are pretty normal these days. Weird in what way?" Lee asked.

"It looked like a boy's face, I'd say. It kind of resembled her. Similar short haircut. Normal features," he replied.

"Did you hear anyone call her by name?"

He shook his head. "Sorry."

"Thanks," Lee said. "Any idea where the protesters hung out when they weren't here?"

The guard shrugged. "Try the coffee shop down the street. The Daily Grind. They spent a lot of time there."

Lee thanked him and walked to the coffee shop. Inside, she approached the counter where a young woman with bright blue hair stood near the cash register.

"I'm looking for a friend who might have been here during the protest at the research park." She showed the barista Reacher's photo. "Have you seen him?"

The barista shook her head. "Sorry, don't recognize him. But we had a lot of protesters in and out for a couple of days."

Lee nodded, looking disappointed. "He's always getting involved in causes. I was hoping to catch up with him. Did you notice anyone who seemed to be leading the group? Maybe someone older than the students?"

The barista's eyes lit up. "Oh yeah, there was this one woman. She wasn't a student. Kept talking about how the cosmetics protest was just the start. Said they had bigger plans."

"That sounds like something my friend would be interested in," Lee said. "Did you hear any details about these plans? Or where they might be headed next?"

"She didn't give details," the barista said. "Just kept saying they needed to think bigger, that small protests weren't enough anymore."

"Tall woman, short dark hair, with a boy's face tattooed on her left arm?" Lee asked as a formality.

She nodded and then hesitated. "I probably shouldn't say this, but I overheard her on the phone. She mentioned something about Grand Cedar. Said they were moving on to the next phase there."

Lee widened her eyes with feigned excitement. "Grand Cedar? That's great, actually. My friend mentioned something about Civil War sites. Maybe that's where he was headed. Thanks so much for your help."

She left the coffee shop thinking the protest seemed minor, but the mention of bigger plans and Grand Cedar was intriguing. It might be nothing, but it was worth checking out, given Reacher's apparent interest.

Maybe she could find photos of the woman with the tattoo. She glanced around the area of the coffee shop attempting to identify CCTV cameras. She didn't spy any. Which didn't mean they weren't there.

CHAPTER 16

Mill River, Virginia

THE ACRID SMELL OF exhaust fumes hung in the air as Lee's eyes locked onto a man in a dark jacket across the street. His face was obscured by shadows as he watched her intently. The hairs on the back of her neck prickled when she met his gaze. He turned away with practiced nonchalance, his movements too smooth to be natural.

A van, paintwork dulled with grime, careened into the parking lot, brakes squealing as it lurched to a stop beside her.

Before Lee could react, the van's side door flew open with an ear-splitting metallic squeal. Two men burst out. The first lunged for her with grasping, meaty hands. Lee ducked, feeling the rush of air as his arm swung over her head.

She drove her elbow upward, connecting solidly with his solar plexus. His breath whooshed in a pained wheeze as he doubled over.

Lee pivoted to grab the second man's outstretched arm and used his momentum to slam him against a nearby car. The impact reverberated through the car and his head bounced off the roof with a resounding crack. He slumped against the vehicle, eyes glazed.

Her escape was cut off by the first man, still gasping for air with a gun leveled at her chest. The barrel looked impossibly large.

"Get in the van," he rasped, his voice raw with pain and barely contained fury.

The street stretched empty in both directions. No potential witnesses or saviors. No convenient weapons, either.

"Okay. Okay," Lee said steadily, as if gentling a rabid animal. She raised her hands slowly, palms out in a gesture of surrender.

The sudden blare of a car horn cut through the tension. A sedan came tearing around the corner, tires squealing as it barreled forward.

The gunman's gaze snapped toward the sound, dividing his attention for a crucial second.

Lee seized her chance.

Her hands blurred into motion, chopping down on the man's wrist with brutal precision.

His gun clattered to the ground and skittered beneath the van out of reach while his eyes widened in shock and pain.

Lee threw a solid punch. Her fist connected with the gunman's face in a satisfying crunch. Blood spurted from his nose as he howled in agony, hands flying up to staunch the flow.

The sedan screeched to a halt, and the passenger door flew open.

"Get in!" the woman yelled, urgent and commanding. She looked harmless enough. Maybe thirty years old, slender, blond hair in a ponytail, wearing jeans and a baseball cap firmly pulled down to shield her face.

Lee sprinted for the sedan and hurled herself into the passenger seat. The leather was cool against her skin.

Before she could fully close the door, the car surged forward, tires spinning on the asphalt. Lee grabbed the door handle and yanked the door shut against the rushing wind.

In the side mirror, she watched as the failed kidnappers stumbled toward the van. Their reflection paled as the sedan sped away, leaving behind the lingering scent of burnt rubber.

"Who are you?" Lee asked, as soon as she could steady her breathing.

"Zoe Seltzer," the woman replied, focused on the road. "I saw what was happening. Couldn't just drive by."

In the mirror, Lee watched the van which was now following them.

They raced through the narrow Mill River streets with the van closing the gap behind them. Zoe must have had some high-speed and evasive maneuvers training because she drove expertly. At the first opportunity, she turned down an alley, tires squealing.

The alley ended at an eight-foot cyclone fence strung tight across the exit. Zoe kept the pedal to the metal and approached at full speed.

"Stop! You can't bust through that fence!" Lee shouted.

Zoe hit the brakes. The car spun sideways and stopped within inches of the barrier to create an additional roadblock.

The van turned into the alley zooming toward them.

Zoe killed the engine. "Run!"

They dashed from the car and squeezed through a gap between the wall and the fence. A moment later, the van reached the alley's end and screeched to a full stop, inches from Zoe's sedan.

Before the goons could get out of the van, both women ran toward a busy street. Zoe took the lead. She entered a six-story building, found the staircase, and climbed to the roof. Lee followed close behind.

At the rooftop, they paused for a moment.

Breathing hard, Lee said, "Thank you. But why did you help me?"

Zoe's eyes narrowed. "I've seen those men before. They were at the Radiant Labs protest."

Lee studied Zoe's sweat-stained face. Her spiky brown hair and the tattoo on her right biceps matched the description of the protest leader from the coffee shop.

"You were there?" Lee asked.

Zoe nodded. "And I heard things. Plans. I think you just got caught in the middle of it."

"What kind of things?" Lee asked.

Before Zoe could answer, Lee heard two sets of heavy shoes pounding up the stairs.

Zoe grabbed Lee's arm and pulled her toward a utility shed on the other side of the roof.

"Quick, in here," she whispered urgently.

They squeezed inside the small structure just as the roof door burst open.

Through a crack in the shed's door, Lee watched the two goons fan out across the roof.

"Where'd they go?" one man growled.

"Stop yapping and search. They have to be here somewhere," the other replied angrily.

Lee felt Zoe tap her shoulder. She turned to see Zoe pointing at a maintenance ladder inside the shed. It led down into the building.

With Zoe leading the way and as quietly as possible, they began to descend the ladder. Lee had to hope the noise of the two men searching would mask any sound they made.

Just as she reached the floor below, she heard a shout from above.

"The shed! Check the shed!"

Zoe's eyes widened. "Run!" she mouthed silently.

They took off down the hallway, the sound of footsteps pounding down the ladder echoing behind them.

Lee and Zoe raced away, footsteps echoing off the bare walls. They reached a stairwell and descended, taking the steps two at a time.

"We need to split up," Zoe said between breaths. "I'll lead them away. You get to safety and call for help."

Before Lee could protest, Zoe burst through a door on the next landing, deliberately making noise. The shouts from above grew louder, following Zoe's path.

Lee continued racing down the stairs.

She reached the ground floor and cautiously peered out of the stairwell door. The lobby was empty.

Lee slipped out and headed for the main entrance.

Just as she reached for the exit, a hand grabbed her shoulder. Lee spun around, ready to fight.

"Wait!" Zoe hissed, snatching her hand away as if touching Lee had burned her. "They're outside."

Through the glass doors, Lee saw the van parked across the street. The two men were scanning the area like heat-seeking missiles.

"There's another way out," Zoe whispered. "Through the basement. Come on."

Reluctantly, Lee followed Zoe back to the stairwell and headed below ground.

They descended to the basement level, eventually emerging into a dimly lit parking garage.

"My car's here." Zoe led the way to a nondescript sedan. "We need to get out. Fast."

Lee hesitated. "I can't just leave. What about my car?"

Zoe's expression hardened. "Those men are dangerous. Armed muscle like that goes way beyond a small-town college kid protest."

"What do you know about it?" Lee demanded.

"We need to go. Now." Zoe glanced nervously at the garage entrance. "I'll tell you everything once we're on the road."

Lee weighed her options. Zoe had just saved her life, but she was also involved in whatever all this was about.

The sound of a door slamming echoed through the garage. Footsteps approached.

"Decision time," Zoe said, her hand on the car door. "Are you coming or not?"

CHAPTER 17

Mill River, Virginia

THE SEDAN'S ENGINE ROARED as Zoe weaved through traffic, her eyes flicking between the road ahead and the rearview mirror. Her short, dark hair, styled in an edgy undercut with a wide pink streak in the front, whipped around her face as the wind rushed through the partially open window. The sleeve of her leather jacket rode up, revealing intricate tattoos snaking up her forearm.

Theresa Lee, still catching her breath in the passenger seat, took a hard look at Zoe's sharp, angular features displaying her intense concentration. Piercing eyes scanned for any sign of pursuit. She seemed impossibly young. Mid-twenties at most.

When Zoe slowed and turned onto a side street, Lee broke the tense silence. "Who are you? And why are you helping me?"

Zoe's grip tightened on the steering wheel, her knuckles whitening. She gave Lee a quick glance, wary and determined. "Let's just say I've got a vested interest in keeping you alive."

Lee's eyebrows shot up. "Why?"

A bitter smile played across Zoe's lips. "I've been tracking EcoGuard's operations for the past three years."

"Ever since what?" Lee pressed, sensing a personal connection.

Zoe took a deep breath with barely contained emotion. "Ever since their goons killed my little brother at a protest. Cameron was only seventeen. He was just a kid standing up for what he believed in, and they gunned him down like he was nothing."

Lee's expression softened. "I'm so sorry. That must have been devastating."

Zoe nodded, her eyes glistening. "It was. But it also lit a fire in me. Gave me a purpose I didn't have before. I've dedicated my life to exposing and taking down these charlatans. I've infiltrated activist groups, gathering intel, and I'm building a case. If I can't get the government interested in prosecution, I'll go to the media."

"You're an activist?" Lee realized Zoe's youthful appearance and edgy style would help her blend in with those crowds.

"That's the cover, yeah," Zoe replied, a hint of pride in her voice. "I've made a name for myself in those circles. It's given me access to information I'd never get through official channels."

As she pulled into an underground parking garage, Zoe finally allowed herself to relax slightly. She turned to Lee, "Look, I know you've got no reason to trust me. But I've been watching EcoGuard's crew. They're not at all what they want you to believe. When I saw them go after you, I couldn't just stand by and let it happen."

Lee studied her for a long moment. "Thank you. For saving me back there, and now that you've explained things, I think we might be able to help each other."

"That's what I'm counting on. Together, we might just have a shot at bringing these thugs down once and for all." Zoe smiled, reaching into her pocket. She pulled out a small object, palmed it briefly, and then handed it over.

Lee took the zip drive. "What's this?"

"Everything I've gathered so far. Solid evidence of enough crimes to keep the courts busy. At the very least, we can get these jerks off the money train. Heads should roll," Zoe said. "If anything happens to me, will you see that it gets to the right people?"

"Who are the right people?" Lee asked, frowning.

"Take it to my boss. He'll know what to do with it," Zoe replied.

Lee stuffed the zip drive into one of her pockets before Zoe could change her mind and ask for it back. "Who's your boss?"

"He's on the zip drive, too," Zoe said. "Don't worry."

"Okay. What are we doing now?"

"You're getting out here," Zoe replied. "I'll lead those guys away from you, to give you a chance to escape."

"Will you be okay on your own?" Lee asked, truly worried for the young woman.

Zoe grinned. "Don't worry about me. I've been doing this for a long time now and nothing bad has happened to me yet."

Lee gave Zoe her cell phone. "Put your digits into my phone. I'll call you as soon as I know anything."

Zoe accepted the phone and put her phone number into it, but she didn't take any contact information from Lee. Which was not a good sign.

Lee shook her head but said nothing more. She left the car and Zoe sped off, heading out to play cat and mouse with more eco-warriors, Lee supposed.

Zoe was young. She felt invincible. Lee remembered that feeling. The last time she'd had it was decades ago.

As Zoe peeled out of the underground garage, Lee hustled to a quiet corner to make a phone call. He picked up on the third ring.

"How's it going?" Senator Sansom asked.

Lee told him about the attempted kidnapping, Zoe Seltzer, the zip drive, and Zoe's desire to bring down ecoterrorists to avenge her brother.

When she'd finished, Sansom said, "I see. I'll look into it. Get some details. Keep this to yourself for now."

"Don't tell Otto and Smithers, you mean?" Lee asked.

"Agreed."

CHAPTER 18

Mill River, Virginia

SMITHERS WAS DRIVING BECAUSE Kim was the lead agent and Smithers was number two. Number two always drove. Simple as that. Kim had rebelled against the idea when Gaspar first insisted. But over the months that she'd been hunting Reacher, she'd come to appreciate having a driver.

The hot July sun baked the asphalt sending up heat shimmers as they drove into Mill River. Smithers turned off the main street toward a local park and pulled into a shaded spot and shut down. The engine ticked as it cooled.

Kim spied Theresa Lee waiting on the weathered bench under an ancient oak. Lee's dark hair was pulled back tight, and her face was set in its usual no-nonsense expression.

"What've you got?" Kim asked as they approached.

Lee handed them each a bottle of water. The plastic was slick with condensation. "Reacher was here. A few days ago. He acquired an SUV and disappeared."

"Yeah, you mentioned that." Smithers twisted the cap off his water and took a big gulp.

Lee's eyes narrowed. "There was an incident at O'Malley's Bar the night before he left."

"What kind of incident?" Kim asked after she sipped the cool water.

"I haven't followed up on that yet. Thought you might want to be there," Lee replied.

Before she could reply, Kim's phone buzzed. She glanced at the screen and then picked up the call.

"Gaspar." She listened, her face blank. "Got it. Thanks."

She turned to the others. "Gaspar's been checking video footage from traffic cams. He found one showing Reacher's SUV heading south out of town."

"South?" Smithers asked. "Toward North Carolina?"

Kim nodded.

"We need to get going. He's putting too much distance between us. We don't want to lose him again," Lee said.

"There are lots of places south of here where he could be. No reason to go rushing in the wrong direction. Gaspar's trying to find him again. When he does, we'll head out," Kim replied. "Meanwhile, let's talk to local law enforcement. See what they know about the bar incident. Before we go in there, I'd like to have a few facts."

Lee seemed annoyed, but she didn't voice her concerns. Which was okay with Kim.

Smithers drove the SUV to the Mill River Police Station, a squat brick building with a faded flag. Inside, the air-conditioning hit them like a wall of ice. Smithers flashed his badge at the paunchy desk sergeant.

"FBI? What brings you folks to Mill River?" He asked while raising his bushy eyebrows for emphasis.

"We're looking for information about a disturbance at O'Malley's Bar a few nights back," Kim said pleasantly. "Mind filling us in?"

The sergeant leaned back. His chair creaked as if it might sink to the floor. "Nasty business. Drunk husband came in swinging at his wife. Big guy stepped in, laid the husband out cold."

"This the big guy?" Smithers asked, showing Reacher's photo on his phone. "About six-five and two-fifty? Fair hair. Blue eyes."

"Left before we arrived." The sergeant took a brief look and shrugged before handing the phone back to Smithers. "I didn't see him personally. But sounds like that could be him from what the witnesses said."

"What about the husband?" Lee asked. "Did you arrest him?"

The sergeant shook his head. "We took him to the hospital. Wife wouldn't press charges. Besides, he was in no shape to go to jail when your guy finished with him."

Kim exchanged glances with Smithers and Lee. "We'd like to talk to the bartender and the victim first, and then the husband."

"Bartender's probably at O'Malley's now. Victim's still at County General, far as I know," the sergeant said as he jotted the names down and handed them to Kim. "Husband's probably still there, too, given how bad he was mauled."

They thanked him for the information and left the station. Outside, they split up. Kim and Lee headed to the bar while Smithers went to the hospital.

O'Malley's was dim and cool and dark. The smell of stale beer hung in the air. The bartender, a heavyset man with graying temples, looked up as they entered.

"What'll it be?" He swiped a beer glass with a rag while he waited for their orders.

Kim showed her badge. "We're looking for a guy involved in an incident here a few nights ago."

The bartender's face darkened. "Damned shame, what happened to Sarah."

"Tell us about the man who intervened," Lee said as she leaned against the bar.

"Big guy. Quiet. Drank his coffee and minded his own business. Until Ted started wailing on Sarah. Then he moved fast." The bartender's expression suggested he was a little in awe of how fast the guy moved.

Kim leaned in. "What exactly did he do?"

"Grabbed Ted's arm mid-swing. Twisted it high and hard behind his back. I thought he'd pull the arm right out of the shoulder socket. Ted howled like a stuck pig. Then the guy shoved Ted to the floor and told him to stay there or he'd come back for more."

"Ted did as he was told, right?" Lee said.

"Bet your ass. Any fool would have," the bartender replied. "Then the guy went over and said something to Sarah, real quiet-like. She nodded and rushed out."

"What happened after that?" Lee asked.

The bartender shrugged. "Not much. Sarah was gone. Ted was writhing on the dirty floor. The guy came back and paid for his coffee. That was about it."

"Did the man say anything else?" Kim pressed.

"Not much. But he'd asked about bus schedules earlier."

"Did you hear what he said to Sarah?" Kim wanted to know.

The bartender shook his head. "Nah, the conversation was too quiet. We had a few folks in here that night, so it was noisy. But Sarah looked relieved, I guess. Like she finally had a way out."

"How often did Ted come in here?" Lee asked.

"Too often." The bartender's face hardened. "Always looking for Sarah. Always drunk. Always trouble."

Kim nodded. "Did the big guy seem to know Ted or Sarah?"

"Nah," the bartender said, shaking his head. "None of us ever seen him before. Seemed like he was just passing through."

"Anything else you can remember?" Kim asked. "Any little detail could help."

The bartender thought for a moment. "Yeah, now that you mention it. After Sarah left, the big guy asked me something strange. Wanted to know if I'd heard of any similar situations in towns south of here."

Kim and Lee exchanged glances. "And what did you tell him?"

"Said sure, I'd heard rumors. Guys beat on their wives. It happens everywhere, doesn't it?" the bartender replied. "He just nodded and left."

Kim's phone buzzed with a text from Smithers. *Victim checked out yesterday. No forwarding address. Ted's still here though. Broken arm, bruised ego.*

Lee read the message over Kim's shoulder.

Kim turned back to the bartender. "Did you see which way the man went afterwards?"

He shook his head. "Like I said, paid his tab and walked out."

"Do you have CCTV in here?" Kim asked, just in case. She'd scanned the room for cameras when they arrived and found none.

"Wish we did sometimes." He shook his head again. "People don't want to be watched while they drink. They come in here to get away from all that. Have a little fun. Cut loose a bit, you know?"

CHAPTER 19

North Carolina

MOLINA'S SPRAWLING NORTH CAROLINA property was a perfect incubator. A crude replica of the dam's control building stood amid the surrounding wilderness.

Plywood walls, hastily painted gray, formed a maze-like structure. Chalk outlines on the packed dirt ground marked doorways and obstacles. The scent of pine and recent rain permeated everything.

Sally Jane knelt beside the explosive vest, focused in concentration. She meticulously checked each wire, her fingers tracing the connections with practiced precision. The inert detonators received the same careful scrutiny. Though the vest was a dummy, Sally Jane treated it with the gravity of a live explosive.

Molina stood nearby, his arms crossed as he observed her work. His eyes, sharp and calculating, missed nothing.

"Good," he said, his voice cutting through the ambient forest sounds. "Now for the run."

He moved to the edge of the makeshift course, gravel crunching under his boots. The stopwatch in his hand gleamed in the fading sunlight. "Ready?" he called out.

Sally Jane rose, her movements deliberate as she strapped on the heavy vest. The weight settled on her shoulders. She nodded, her jaw set with determination.

"Go," Molina said, his thumb clicking the stopwatch.

Sally Jane burst into motion. She sprinted into the mock-up, her footfalls echoing off the plywood walls. She ducked under a low-hanging pipe, the move well-practiced and smooth. Vaulting over a chest-high barrier, she landed with a soft thud and continued her charge through the twisting "hallways."

From her vantage point near a gnarled oak tree, Melissa watched intently. Her eyes tracked Sally Jane's progress, assessing every move.

Sally Jane's breath came in controlled bursts as she navigated the final stretch. With a final surge of speed, she burst through the last doorway. Her hand slapped down hard on the red X marked "Control Room" on a makeshift console.

Molina's voice rang out. "Excellent. Three minutes, twelve seconds."

Bent over with hands on her knees, Sally Jane gulped in air. Sweat beaded on her forehead, and a few strands of hair had escaped her tight ponytail.

"Good work," Molina said, approaching her. His tone carried genuine approval. "You'll shave off more time in the real building."

Sally Jane straightened, still catching her breath. "Thank you," she managed between gasps. Her eyes, filled with a mix of exhaustion and fierce dedication, met Molina's. "I won't let you down."

Molina nodded, then turned to Melissa, who had approached after the run. In a low voice, he said, "I've made a change to the plan. The vest will detonate automatically after thirty minutes."

Melissa's eyes narrowed. "Why the change?" she asked, her voice equally hushed.

"Daisy Hawkins," Molina replied. "Her failure at the Atlanta airport two weeks ago. We can't risk another hesitation."

Before Melissa could respond, a shrill alarm cut through the air. It came from the direction of the main house, distant but unmistakable. Sally Jane's body tensed instantly, her hand moving reflexively toward the mock detonator on her vest.

Molina watched her reaction closely. The vest was harmless, but Sally Jane's instinct troubled him. In the fading light, his expression darkened. A single question loomed in his mind: When the moment of truth arrived, would she maintain her composure, or would she falter like Daisy Hawkins?

The alarm's piercing wail faded as quickly as it had begun, leaving an uneasy silence. Molina's eyes remained fixed on Sally Jane, studying her every micro-expression. Her initial tension ebbed, replaced by a forced calm that didn't quite reach her eyes.

"False alarm," Melissa announced, lowering her hand from her earpiece. "Perimeter sensor malfunction. They're resetting the system now."

Molina nodded, his gaze still locked on Sally Jane. In a carefully neutral tone, he said, "Your reaction time was impressive. But remember, hesitation of any kind could jeopardize the entire operation."

Sally Jane swallowed hard. "Understood, sir. It won't happen again."

"See that it doesn't," Molina replied and turned to Melissa. Quietly, he instructed, "Increase her stress training. I want to see how she performs under intense conditions."

Melissa nodded, a hint of concern flickering across her features. "Are you sure that's wise? We're so close to deadline."

"Exactly why we can't afford any surprises. Just do it," Molina cut her off, watching Sally Jane removing the dummy vest. Her fingers trembled slightly as she worked the straps. He approached her, his footsteps deliberately heavy on the gravel to announce his presence.

"Walk with me." He didn't wait for her response before striding toward the tree line.

Sally Jane fell into step beside him, matching his brisk pace. They walked in silence for several moments into the dense forest. Sunlight filtered through the canopy, raising the stifling heat to uncomfortable levels on the forest floor.

Finally, Molina spoke. "You've come a long way, Sally Jane. Your dedication to our cause has been admirable."

"Thank you, sir," she replied with only a slight waver in her voice.

Molina stopped abruptly and turned to face her. "Dedication alone isn't enough. What we're about to do will change the world. There can be no room for doubt, no moment of hesitation."

Sally Jane met his gaze. "I understand the stakes, sir. This is the most important thing I'll ever do in my life. I'm ready."

"Are you? Really?" Molina's gaze bored into hers searching for any hint of uncertainty. He leaned in closer and dropped his voice to a near whisper. "Because once you're inside that dam, there's no turning back. No last-minute changes of heart. You'll do what needs to be done."

Sally Jane squared her shoulders. "I won't fail you, sir. Or the cause."

A long moment passed before Molina nodded, seemingly satisfied. "Good. Get some rest. Tomorrow's training will push you to your limits."

They walked back to the clearing where Melissa was overseeing the dismantling of the mock-up. She caught Molina's eye as he emerged from the tree line, a silent question in her gaze. He gave an almost imperceptible nod, and Melissa's shoulders relaxed slightly.

"That's enough for today," Molina announced. "Everyone get some food and rest. We start again at oh-five-hundred."

When the small group dispersed, Sally Jane lingered for a moment, her gaze drawn to the dummy vest lying on a nearby table. With a deep breath, she turned away and followed the others toward the house.

Molina watched her retreat. In his mind, contingency plans began to take shape. He had come too far, sacrificed too much, to let anything or anyone jeopardize what was to come.

CHAPTER 20

Mill River, Virginia

AS IF HE KNEW she'd be finished with the bartender interview, Gaspar called Kim's phone again. Sometimes she found it reassuring to know she was being watched twenty-four seven. Other times, not so much.

"I've been analyzing the traffic cam footage." Gaspar launched right into the reason for his call. "Reacher's SUV passed through three towns south of Mill River in the last few days. Each town has police reports of a similar incident: a bar fight where a big man intervened in a domestic dispute."

Kim's heart sped up a couple of beats. "Are you sure?"

"Positive," Gaspar replied. "It's like Reacher's following some kind of trail."

"Okay. We're almost done here. Keep me posted."

"What is it?" Lee squinted in the bright sunlight as she donned her sunglasses.

Kim relayed Gaspar's report and Lee seemed surprised. "What the hell is Reacher doing?"

"Dunno." Kim shrugged. "He sometimes gets involved in local disputes, but he doesn't usually go looking for trouble. It's usually the opposite. Trouble finds him."

"Unless he's got a good reason to go looking," Lee replied, as if she knew something about Reacher that Kim didn't. Which she probably did. Probably more than one thing.

"Why did he get involved in your subway case back in New York?"

"Pretty simple. He felt guilty. The woman on the subway killed herself. He felt responsible," Lee replied easily. "He was standing right there when she did it. He felt like he could have and should have stopped her."

"Could he have stopped her?" Kim asked, cocking her head.

"Probably not. Which I told him. Several times." Lee shrugged this time.

"He disagreed with you?"

"He said he knew I was right. But that didn't stop him from hunting down those who were actually responsible for getting the woman in such a state that she saw no other way out," Lee replied.

"We need to find out what's really going on here," Kim said as Smithers pulled up to the curb in the SUV and they stepped inside.

They settled into their seats, and she gave Smithers a quick rundown of what they'd learned.

Wiping sweat from his brow, Smithers then reported his results. "Hospital was a dead end for Sarah. Took me a while to find out that she'd checked out. You know how hospitals are about sharing information on patients."

Lee said, "What about the husband?"

"Ted's still there. Broken arm, bruised ego, from what the orderly told me. I didn't have a chance to chat him up before you called. Might be worth another try."

"Good idea. And we should track down Sarah," Kim replied. "The bartender mentioned Reacher asked about bus schedules. There's a women's shelter one town over, right?"

"Yeah," Lee confirmed. "Worth checking out."

"All right," Kim said. "Smithers, you and Lee head to the shelter. Drop me at the hospital. I'll have a chat with Ted. Then we'll regroup and follow Reacher's trail."

Smithers dropped Kim at the main entrance to County General Hospital and headed north. Kim got a visitor's pass from the volunteer at the front desk, who gave her directions to Ted's room on the second floor.

When Kim approached, she saw a uniformed officer stationed outside.

"FBI. I need to talk with the patient," Kim said, showing her badge. The officer nodded and stepped aside. Virginia was close to Washington, DC. Local cops were used to federal agents wandering around, she guessed.

Ted lay flat in the bed, his right arm in a cast. His face was a mess of bruises, and his jaw was wired shut. He glared at Kim as she entered.

"Here to arrest me?" he growled between his artificially clenched teeth.

Kim pulled up a chair. "I'm here about the man who did this to you."

Ted's eyes narrowed. "That bastard had no right to interfere. When you catch him, I'll be glad to testify. He's a thug. He belongs in prison."

"Tell me what happened." Kim kept her voice neutral.

Ted recounted the bar fight casting himself as the victim of his wife's bad behavior, insisting Reacher had been the aggressor. "I didn't even look at the guy. He just came after me for no reason and beat the crap outta me."

Before she could reply, Kim's phone buzzed. A text from Smithers. *Found Sarah at the shelter. Says a woman approached her after Reacher left. Offered her a "way out" and a "chance to make a difference."*

Kim digested the intel and turned back to Ted. "Did the man say or ask you anything?"

Ted frowned. "Yeah. Asked if I knew anyone named Melissa. Said it was important. I didn't even have a chance to answer him before he started in on me."

She cocked her head. "And do you? Know anyone named Melissa?"

"Hell, I don't know. Probably. Melissa's a common name," Ted scowled as he answered.

"Okay." Kim stood to leave. "Thanks for your time."

"You arrest that bastard, you hear? Come back and tell me you did it and I'll show up to testify. Any time, any place. And tell my wife to get her ass home," Ted growled as she left the room.

What a jerk. If his wife ever went back to him, she'd be a fool. Ted's kind never changed. But Kim held her tongue and kept walking.

Outside, she called Smithers. He spoke first. "On our way. Be there in five."

She waited at the curb until he pulled up. She hopped into the passenger seat and buckled up.

When they were on the road, following the route Reacher probably took heading south, Kim filled them in on what she'd learned from Ted.

"So Reacher asked about someone named Melissa?" Lee asked from the backseat. "Wonder what that's about?"

"Dunno," Kim replied. "But if we could find Melissa, we might get that much closer to Reacher."

Smithers gripped the wheel tighter. "On a slightly different topic, was Daisy Hawkins an abuse victim?"

"Good question," Lee said. "We didn't find anything like that during our deep dive into her background. But a lot of domestic abuse goes unreported. So it's possible."

"You're thinking abused women are a common denominator here?" Kim asked just as her phone rang with a call from Gaspar. "Hey, Chico. What's up?"

"Traffic cameras picked up Reacher's SUV heading into a town called Grand Cedar, about sixty miles south of your position," he said.

"Thanks. That'll be our next stop," Kim said. "Meanwhile, I know you're already up to your ears in alligators. But can you check to see if there's any record of domestic abuse in Daisy Hawkins's background?"

"Domestic abuse? Why? Is it relevant?" Gaspar replied.

"Not sure. But it could be."

"Okay. I'll add it to the list, Suzy Wong," Gaspar teased as he hung up.

As they sped down the highway, Kim wondered what Reacher had uncovered. Where was it all leading?

One thing was clear. Finlay and his horde of agents were behind the curve.

Catching up with Reacher and whatever was going on before something worse developed might already be impossible.

CHAPTER 21

Grand Cedar, Virginia

THE SUN WAS SETTING as Smithers drove past the sign welcoming them to Grand Cedar, another seemingly picturesque but quiet small town south of Mill River.

"Where do we start?" Smithers asked as they cruised down Main Street hoping to find Reacher or his SUV or, at the very least, an indication that he'd been there.

Kim spotted a rundown bar at the edge of town. The neon sign out front proclaimed the *U & I Bar and Grill*. A familiar-looking older model SUV was parked outside.

"There," she said. "That's where we start."

They pulled up next to the SUV. Kim checked the plate.

"It's Reacher's." Kim willed her stomach to stop churning and patted her holster for reassurance. "Let's go in. See what we can find out."

Lee said, "This is exactly the sort of place he'd look for if he were searching for a particular type of person. If he's in there, I'll take the lead."

"Good plan. He probably won't attack you, and maybe you can distract him from attacking us," Smithers chuckled.

Kim gave him a scowl, even as she understood the wisdom of his words. She'd stopped fearing Reacher a while ago, after he saved her life. He wouldn't have saved her back then if he'd meant to kill her later, she reasoned. But it was just a theory. One that, so far, hadn't been tested.

The U & I Bar and Grill stood at the edge of Grand Cedar like a weathered sentinel. The old red bricks held the front façade in place, but the wood trim was splintered and faded from the harsh summer sun.

A neon *Open* sign flickered weakly beside the door. Half its letters were not lit up so in the dark it would say simply *en*. A couple of rusted pickup trucks were also parked on the street out front.

Kim pushed open the creaky door and they entered the dimly lit bar, Kim in the lead, Lee and Smithers close behind. A few patrons glanced up from their drinks, eyeing the newcomers warily before returning to their conversations.

A wave of stale air hit Kim's nostrils. The pungent mix of decades-old cigarette smoke, spilled beer, and greasy bar food combined to emit a revolting odor. She opened her mouth to breathe instead of inhaling the stench. The maneuver provided only modest improvement.

The bar's dim interior was a patchwork of shadows and amber light from the dusty light fixtures, revealing scarred wooden booths and a long bar polished smooth by countless elbows.

A jukebox in the corner wheezed out a tinny country ballad, barely audible over the low murmur of conversation and the rhythmic clack of pool balls. The floorboards groaned underfoot, sticky in places from spilled drinks.

The wall near the exit was covered in layers of tacked-up dollar bills, yellowed news clippings, and faded photographs.

Kim scanned the room searching for any sign of Reacher. No luck. She wasn't surprised and not entirely disappointed. When she finally confronted Reacher, she'd rather do it on her own terms in a place she'd already secured.

The clink of glasses hitting the draft beer pulls punctuated the bartender's movements as he poured another round for the regulars, adding the unmistakable scent of fresh beer to the barely breathable mix.

Kim approached the bartender, a grizzled man in his sixties who seemed to blend in with the woodwork. He was as worn, dark, and tired as the rest of the place.

She pulled out her phone to show Reacher's photo. "We're looking for this guy. Tall, well-built, probably came in here recently."

The bartender's expression remained neutral. "Lot of people come through here. Can't say I remember anyone specific."

Kim leaned in closer, still holding out the photo and lowering her voice. "The man we're looking for might have asked about a woman named Melissa. Ring any bells?"

Recognition flickered across the bartender's face before he stifled it. "Listen, I don't want any trouble. Guy was here and left. Didn't even order a beer."

"What did you tell him when he asked about Melissa?" Kim pressed.

He shrugged. "Nothing to tell. I don't know nobody named Melissa."

"What about customers or visitors? Got any Melissas coming in here lately?" Lee asked.

"How would I know?" he replied. "I don't ask folks anything personal. They pay me for the drinks and I respect their privacy."

"Did he say where he was headed?" Smithers chimed in.

The bartender shook his head. "He asked about some old apartment complex on the outskirts of town. Abandoned place, been shut down for years. Grove Apartments. One of those housing projects that turned into a drug dealers' hell before they shut it down. Gotta be hundreds of similar places around the country."

Kim exchanged glances with Smithers and Lee. "Did he say anything else? Why he wanted to know or what he planned to do there?"

The bartender shook his head. "Not a word. Didn't say much at all. I've had better conversations with the alley cats out back."

Lee approached the group playing pool, but it looked like she wasn't making any progress there, either.

Smithers headed to check the men's room and the back alley.

Kim had kept the bartender occupied while they completed the recon, but they both returned shortly, shaking their heads to confirm nothing gained.

"Okay. Looks like he's not here," Kim said when Smithers and Lee returned to the bar.

"That's what I told you. Save yourself some trouble if you accepted the truth when it's offered," the bartender said, clearly annoyed now.

"There's a black SUV parked out front," Kim said.

"So? It's mine. I park it there every day. Never had a parking ticket yet," he said.

"You sure? Because the guy we're looking for is driving one just like it," Kim said.

"Big deal." The bartender shrugged again. "It's a Chevy. Millions made every year."

"What about the license plate?"

"What about it?" He was getting more defensive by the moment.

"It's registered to a rental company in Mill River," Kim lied. She figured Reacher had probably stolen the plates. But the bartender shouldn't know that.

"Not possible." The bartender huffed before he threw his towel down and stomped from behind the bar all the way to the front door and outside.

Kim followed him out into the hot, blinding sunlight. He glanced at the front license plate on the SUV and then marched around the vehicle and stared incredulously at the back plate.

"What the unholy hell?" He demanded as if the gods might answer him personally.

"You're saying the SUV is yours but the plates are not?" Kim asked, just to be clear.

"Damned straight."

"Got your keys?" Kim asked.

He fished around in his pocket and retrieved the fob. He pushed the button to unlock the doors. All four locks popped up.

He opened the passenger door allowing the heat to pour out in waves and wash over them. He stuck his head inside and looked around. He grabbed a stainless-steel insulated coffee mug and brandished it toward Kim.

"World's Greatest Dad," he said, waving the cup and its logo. "See? That's mine. The SUV is mine. And tell that asshat who stole my plates he'd better stay out of my sight."

"Show me your registration," she said.

He ducked his head inside the sauna again and came out with a small white card, handing it to Kim. "You're Albert Bowling?"

He stuck his chin out. "All my life. What of it?"

She used her phone to take a photo of the registration and a quick photo of Bowling. Then she handed the registration back to him. He tossed his mug onto the passenger seat, slammed the door, and stuffed the registration along with the fob into his pocket.

"You got any more questions, you bring the police with you. Got that?" Bowling demanded angrily as he turned and stalked back into the bar.

Smithers arched his eyebrows and grinned. "Was it something we said?"

CHAPTER 22

North Carolina

MARCUS MOLINA'S FINGERS TAPPED an anxious rhythm on the edge of the map-covered table. The room, a converted basement in an old barn on the far corner of his property, felt claustrophobic despite its size.

Long ago, when this was a working farm, tobacco had been stored here. Now, it appeared to be abandoned if anyone bothered to find it.

Harsh fluorescent lights cast a sickly glow over everything, deepening the shadows under Melissa Black's eyes as she paced.

"We're running out of time," she snapped, breaking the tense silence. "The world isn't going to save itself, Marcus."

Molina nodded, forcing himself to focus. "Right. Let's start with the obvious targets."

"GlobOil in Houston," Black said, her voice cold and precise. "The heart of the fossil fuel industry."

Molina placed a black pin on Houston, the soft click oddly final. "Agreed. What about the West Coast?"

"The Port of Los Angeles," Black replied without hesitation. "It's a symbol of overconsumption and global trade exploitation."

As Molina marked Los Angeles, he felt a twinge of doubt. "The casualty count there could be significant. Are we certain?"

Black's hand slammed down on the table, making Molina jump. "Casualties are inevitable, Marcus," she hissed, leaning in close. Her eyes burned with a fervor that both captivated and terrified him. "Remember why we're doing this. Remember the millions who will die if we don't act now."

Molina swallowed hard, nodding. "You're right. It's a lot to process all at once."

Black's expression softened fractionally. "I know. But we can't afford doubt now. Not when we're so close."

Molina took a deep breath, steeling himself. "Okay. Washington, DC is next. The Department of the Interior."

"Perfect," Black nodded. "They control federal land use. It sends the right message."

They continued their selection process, debating each location. New York's Financial District made the list, along with a major fracking operation run by ShaleForce in Pennsylvania.

"What about the Midwest?" Molina asked, studying the map.

Black pondered for a moment. "MidwestPower's coal plant in Minnesota. And that massive BeefCorp feedlot in Nebraska."

Molina placed the pins, frowning as he stepped back to see the full map at once. "We're missing one. We need to choose an unexpected target to shake them to the core."

A slow, cold smile spread across Black's face. "The headquarters of EcoHarmony Foundation in San Francisco."

Molina's gaze snapped up. "What? They're environmental advocates. They're on our side."

"Are they?" Black's voice was soft, dangerous. She moved around the table, standing uncomfortably close to Molina. "They preach moderation. Working within a broken system. What has that ever achieved? We'll show the world that's not enough."

Molina wanted to argue, but the intensity in Black's eyes stopped him. She was right.

After years of peaceful protesting, progress had been glacial. It was time for a big disruptor. Forced change was lasting change.

He placed the final pin with a firm hand.

"It's done," he said, admiring the choices before them.

Black's eyes gleamed with triumph. "Now, we assign our soldiers."

Molina reached for the folder containing the bombers' profiles. Ten faces stared back at him, each willing to die for the cause. He spread the photos on the table, next to the map.

"Sarah for GlobOil," he began, picking up the photo of a stern-faced woman with close-cropped hair. "She has the military background to handle their security."

Black nodded. "Good. Give David the EcoHarmony Foundation. His youth and idealism will help him blend in."

One by one, they matched bombers to targets. Each decision felt like sealing fate. Because it was.

"What about James?" Molina asked, holding up the photo of a middle-aged man with kind eyes. "He seems less committed than the others."

Black's expression hardened. "James understands the stakes. They all do. Doubt is a luxury we can't afford."

As they finished the selections, Molina leaned back. Exhaustion etched his face. "It's done."

Black placed a hand on his shoulder, an unusually gentle gesture for her. "You've done well, Marcus. This is the moment we've worked toward for years."

Suddenly, Molina's phone buzzed. He frowned, pulling it out. Only a handful of people had this number, and they knew not to use it.

The text message was from Cannon, his right-hand man. It simply said "David's missing. Off the grid. Call me."

"We have a problem," Molina said, looking up at Black. "What is it?"

Molina swallowed hard. "It's David. Our EcoHarmony Foundation patriot."

"What about him?" Black's voice was dangerously soft.

"He's gone dark. Completely off the grid. Cannon can't reach him."

Black's face hardened into a mask of fury. "We need to find him. Now."

"We're working on it." Molina dialed Cannon's number. He put the call on speaker.

"Report," he said when Cannon answered.

Cannon's voice blasted through the speaker. "We've been trying to reach David for the past three hours. His phone is off, and he missed two check-ins."

Black leaned in. "What was his last known location?"

"A coffee shop two blocks from EcoHarmony's local office," Cannon said. "He vanished after that. We're scanning security cameras in the area, but so far, nothing."

Black swore viciously. "Keep looking. Use every resource we have. Understood?"

"Copy that," Cannon replied before the line went dead.

Molina met Black's gaze, seeing her panic.

"What if he's been compromised?" she asked.

Molina's jaw clenched. "Then we move to Plan B. We can't let one weak link destroy everything we've worked for."

"Plan B?" Black arched her eyebrows. "We are a long way from ready for the nuclear option."

"We're prepared for every contingency," Molina cut her off. "Now, we need to make those calls. We need to know if this is an isolated incident or if we have a bigger problem."

As Molina began the calls, one thought kept repeating in his mind. Had David lost his nerve, or worse, had he been caught?

Either way, the entire operation and the revolution they'd fought so hard to achieve was suddenly balanced on a knife's edge.

CHAPTER 23

Grand Cedar, Virginia

"NOW WHAT?" SMITHERS ASKED after they'd piled into the stifling hot SUV. He restarted the engine and turned the air conditioning on full blast.

Kim pulled the seatbelt away from the retractor and snugged her alligator clamp onto the webbing and Smithers started to roll.

As if she actually expected answers from the universe, she said, "Why would Reacher be interested in an abandoned apartment complex? What's he up to, anyway?"

"He was here. We know that now. He switched the plates on the SUV, so he must be planning to keep it a while," Smither said.

"Or he could have acquired another vehicle somehow," Kim replied. She texted the registration and Bowling's photo to Gaspar along with a quick note explaining the situation and asking him to check traffic cams for a vehicle sporting the stolen plates.

"I've got satellite imagery of this area." Lee had resettled in her seat and pulled it up on her phone and rattled off the address. "Grove Apartments is about five miles east of here. Photos fit the bartender's description."

"That's got to be it," Kim said as she punched the address into the SUV's navigation system. Smithers followed the directions.

As they approached the outskirts of town, the looming silhouette of the abandoned Grove Apartments complex came into view. Five clapboard buildings, each four stories high positioned at angles forming a lopsided pentagon. Like a child's attempt at geometry.

The buildings had been painted white with black shutters and black roofs. Now, they were gray and dirty, the paint was peeling or nonexistent, and the remaining roofs were missing half their shingles.

Three of the buildings had partially collapsed after urban decay and the ongoing demolition. Rubble had spilled into the center courtyard. The other two buildings were still relatively intact.

Smithers avoided piles of debris as he maneuvered around the potholed drive encircling the buildings. Heavy construction equipment had been gathered in one location when the crew knocked off for the weekend.

No cars or other personal vehicles were parked in the lots. No black SUVs other than the one Smithers was driving.

"Looks like Reacher's not here," Smithers said when they'd completed the bumpy circular drive.

"Let's park and take a look," Kim said.

Smithers found an isolated spot hidden from view a short distance away and killed the engine.

"How do you want to play this?" Lee asked, her hand instinctively moving to her weapon.

Kim considered the options. "We go in quiet. For all we know, Reacher could be in there right now. And he might not be alone."

They approached the complex cautiously. Gravel crunched under their feet sounding unnaturally loud in the stillness.

As they neared the main entrance, Kim noticed fresh tire tracks in the dirt. "Someone's been here recently."

Suddenly, a muffled sound came from inside the building raising the hairs on the back of her neck. It could have been a voice, or machinery, or simply the wind playing tricks on her.

"Watch yourselves. We don't know what we're walking into." Kim drew her weapon. Smithers and Lee did the same.

Kim reached for the exterior door handle and slowly pushed the door open, wincing at the loud creak of rusted hinges. They entered the dilapidated apartment building slowly to allow their eyes to adjust.

Brief streaks of sunlight filtered through broken windows casting eerie shadows across peeling wallpaper and debris-strewn floors. Empty fast-food wrappers, soda and beer bottles, and discarded drug paraphernalia cluttered the filthy threadbare carpet.

They moved silently through the hallway alert for any type of movement. As she approached a stairwell leading to the upper floors, Kim heard the muffled sound again. It was a faint voice, definitely human.

She gestured to Smithers and Lee, pointing upward. They nodded understanding of the plan.

Carefully, Kim ascended the creaky stairs, each step calculated to minimize noise. At the top, a dim light spilled from beneath a closed apartment door. She pressed her ear against it, straining to hear words as well as sounds.

She took a deep breath, weighing her options. She signaled to Smithers and Lee, positioned on either side of the door.

With a nod, Kim stood to one side and knocked firmly. "Hello? Is anyone in there?"

There was a moment of silence followed by shuffling sounds from within the apartment. The door creaked open, revealing an unkempt middle-aged couple, both looking terrified and confused.

"Please," the woman said, her voice trembling. "We just needed a place to stay. We have nowhere else to go."

Kim kept her weapon in her hand but lowered it to maintain a less threatening posture. "We're not here to cause you any trouble. We're looking for someone who was supposed to be here."

The couple visibly relaxed but remained wary.

"I'm Kim," she said in a friendly tone hoping to draw them out. "These are my colleagues, Reggie and Theresa."

The man nodded. "I'm Tom Grayson, and this is my wife, Linda."

"The man we're trying to find may have been here recently," Kim said, pulling out her photo of Reacher and showing it to the couple. "He's tall, well-built, athletic. Have you seen him?"

Linda's eyes widened with recognition. "Yes, actually. He came through here and asked us some questions."

Kim leaned in, intrigued. "What kind of questions?"

Tom frowned, recalling the encounter. "He was looking for a woman named Melissa. Wanted to know if we'd heard anything about her or seen her around."

Linda picked up the tale as if she were eager to get rid of them. Which she probably was. "We hadn't seen any Melissa or heard of her, so he left."

"Did he say where he was headed next?" Smithers asked.

Linda replied, "He asked us if we knew anything about people living in Grand Cedar, but we don't. We're not from around here."

"Thank you both," Kim said, realizing they had nothing significant to offer. "I'm sorry about your situation. Is there anything at all we can do to help you?"

"They're tearing this building down in a few days. We'll be going to a local shelter. We just wanted to stay in our own place as long as we could," Linda replied, her eyes glassy with tears again.

"Good luck to you," Kim said as she led the others back outside.

As they walked back to the SUV, Lee said, "At least we know we're on the right track with Reacher. We need to catch up with him."

They piled into the car, with Smithers behind the wheel once again. Kim's phone vibrated in her pocket with a text from Gaspar.

Ran background on Melissa. Multiple hits. Most promising is Melissa Carlyle Black, 32, former social worker. Reported missing by neighbor 6 months ago. Last known location Grand Cedar, VA.

He'd included Melissa Black's address and a driver's license photo. Kim read the text to her teammates and punched the address into the SUV's navigation system. Melissa Black's home was close.

"Let's check out the house. Maybe talk to the neighbors," Kim said.

"Will do," Smithers replied.

He followed the navigation instructions off the main street into a modest neighborhood of small ranch homes with detached garages. Single story layouts sprawled across the modest lots sporting earth-toned brick or wood siding. Low pitched roofs and large picture windows also suggested the development was built in the mid-seventies.

Smithers drove slowly past Melissa Black's address. The house was dark and seemed to be unoccupied. The lawn was overgrown. Weeds choked the flowers beds. A few flyers were piled on the stoop at the front door.

"Nobody's living there," Lee said. "She's been missing six months, Gaspar said. Looks like the place could have been neglected at least that long."

"Let's go around to the alley and see if there's a way in," Kim said.

Smithers slowed at the next block and turned left. Halfway down the block, he turned into the alley and bounced along the rough pavement to Melissa Black's backyard.

The row of cookie-cutter houses had probably been built by a single developer. Each had a detached garage and a four-foot cyclone fence across the back property line typical of the era. A few of the gates had locks, but most did not.

Trash Dumpsters lined up against the backs of the garages waiting for pickup. Melissa Black's Dumpster was empty, as if her trash had been collected and she'd never added more to the bin.

"Now what?" Smithers asked.

"Wait here. I'll take a look," Kim said as she unbuckled her seatbelt, opened the door, and slipped to the ground. Before Kim could stop her, Lee followed close behind.

Kim approached the gate at the corner of the garage. A simple fork latch held the gate closed. She stopped there and peered into the backyard, which was even more neglected than the front. Shades covered the windows, blocking the interior from view. A small concrete patio at the back door was cluttered with unused furniture and gardening supplies.

"Let me. I'm not a cop. I'm not required to have a warrant," Lee stepped up beside Kim, opened the gate, and walked through.

"Maybe you're not a cop anymore, but you're still trespassing," Kim said as she followed and relatched the gate behind her.

CHAPTER 24

Grand Cedar, Virginia

THE OVERGROWN GRASS WHISPERED against her legs as Kim picked her way through Melissa Black's neglected backyard.

Her gaze darted from window to window, all shrouded. "Looks like no one's been here in months," she murmured. "There's no indication that Reacher has been here, either."

Lee nodded, already kneeling by the back door. "Let's see what Melissa left behind."

She manipulated her lockpick set while Kim kept watch for a tense minute.

"We're in," Lee whispered, easing the door open. She unholstered her gun, holding it at the ready. "Clear the rooms?"

Kim nodded and drew her weapon.

The smell of stale air and abandonment hit her even before she stepped inside. Dust motes danced in the thin shafts of light piercing through gaps in the shades.

Typical of the era in which it was built, the house had an open floor plan connecting the kitchen, dining, and living areas. Wood cabinets, laminate counter tops, shag carpeting, and linoleum flooring were all anachronistic now.

Pale light filtered through grimy windows in the dim, dusty kitchen. The space seemed frozen in time. Unwashed dishes cluttered the sink. A thin film of mold formed on a plate's surface. A half-empty coffee mug sat on the countertop, contents evaporated to a dark stain.

Kim's boots left the only footprints visible in the thick dust on the linoleum floor.

They moved into the living room. A sagging couch faced a small TV. The dark screen reflected their distorted figures. Picture frames lay face-down, as if Melissa couldn't bear to look at the memories. Magazines were strewn across a coffee table. Heavy curtains blocked the windows. Dust coated everything. Only tiny insect tracks disturbed it.

Kim moved toward the narrow hallway. She passed a small bathroom. The medicine cabinet hung open. Someone had ransacked its contents. A toothbrush lay forgotten in the sink.

The next room seemed to double as a guest room and office. A desktop computer sat silent. Boxes were stacked in one corner. Melissa might have been packing or unpacking when she fled.

Kim reached the master bedroom last. An unmade bed dominated the space. The sheets looked twisted. Closet doors stood open. Hangers hung askew. Several garments lay dropped on the floor. A dresser with half-open drawers filled most of the adjacent wall.

"Clear," Lee announced as she lowered her weapon.

Kim holstered her gun, gloved up, and began a more thorough examination.

She noticed a faint rectangle on the nightstand. A photo frame had occupied that spot.

"What do you think?" she asked, surveying the jumble of discarded clothes and open drawers.

Lee's eyes narrowed as she gloved up and moved to the bedside table. "She left in a hurry but look at this."

Kim peered over her shoulder. A small notebook lay open, a pen beside it as if Melissa had been writing just before she vanished.

"What does it say?" Kim asked.

Lee picked up the notebook, frowning as she deciphered the hurried scrawl. "It's a series of dates and locations. The last entry is interesting."

Kim looked over Lee's shoulder and read aloud. "*Jack's getting close. I have to move again.* Is she talking about Reacher?"

"Jack's a common name. Could be anyone, I guess." Lee flipped through the earlier pages. "It's all here. She's been tracking Jack's movements, staying one step ahead."

"So Jack's not just trying to find her," Kim mused, "he's hunting her."

"And now we know why Melissa's running," Lee added. "Question is, what does Jack want with her?"

Kim scanned the room again. "Whatever it is, it was enough to make her abandon her whole life."

Lee nodded, carefully bagging the notebook as evidence. "Let's hope this gives us the lead we need."

Kim noticed a small safe in the back corner of the closet, door slightly ajar. She pushed it open. "I think we've got something here."

She reached into the safe and pulled out a small duffel bag. She unzipped the bag, flipping through the items inside quickly. "This doesn't make sense."

"What do you mean?" Lee asked from across the room where she was checking under the bed.

"It looks like a go-bag. Something she set up so she could just grab it and go." Kim catalogued the bag's contents as she studied each item. "Cash for expenses. A fake passport for crossing borders. A journal that might contain important information. A USB drive that could hold digital evidence. The gun for protection."

"Those are exactly the things she'd take if she were running. And those photos," Lee added, pointing to a couple of yellowed snapshots. "Likely the man she's running from or watching out for. Reacher's not in them. So maybe it's another Jack she's worried about."

Kim frowned. "So why leave it all behind?"

"Looks like she was in an extreme hurry," Lee replies.

"Or someone made her leave," Kim suggested. "Maybe she didn't have a choice."

Lee looked around the room again. "No signs of a struggle though."

"What if," Kim said slowly, "this isn't Melissa's real go-bag? What if it's a decoy?"

Lee's eyes widened. "A false trail. Clever. Leave behind what looks like emergency supplies in case someone comes looking."

"While the real escape kit is somewhere else," Kim concluded. "We might be looking at her backup plan for her backup plan."

Melissa Black was proving to be more resourceful than Kim had anticipated. Which made her wonder. Why was Reacher hunting her? And why was she running?

"We should check for hidden compartments," Lee suggested. "False bottoms in drawers, hollow books, loose floorboards."

Kim nodded. "Whatever spooked Melissa was serious enough to cause her to abandon everything and run."

They began a meticulous search of the house. Kim pulled out a drawer from the desk. "Take a look at this."

Inside was a stack of folders. Lee picked one up and flipped it open. "Case files?"

"Looks like social work records," Kim said, examining another folder. "Detailed notes on troubled individuals. Mostly young men, some women. They all have histories of depression, isolation, religious extremism."

Lee frowned. "Why would she have possession of these? Medical records like this are highly confidential. She's breaking about a dozen laws and ethical rules by leaving them here."

Kim shrugged. "Maybe she volunteered at a clinic or a halfway house? Did some social work at home?"

"Possible," Lee said, but she sounded unconvinced as she scanned the contents of the files. "There's something off about these notes though. They're too detailed. Too focused on vulnerabilities."

Lee grabbed the files and stuffed them into another bag while Kim made one last sweep of the house, using her camera to video all of the rooms, just in case she needed a virtual visit later.

"Time to go," Kim said, heading toward the back exit.

"Go where?" Lee replied, following.

CHAPTER 25

Grand Cedar, Virginia

KIM STEPPED OUT OF Melissa Black's house. Lee followed close behind, carrying the files tucked under her arm, and carefully relocking the back door.

They crossed the backyard in the shadows and exited through the chain link gate to the alley where Smithers was waiting. As Kim approached the SUV her phone vibrated in her pocket demanding attention.

She waited in the steamy heat until Lee was inside the SUV to take the call in case Gaspar had something confidential to report. "Hey, Chico. Whatcha got?"

"An interesting development in Leland, North Carolina," Gaspar's voice crackled through the iffy connection. "I turned up a police report from two nights ago. Bar fight at a place called Boone's Tavern. Apparently the fight broke out when some jerk was manhandling a woman sitting alone at the bar. The jerk is in the hospital now. Probably has a huge bruise on his forehead to go with a few broken bones."

Kim felt the familiar jolt of electricity along her spine that only Reacher seemed to cause. "Sounds promising. Did the locals arrest either of them?"

"Nope. Guess the injured fellow has a rep for being a hothead and a troublemaker. And the second guy walked away. He was long gone by the time the cops arrived," Gaspar said, describing a familiar pattern.

Reacher was the Teflon man. He'd committed all manner of assaults and worse over the years, but never seemed to suffer any lasting consequences from the justice system.

Kim nodded as she took it all in. "Any more details?"

"Eyewitnesses described a big guy, well over six feet. Blond, blue eyes, built like a Mack truck, they said. Bartender remembers him paying cash," Gaspar said with a hint of satisfaction. "He also overheard a couple of guys call him 'Jack.' Probably just general slang, but it could be something."

Kim glanced back at Melissa Black's house, recalling the diary entries about a man she'd identified as Jack. "Any visuals?"

"CCTV footage from the bar. Quality's poor, but it shows the big guy talking to another man. Can't make out either man's face. His name isn't on the police report, but I can probably find out."

Kim dabbed the sweat from her brow with her forearm. "What else you got?"

"You're never satisfied, are you Suzie Wong?" Gaspar teased. "As it happens, there was an ATM withdrawal using Reacher's card half a block from the bar."

Gaspar paused, probably for emphasis, but Kim's entire body already felt electrified.

An ATM withdrawal using Reacher's card coupled with the video from the bar and the eyewitness descriptions were conclusive enough for her.

After all these months, she was closer to Reacher than she'd ever been. The knowledge was exhilarating. And terrifying. All at once.

Gaspar was still talking, but Kim had zoned out. So she asked him to repeat what he'd said.

"Get your head in the game, Otto," he chastised her before repeating. "I'm still searching for outside video in the area of the bar. I'd like to have a clearer picture of Reacher, if it was him. Barring that, the big guy getting into a black SUV could help us."

"Yeah, that would be good. But this is plenty for now," Kim replied. "How far is Leland from here?"

"About three and a half hours southwest across the state line," he said and then gave her the physical address for Boone's Tavern.

Kim checked her watch noting the second hand ticking away precious time. "Alright, send everything you've got. We're heading there now."

"Already done. It's all waiting in your secure server."

"Thanks, Chico. I couldn't do this job without you."

"Damned straight," he replied with a laugh just before he ended the call with a final warning. "Watch your six. Cooper finds out what you're doing and he'll come down on you with a vengeance."

The warning hit home hard. Gaspar was right. And Cooper watched her like a hawk watches a field mouse. Which meant he probably knew already.

But at some point, she'd need to tell Cooper. She hoped it could wait until after she'd found Reacher to avoid the worst of the fallout. The last thing she needed was Cooper micro-managing her actions. Which he would absolutely do if she allowed him to interfere.

Kim slipped the burner phone into her pocket and climbed into the SUV. Reggie turned his attention from Lee and asked, "Anything useful?"

"A promising lead in Leland, North Carolina. It's forty-eight-hours old. We need to get moving." She punched the address for Boone's Tavern into the navigation and the fastest route showed up on the screen. "We're headed there."

"You planning to share the intel or not?" Lee asked from the backseat where she was reading the social work files she'd collected in Melissa Black's house.

Kim said, "Looks like Reacher might have been involved in another bar fight. The eyewitnesses described him, and it sounds like Reacher. We've got grainy video that could be him."

"Can we see it?" Lee's question was impatient and eager.

"Yeah. I need to download it. Hang on." Kim pulled her laptop and her secure hot spot from her bag and connected to her private server. She downloaded the video and queued it to play.

Smithers pulled over onto the shoulder to watch. Lee leaned forward between the seats. Kim pushed the play button.

The video was brief. Less than thirty seconds. It showed a guy manhandling a woman seated at the bar. He grabbed her arm and jerked her hard. She struggled against him and ended up on her ass on the floor.

Before the man could grab her again, the second guy moved swiftly into the frame and shoved the first man aside. Which infuriated the first man.

He yelled something that might have been, "What the hell are you doing?"

Whatever the first man said was lost to the noise inside the bar. But the first man didn't wait for a reply. He took a big, roundhouse swing aimed at the big man's jaw.

The big man simply raised his giant-sized hand, caught the punch in his palm, and held onto the fist. The first man spewed a string of curses.

The first man struggled to free himself, with zero effect on the big man.

It seemed like the big man had tired of the game after a few seconds, so he adjusted his stance and, while holding onto the first man's fist, delivered a hard, straight head butt to his face.

The blow laid the first man out flat on the floor.

The big man tossed a few bills onto the bar while he said something to the bartender that couldn't be heard on the video. Then he left the bar.

"So what do you think? You've met Reacher. Talked to him," Kim said to Lee. "Is that guy Reacher or not?"

"Looks like Reacher. Walks like Reacher. Acts like Reacher." Lee nodded once for emphasis. "Who else would it be?"

"We've also got an ATM withdrawal near that bar from Reacher's personal bank account using his ATM card," Kim said. "There's no evidence that Reacher's ATM card has been stolen."

Lee said, "You got a warrant to search Reacher's bank account?"

Kim said nothing.

"Safe to assume Reacher used the card himself," Smithers said flatly. "Sounds like we're making progress."

"Let's get through these files while we're driving. Be ready to hit the ground running when we reach Leland," Lee suggested, handing half the files to Kim.

The sun was sinking toward the horizon, painting the sky in shades of orange and purple. It would be full dark before they reached Leland.

Reacher was probably long gone by now. Which was okay. She wasn't keen to engage Reacher in the darkness.

Half an hour later, Kim was deep into a file about one of Melissa Black's clients with a history of erratic behavior when Smithers spoke up.

"We've got a tail," he said quietly, his eyes flicking to the rearview mirror.

Kim looked up, instantly alert. "What do you see?"

"Government-issue sedan, two cars back. It's been with us since we left Black's neighborhood."

Lee twisted in her seat to look. "Another agency working the case?"

Kim cocked her head. "Possible. We know there are other teams investigating Daisy Hawkins. They probably had Black's house under surveillance."

"Should we lose them?" Smithers asked, hands tightening slightly on the wheel.

Kim considered the suggestion seriously for a moment. "They don't know who we are, and we don't want to raise suspicion. If they keep following us, we'll lose them."

Smithers nodded, maintaining their speed and position on the highway. For now.

"This complicates things," Lee muttered, turning back to her files.

"It does," Kim agreed. "But it also confirms we're on the right track with a connection between Hawkins and Black."

"Yeah," Smithers replied. "As long as they don't bigfoot us."

Kim said nothing. Her misgivings intensified, sending the snake in her stomach into fits of writhing she could barely control, even after chewing three antacids all at once.

She was closer to finding Reacher than she'd ever been. Which was more than okay.

But Reacher had been a military cop for thirteen years and a damned good one by all accounts.

He knew most bars had CCTV.

He knew ATM withdrawals could be traced.

He knew vehicles and license plates could be identified and tracked.

He also knew that bar fights were a nightly occurrence in dive bars around the country. If serious bodily injury resulted, Police were called and filed electronic reports.

Reports that could be accessed by a good investigator with the right connections.

The whole setup made her extremely uneasy.

It felt like Reacher was leaving her a trail of breadcrumbs to follow. Which was not okay. Not even remotely.

What the hell was he doing?

CHAPTER 26

North Carolina

"DAMMIT." MARCUS MOLINA SLAMMED his fist on the steering wheel. The clock on the dashboard mocked him: 10:00 p.m. David had been off the grid for over six hours now.

Beside him, Melissa Black sat stone-faced, her eyes fixed on the road ahead.

"We need to find him," she said, her voice unnervingly calm. "Now."

"No kidding," Molina replied with heavy sarcasm. "We've looked in all the obvious places. Let's check his apartment."

Twenty minutes later, they pulled up to the curb outside a dilapidated building on the outskirts of town. Molina killed the engine and turned to Black. "Stay here. I'll check it out."

"Be quick," she replied, scooting into the driver's seat, when Molina stepped out and closed the door.

He watched as she pulled away from the curb. He glanced around the immediate vicinity for surveillance gear, hoping his luck would hold. The last thing he needed was a stray video capture of him or his vehicle.

This wasn't the sort of neighborhood where homeowners installed doorbell cameras. There were no businesses on this block, either. He might escape notice here if he didn't linger.

Molina strolled up the sidewalk to the front door and walked inside the building as if he were an invited guest.

Inside, he jogged up the stairs to the third floor. He knocked on David's door. No answer. He tried the handle. Locked.

After a furtive glance around and finding no potential witnesses, Molina pulled out a lockpick set. Seconds later, he was inside.

The apartment was sparsely furnished, almost monastic. A single unmade bed, a small desk covered in environmental justice pamphlets, and walls plastered with protest posters instead of photos of music idols or vacation spots.

Molina riffled through drawers and checked under the mattress. He found a couple of things suggesting David had been here earlier in the day. His toothbrush was in a glass on the bathroom sink. The floor of the shower was still damp.

But nothing revealed David's current whereabouts.

Molina sent Melissa a quick text. After giving her a few minutes to return, he left the apartment and made his way outside to the vehicle.

As he climbed in, she gave him a questioning look and he shook his head.

"He's not here now. But he was here a few hours ago. He can't have gone far. He doesn't own a vehicle, and he's got no money to rent one," Molina said.

"Where to next?" she asked, still seated behind the steering wheel.

Molina thought for a moment. "The university. He spends a lot of time in the environmental science building."

"It will be closed at this time of night."

"You have a better idea?" Molina asked impatiently.

Black shook her head. "Unfortunately not."

They rode in tense silence all the way to the university. As Black had warned, the buildings and the campus seemed deserted. She dropped Molina off in front of the environmental science building and drove away.

Molina pulled his hoodie on. Walking with his head down and hunched over to obscure his identity, he hurried inside.

He searched empty classrooms and laboratories. A few students were gathered in common areas, but he found no trace of David.

He texted Black to pick him up and returned to the car once again empty-handed.

"This isn't working." Black's patience had worn thin. "We need to think like David. He's a total loner. No family. No friends outside our group. Where would he go if he was having doubts?"

Molina shook his head. "David wouldn't have doubts. You saw how committed he was during the training sessions. He was always the most enthusiastic, the most driven."

Black nodded. "That's why I chose him for EcoHarmony. His passion, his youth. He's perfect for infiltrating their ranks. And he'll make an ideal martyr for the cause."

"So why has he gone dark?" Molina asked rhetorically.

Black's eyes narrowed. "That's what we need to figure out. And fast."

Molina racked his brain, thinking back to his conversations with David. Something nagged at the edge of his memory.

"It's a long shot," he said suddenly.

"Whatever it is, we don't have anything better," Black replied.

Following Molina's directions, Black drove to a small, overgrown cemetery on the outskirts of town. The town was small, but it was more than a hundred years old. Hundreds of people had died there over the years. The municipal cemetery covered a few acres of land.

As they pulled up to the entrance, Molina said, "Drop me off here. I'll call when I'm ready to be picked up."

He pulled his hood up again and left the vehicle. Black drove away.

Continuing to play his hunches, Molina hustled along the gravel trail from the front of the cemetery where the graves dated back to the early eighteen hundreds. As he moved deeper into the headstones, he felt like he was marching through time. The Civil War dead filled a large section, followed by those who had died during other wars.

As he entered the twenty-first-century sections, he spotted a lone figure hunched over a fresh grave in the pale moonlight. He slowed his jog to a quieter approach, barely making enough noise to announce his presence.

He didn't want to startle David. But David didn't turn.

"I thought I might find you here," Molina said softly as he reached the gravesite.

David's shoulders tensed. "How did you know I'd be here?"

Molina stopped beside him, looking down at the simple headstone. *Daisy Hawkins*, it read. Nothing else.

"You mentioned her once. Not by name, but I could tell she was important to you."

David nodded, his eyes never leaving the grave. He whispered, "We were going to change the world together."

Molina chose his next words carefully. "You still can, David. We can't let Daisy's sacrifice be in vain."

Finally, David looked up. His eyes were red-rimmed but burning with intensity. "What do you mean?"

Molina took a deep breath. "We've chosen the targets. You've been selected for a special mission. One that will shake the very foundations of the environmental movement."

David stood up from his crouch by the gravesite, suddenly alert. "Tell me."

"EcoHarmony Foundation. Their headquarters in San Francisco."

David's eyes widened. "But they're supposed to be on our side."

Molina shook his head. "They preach moderation when the world is burning. They're part of the problem, David. And you can show everyone the truth. Make Daisy proud."

For a long moment, David was silent. Then, slowly, a smile spread across his face. It was a terrible thing to behold.

"Yes," he said. "Yes, I'll do it. For Daisy. For the planet."

Molina nodded, relief flooding through him. "Come on. We have work to do."

As they walked back to the car, David suddenly stopped. "Wait. My phone. I turned it off. I needed to be alone. I'm sorry if I worried you."

Molina waved off the apology. "It's fine. Just don't do it again. We need to be able to reach you."

They reached the car. Black's eyes narrowed as she saw David.

"Is everything set?" she asked.

Molina nodded. "We're back on track."

As they drove back to headquarters, Black turned to face David in the backseat.

"You understand the importance of your mission, don't you, David?" she asked.

David nodded fervently. "Yes. EcoHarmony needs to be exposed for the frauds they are. Their half-measures are dooming us all."

"Exactly." Black smiled her reassurance, as if David were a particularly apt pupil. "That's why we chose you.

Your passion, your conviction is exactly what we need for this mission."

David leaned forward, his eyes blazing with a convert's zeal. "Tell me more about the plan. I want to know everything."

As Black began to outline the details, Molina felt a twinge of something he couldn't immediately identify. Unease? Guilt?

He pushed the twinge aside. They had David back. The plan was moving forward. That was all that mattered.

When they returned to headquarters, they gathered around the map. David studied it intently, his finger tracing the path to San Francisco.

"When do I leave?" he asked.

"Soon," Molina replied. "We need to move fast."

David nodded like a child at the carnival. "I'm ready."

As they finalized the details, Molina marveled at David's transformation. The lost, grieving man he'd found at the cemetery was gone, replaced by an impatient soldier ready for battle.

Later, after David left to prepare for his mission, Black pulled Molina aside.

"Close call and a near miss," she said. "We can't have a repeat of this. No more patriots going dark. No more doubts from the top if we want to keep the others on track."

"Correct." Molina nodded. "They know you well. Check in on each of them. Make sure they're revved up and ready to launch."

"Will do," Black said firmly.

Molina felt a chill run down his spine. They had averted disaster today, but at what cost?

The young man marching off to his fate bore little resemblance to the idealistic student Molina had first recruited. Even his parents wouldn't recognize him now. David was no longer a kid. He was a martyr.

The plan was in motion, and there was no turning back. Very soon, the world would change forever. David and the other martyrs would be at the heart of it all, perfect weapons forged from grief and rage.

Molina only hoped they could control the fire they had ignited.

CHAPTER 27

Leland, North Carolina

THERESA LEE PUSHED OPEN the heavy wooden
door of Boone's Tavern. A wave of warm, stale air hit her.
The sharp tang of spilled beer mixed with the acrid bite of
cigarette smoke irritated her nose.

She blinked to help her eyes adjust and the dim interior
came into focus. Floorboards creaked under her feet, cutting
through noisy patrons and clinking glasses

Otto stepped in behind her. The two women stood still
and scanned the room for potential threats.

Worn wood paneling covered the walls. Neon beer signs
glowed dimly. A battered foosball table stood in the center of
the open space. A few locals hunched over their drinks at the
bar. Country music played softly from an ancient jukebox.

Otto nodded to Lee and moved to chat with the patrons.
Lee approached the bartender, a bald man with a full beard
and massive arms.

"Evening," Lee said, smiling warmly. "Rough night?"

The bartender shrugged. "Same as any other."

"I'm Theresa. And you are?"

"People call me Wes."

Lee leaned on the bar, keeping her tone casual. "Wes, something happened here a couple nights ago and a friend of mine might've been involved. I'm worried about him."

Wes seemed mildly surprised. "Couple of guys got into a fight. One went to the hospital. Is that what you mean?"

Lee nodded. "That's the one. My friend's a big guy, keeps to himself mostly. Sound familiar?"

"Yeah," Wes said. "He came in, minded his own business. Then Donnie started running his mouth."

"Donnie sounds like trouble," Lee said.

"You don't know the half of it." Wes snorted. "He was hassling his girlfriend, Penny. Timid little thing he found in the hills somewhere. Thinks he owns her now."

As Lee chatted with Wes, she noticed Otto moving around the room. Lee kept her focus on the bartender, hoping to build enough rapport to get more information.

"Sounds like quite a night," Lee said. "I don't suppose you remember anything else about my friend? Or Donnie and his crew?"

Lee nodded, encouraging Wes to continue.

"Your friend," Wes said, "he handled himself. But Donnie and his crew, they're bad news. Especially for Penny."

"Sounds like Penny could use some help," Lee suggested carefully.

Wes's expression hardened. "Lot of folks around here could use help. Doesn't mean they get it."

Lee was about to respond when she caught Otto's eye across the room. The subtle head tilt indicated she'd found something.

"Excuse me a moment," Lee said to Wes. She made her way over to Otto, who stood near a cork bulletin board near the dart games.

"What is it?" Lee asked quietly.

Otto pointed discreetly to a grainy image pinned to the board. It showed the front entrance, timestamped from two nights ago. Despite the poor quality, Lee recognized Jack Reacher immediately.

"Yep. That's him," Lee said quietly.

"Agreed." Otto used her phone to take a photo of the entire corkboard and take a closeup of the Reacher image.

Lee turned back to Wes again. Casually, she said, "That photo on the corkboard. You take pictures of everyone coming and going?"

Wes tensed slightly. "Safety measure. Helps me prove I'm not serving minors when the liquor control squad comes around."

"Smart. Must come in handy sometimes." Lee nodded, keeping her tone light. "Any chance you have more from that night? Might help me piece together what happened with my friend."

Lee waited as Wes considered her request. His gaze darted to the security camera above the door, then back to her face. She didn't rush him.

"Maybe I do," Wes finally said. "What's it worth to you?"

She reached into her pocket and pulled out a fifty-dollar bill. She placed it on the bar, her fingers resting lightly on top.

"This is just to look," she said. "If I need copies, we can discuss a fair price."

Wes eyed the money. He glanced around the bar, then nodded.

"Wait here," he said.

Lee watched Wes disappear into a back room. She caught Otto's attention and gave a small nod. Otto resumed her conversation with a patron, but Lee noticed her hand had moved closer to her weapon.

Wes returned with a manila envelope. He set it on the bar next to Lee's hand.

"These are from that night," he said. "Don't make me regret this."

Lee opened the envelope. Inside were several grainy printouts from the security camera. She spread them out, her eyes scanning each image.

"Tell me about these people," she said to Wes, pointing to a group of men clustered around a young woman.

Wes leaned in to examine the photo. "That's Donnie and his crew. The woman's Penny."

Lee studied the image. Penny looked small, almost lost among the group of men. Her body language screamed fear.

"And this one?" Lee pointed to another photo, showing Reacher at the bar.

"That's your friend," Wes said. "Like I said, he kept to himself until Donnie started trouble."

Lee nodded. She flipped through more photos, organizing them in order of the timeline that unfolded that night.

"Mind if I keep these?" Lee asked.

Wes shrugged, which she took for permission.

Lee slid the photos into her pocket. She glanced toward Otto and noticed a shift in the bar's atmosphere. The other patrons had grown quiet. Attention had fixed on the two unfamiliar women.

Otto joined Lee at the bar just before the bar's front door banged open. Lee's hand moved instinctively toward her gun as she turned to face the newcomer.

A tall, broad-shouldered man stepped into the bar. Unkempt beard, bloodshot eyes glaring as he scanned the room. A jagged scar ran down his left cheek.

Two other men flanked him, both sporting similar looks of barely contained aggression.

The bar fell silent. Wes straightened up behind the counter.

"Bubba," he said, his voice low. "Didn't expect to see you here tonight."

Bubba's gaze fell across Lee and Otto. His eyes narrowed.

"Who the hell are you?" he growled.

Lee kept her voice calm. "Just passing through. Having a drink."

Bubba took a step closer. "Funny. Looks to me like you're asking questions. Poking around in business that ain't yours."

Otto shifted slightly, positioning herself to get a clear line of sight between Lee and Bubba. Lee could feel the tension in the room ratcheting up.

"We don't want any trouble," Lee said.

Bubba sneered. "Too late for that. You ladies picked the wrong bar to stick your noses in. Donnie might be laid up, but I'm here to make sure things stay how they should."

Lee assessed the options. Smithers was outside, but calling for backup would escalate the situation. She needed to defuse this, fast.

She met Bubba's glare steadily. "Look, we're not here to cause problems. Just having a drink and leaving."

"Yeah? Then what's ole Wes here got to say that's so fascinating?" Bubba took another step forward as he gestured toward the bartender. "I've known Wes all my life. Believe me, he's not that interesting."

Wes started to gather the glasses off the bar, but Bubba's hand shot out, grabbing his wrist.

"Leave 'em," Bubba growled.

Lee felt Otto tense beside her. The other patrons edged away, leaving a clear space around them.

"Those are mine," Lee said, her voice firm. "Private business."

"Gimme the usual," Bubba said, lips curled into a sneer. "Nothing's private in this town. Not from us."

He reached for the glass when Wes placed it on the bar in front of him. Lee's hand clamped down on his wrist, stopping him.

For a moment, nobody moved. The air crackled with tension.

Then Bubba's free hand balled into a fist. He swung at Lee's face.

Lee ducked the punch, feeling the air whoosh past her ear. Otto moved instantly, driving her elbow hard into Bubba's kidney. He stumbled back, colliding with one of his cronies who propped him up until he steadied onto both feet.

The bar erupted into chaos. Lee spun to face Bubba's second homie. He lunged at her, but Lee sidestepped, using his momentum to send him crashing into a table.

Otto grappled with Bubba, who was at least twice her size and twice as heavy. She landed two quick jabs to his ribs before he shoved her away.

"Wes!" Lee shouted. "Call the cops!"

Wes hesitated, his gaze darting between the brawl and the phone behind the bar.

Bubba regained his footing, enraged. "You bitches are dead!"

He charged at Lee. She braced herself, waiting until the last second before pivoting, using the same move as before. Bubba's momentum carried him past her and into the bar. Glasses shattered as he slammed into the counter.

Lee heard the bar's door bang open. She risked a glance and saw Smithers rushing in, his hand reaching for the weapon under his jacket.

"Time to go," Lee called to Otto when she heard the sirens in the distance.

They made for the exit, dodging swinging fists and overturned chairs. Behind them, Bubba roared in anger, but his voice was drowned out by the increasingly loud sirens.

Lee and Otto burst out of the bar, Smithers right behind them. They sprinted across the parking lot.

"SUV. Now," Smithers barked, leading the way to the far edge of the lot.

They reached the vehicle just as the first police car rounded the corner, lights flashing, sirens blasting louder than ever. Smithers moved quickly into the driver's seat, Otto took shotgun, and Lee slid into the back.

The engine roared to life. Smithers threw the SUV into reverse, tires squealing as he backed out of the space. He shifted to drive and floored it causing the powerful vehicle to leap forward.

They sped past the incoming police cars.

"Anyone hurt?" Smithers asked, gaze firmly on the road as he navigated the dark streets.

"We're fine," Otto replied.

Lee took a deep breath, adrenaline still coursing through her veins. "Let's get out of this town. We've got what we came for."

Smithers nodded, guiding the SUV onto the highway. In the rearview mirror, the lights of Leland grew smaller, fading into the night.

When they'd put some distance behind them, Smithers asked, "So was Reacher here two nights ago or not?"

Otto replied. "He was here. We have him positively identified on CCTV."

Smithers nodded, satisfied with the result.

Lee added, "Yeah, he was here. But where is he now?"

A beat passed. Then two.

"Turn around. We need to go back," Otto replied.

Smithers gave her a quick look across the console. "Returning to the scene of the crime is always a bad idea, you know."

"Yeah," Otto said. "But we need to talk to Donnie's girlfriend. Reacher defended her and put Donnie in the hospital. Could be Reacher told her why."

"Which could lead us to where he was going," Lee said, acknowledging the plan. "Her full name and address should be on the police report from the bar fight."

CHAPTER 28

Tuesday, July 2
Leland, North Carolina

KIM OTTO FLIPPED THROUGH the police report of the bar fight on her laptop screen until she found the list of witnesses and addresses.

"Got it," she said as she punched the address into the navigation system. "Penny Wheeler, 1542 Willow Creek Road."

"Nice work," Smithers grinned. "Sometimes locals know everyone, so they skip the details. These cops seem to have been on the ball. Might be worth talking to them."

"Possibly." Lee stifled a yawn. "Penny Wheeler knows what happened at the bar. She could have answers about Reacher. Or Docherty. Or whatever the hell is going on."

The SUV's headlights cut through the darkness as Smithers drove the deserted streets directly to Penny

Wheeler's home on the outskirts of town. The clock on the dashboard read 1:17 a.m.

"Lights are on. She must be a night owl," Kim said as Smithers parked a few houses down deep in the shadows of a giant oak tree.

Penny's home stood back from the road, a small, weathered structure with peeling white paint. A rusted pickup truck sat in the gravel driveway. Overgrown shrubs flanked the porch steps. Faded curtains hung in the windows. A dim light shone through one window and fell across the patchy grass. The house seemed to sag slightly, as if tired from years of neglect.

They walked to Penny's front door. Gravel crunched under their feet, but no one seemed to notice the noise.

Kim knocked firmly. They waited. The porch light came on. Penny's tense face appeared in a narrow gap as she cracked open the door.

"Ms. Wheeler, I'm Special Agent Otto with the FBI. These are my colleagues." Kim said. She showed her badge. "We need to talk about the bar incident. May we come in?"

Penny paused and then opened the door wider to let them inside. "Okay. I guess."

Kim walked inside with Smithers and Lee following behind her. Penny gestured toward a worn sofa. She perched on a tired old chair and fidgeted with the hem of her nightgown.

"Ms. Wheeler, we'd like to ask you about the incident at the bar," Kim said.

Penny's eyes darted between the three of them. "I don't know if I should talk about it."

Smithers ignored her objections and leaned forward. "We need to know so we can help you."

Penny took a deep breath. "It wasn't just some random bar fight. Reacher knew I was in danger before anything happened."

Lee frowned. "You mean like a premonition or something?"

"I don't know," Penny said with a shrug. "But he did."

Kim asked softly, "Penny, do you know Daisy Hawkins?"

Penny stiffened as she nodded slowly. "We met at a retreat. That's all."

"What kind of retreat?" Smithers pressed.

"Just a retreat," Penny said, her voice tight. "For women."

Kim exchanged glances with the others. "We need more details. We're trying to find out what really happened to Daisy Hawkins. You want to know that, too, don't you?"

Penny shook her head. "I can't say more. You don't understand."

Lee asked, "How does Reacher fit into all this?"

"I don't know," Penny replied. "He just showed up that night."

Kim said, "This retreat where you met Daisy, how long ago was it?"

"Six months, maybe," Penny said with a shrug. "She was a nice girl who had a hard life. Abusive boyfriend. We kind of bonded over that, I guess."

"Were you surprised when she took her own life?" Kim asked.

Penny shook her head, and her gaze dropped to her fingers which were still pleating the soft cotton nightgown. Her arms and legs were bare, revealing a few old bruises.

Smithers leaned in and picked up the questioning. "Why weren't you surprised?"

Penny's hands shook. "If it wasn't suicide. What if I'm next?"

"Who would want to hurt you?" Lee asked.

Penny's eyes had widened with fear. Her voice trembled as she replied, "I can't say. They'll come after me."

Kim sat next to her. "We can protect you, Penny. But we need to know what's going on."

Penny opened her mouth to speak, then froze, staring out the window.

"They know where I live. They'll come here again," she whispered.

Kim continued to press her, urgently but calm. "We're not leaving you here to deal with this alone. But we need to know about Reacher. What happened at the bar? What did you two talk about?"

Penny flinched and her gaze darted nervously to the window when a noisy truck backfired as it passed, but she said, "I was at the bar, just trying to have a quiet drink. Reacher came in and sat down next to me. It was like he sensed something was off."

"What do you mean?" Lee pressed.

Penny took a shaky breath. "He bought me a drink, asked if I was okay. Said I looked worried. Then he asked about Daisy."

Kim asked, "What did he want to know about Daisy?"

"He asked if I'd heard from her recently. I told him no, that she'd died. He got this look in his eye, like he already knew she was dead and didn't believe it was suicide."

Smithers interjected, "Did Reacher say why he was interested in Daisy?"

Penny shook her head. "Before I could ask, Donnie showed up."

"Donnie?" Kim asked.

"My ex-boyfriend," Penny explained, her voice trembling slightly. "He came straight at me, grabbed my arm, and tried to pull me off the bar stool."

"That's when Reacher stepped in?" Lee guessed.

Penny nodded. "Yeah. One second I'm being yanked off my seat, the next Donnie's on the floor and Reacher's standing over him. It happened so fast."

"Did Reacher say anything else to you? Anything about where he was going or why he was in town?" Kim asked.

"After the fight, he just told me that Donnie wouldn't hurt me anymore. Then he left."

Suddenly, the sound of tires on gravel cut through the quiet night. Headlights swept across the front of the house, illuminating the room for a brief moment before plunging it back into shadows.

"Oh God, is it Donnie?" Penny whimpered, shrinking back in her chair.

Lee moved swiftly to the window, peering out through a gap in the curtains. "Black SUV, tinted windows. Two men getting out. They don't look friendly."

Kim turned to Penny, her voice low and urgent. "Is there a back way out?"

Penny nodded, pointing with a trembling finger toward the kitchen. "Through there, leads to the backyard."

"Alright, let's move," Kim ordered. She helped Penny to her feet while Smithers and Lee took up defensive positions.

As they made their way to the kitchen, a heavy pounding on the front door echoed through the house.

"Penny!" a gruff voice called out. "Open up! I know you're in there!"

"That's not Donnie," she whispered as her face went pale.

"Okay, change of plans. We need to get you out of here now, but we also need to know who these men are and why they're after you. Can you tell us quickly?" Kim asked.

Penny cleared her throat and spoke in a voice barely above a whisper. "They're connected to the retreat where I met Daisy. It wasn't just a women's support group. It was something else. Something dangerous."

The pounding on the door grew louder, more insistent.

"We'll get the full story later," Smithers said urgently. "Right now, we need to move."

Lee took point, leading the way to the back door. Kim supported Penny, who was visibly shaking. Smithers brought up the rear, his hand on his weapon.

As they reached the kitchen, the sound of splintering wood came from the front of the house. The intruders were breaking in.

"Go, go!" Lee hissed, easing open the back door.

They slipped out into the cool night, crouching low as they made their way across the overgrown backyard. The sound of heavy footsteps and angry voices echoed from inside the house.

"My car's just around the corner," Kim whispered to Penny. "We'll get you somewhere safe, and then you're going to tell us everything about this retreat, Daisy, and why these men are after you. Understood?"

Penny nodded, her face pale in the moonlight. As they reached the street, they could hear the men inside the house, angry shouts cutting through the quiet.

Kim led them quickly to the SUV, helping Penny into the backseat while Lee and Smithers took up defensive positions. As soon as everyone was in, Smithers started the engine and pulled away from the curb.

Kim saw two men burst out of Penny's house, looking around frantically. But by then, Smithers had turned the corner, and they were out of sight.

"Alright, Penny," Kim said steadily despite the adrenaline flooding her system. "We're safe for now. Start from the beginning. What's this retreat, and how is it connected to Daisy, Reacher, and the men who just broke into your house?"

Penny took a deep breath, her hands still trembling slightly. "The retreat wasn't what it seemed. We thought it was a support group for women who'd been through tough times, but it was more like a recruitment center."

"Recruitment for what?" Lee asked, turning in her seat to face her.

Penny hesitated, glancing nervously out the window. "I'm not entirely sure. Some kind of organization. They said they could offer protection, a new life. But the price was too high."

Kim kept her eyes on the road, navigating through the quiet streets. "What do you mean by 'the price was too high'?"

"They wanted us to cut all ties with our past. Family, friends, everything," Penny explained. "And there were tasks. Things they wanted us to do. Illegal things."

Smithers frowned. "Like what?"

Penny shook her head. "I got scared and left before they could tell me more. But Daisy stayed. She was desperate to get away from her ex."

Kim pressed on. "And you think this organization had something to do with Daisy's death?"

Penny nodded again. "After I left, Daisy called me. She was scared. Said she'd discovered something terrible about the group. We were supposed to meet, but it didn't happen."

"That's when she committed suicide," Lee finished.

"Yeah," Penny whispered. "But I don't believe it. And neither did Reacher."

Kim glanced in the rearview mirror. "How does Reacher fit into all this?"

"I don't know," Penny admitted. "Like I said, he just showed up at the bar asking questions about Daisy. It was like he knew something was wrong. And then when Donnie came in, all hell broke loose. Donnie's always had a temper, but that night he was different. More aggressive. I think maybe the organization sent him to scare me."

Kim exchanged a look with Lee and Smithers. "Tell us everything you can remember. Names, locations, anything that might help us understand what we're dealing with."

Penny shrugged again. "Melissa was there. She said the retreat was a safe place. We could stay there forever, if we wanted. Daisy stayed, but I was too scared."

CHAPTER 29

Leland, North Carolina

SMITHERS DROVE THE SUV through the quiet streets. The tires hummed softly on the pavement.

Penny lowered her phone, her fingers trembling slightly as she slipped it into her pocket. "My friend says I can stay with her. She lives on the other side of town."

"What's the address?" Kim asked. Penny gave it to her, and she punched it into the navigation.

Kim twisted in the passenger seat to face Penny. "We'll drop you off there. And we'll set up some protection for you in case Donnie comes around again."

"You think he will? Come at me again?" Penny's voice quivered and she seemed terrified.

"Abusive men don't always quit while they're ahead." Kim replied with as much reassurance as she could offer without lying, "Sometimes it takes a few arrests and a stint in jail for the message to get through."

"Reacher told Donnie he'd come back if Donnie tried to hurt me again. He said he'd kill Donnie," Penny said as if she had mixed feelings about it. "Would he really do that?"

Kim said nothing. The truth was that if Donnie abused Penny again, Reacher would come back. And he'd kill Donnie. Reacher was a man who kept his promises.

In the backseat, Lee filled the silence. "Tell us more about your conversation with Reacher at the bar. What did he say? What did you say?"

Penny's gaze dropped to her lap where her hands were clasped tightly together. When she spoke, her voice was barely above a whisper. "Reacher was very focused. He asked about Donnie first and how long he'd been hurting me."

"What did you tell him?" Kim asked, watching Penny's face.

"I told him it had been going on for years," Penny replied, her voice catching slightly. She took a deep breath before continuing. "Then he asked about Melissa."

Smithers's gaze flicked to the rearview mirror. "Melissa?"

"She's a counselor. She works with the place where the retreat was held." Penny nodded slowly. "That's where I met Daisy Hawkins."

Kim's hand tightened on the door handle. "Reacher knew about Melissa already? Before you told him?"

"Yes. He did." Penny confirmed emphatically. "He knew her name and everything. He asked if she might still be at the retreat site."

"And is she?" Lee pressed.

Penny shrugged. "I don't know, but it's possible. He wanted to know about the other people at the retreat. I told him there were ten of us. He asked if we were all in abusive relationships."

"Were you?" Smithers asked gently.

In a barely audible voice, she replied, "Yes. All of us."

The SUV slowed for a red light. Outside, a few late-night pedestrians shuffled along the sidewalk headed in the opposite direction.

The light turned green, and Smithers rolled forward again. Kim said, "Did Reacher say anything more about his plans?"

Penny shook her head. "He just told me to be careful and then he left. Right after he dealt with Donnie. Before the cops came."

The streets narrowed as they entered another residential area. "Where was this retreat held, Penny?"

Penny visibly tensed. Her shoulders hunched and her voice was strained. "It was in western North Carolina. A beautiful, remote place. It had been a farm at one time, but now it's a rustic resort, I guess you'd say."

"What's the name of the place? The nearest town?" Lee asked. "Can you describe it for us? What does it look like? What sort of buildings and equipment did you see there?"

"I don't know what they call it. We went there on a bus with Melissa." Penny closed her eyes, as if visualizing the scene. "The main building was this grand old mansion. White columns, wraparound porch. It sat on a hill overlooking a valley. Forests all around. The air was so clean and crisp."

"Sounds isolated," Smithers observed.

"It was," Penny confirmed, her eyes still closed. "The nearest town was miles away. We had to take a winding road through the mountains to get there. And we stayed there the whole time."

Kim frowned, trying to find such a place on her laptop. "No one mentioned the name of the place?"

Penny opened her eyes. "They just called it the retreat or the sanctuary."

"How many people were there?" Lee asked.

Penny paused, considering. "Maybe twenty of us. Plus counselors, security, kitchen workers, a couple of maids."

The SUV slowed as they approached a small, well-kept bungalow. A single light burned in one of the front windows. Smithers eased the SUV to a stop at the curb.

"Is this where your friend lives?" Kim asked. Penny nodded. "What's her name? We'll put her on the protection detail."

"Jeanie Turner."

"Did she attend the retreat with you?" Smithers asked.

"No."

Kim pulled a card from her pocket and held it out to Penny. "If you remember anything else, or if you feel threatened in any way, call me immediately. We'll be watching the house, too, just in case."

"Thank you." Penny took the card. "Be careful."

Lee stepped out of the car and opened Penny's door, offering her hand. Penny moved hesitantly as she emerged from the vehicle. She glanced around the neighborhood as if Donnie might be waiting.

Penny stood on the sidewalk, clutching her small overnight bag. Lee placed a reassuring hand on her shoulder. "We'll do everything we can to keep you safe, Penny. Try to get some rest. No matter what, don't go back to your house until Donnie is safely in jail."

Penny took a deep breath, squared her shoulders, and started up the short path to the front door. Before she reached it, the porch light flicked on, and the door opened. A woman about Penny's age stood there, presumably Jeanie Turner.

Kim watched the two women embrace and then disappear into the house. Penny closed the door, and the porch light went out.

Lee slid into the backseat and Smithers pulled away from the curb.

Kim broke the silence. "What do you make of all this?"

Lee exhaled slowly. "This retreat sounds like some kind of safe house for abuse victims. But why is Reacher so interested in finding this Melissa? And is she Melissa Black?"

"Melissa is a common enough name. Could be it's not Black," was Smithers's response. "But why is Penny so scared to talk about it all?"

"Let's go with the obvious for now. As a working hypothesis, Melissa Black is the social worker that Reacher is interested in," Kim said. "And it's no coincidence that both Daisy Hawkins and Penny Wheeler were Melissa's clients and attended the retreat together."

"Okay. I can buy all of that. But where are Melissa and Reacher now?" Lee asked.

Smithers replied, "And is all of this connected to Docherty's death in some way? Is Reacher hunting Docherty's killer?"

"At this point, we all need sleep. We passed a motel about a mile back. Let's get some shuteye," Kim said. "We'll hit it hard again after sunrise."

"You're my captain," Smithers joked as he turned the SUV around and headed back.

CHAPTER 30

Leland, North Carolina

THERESA LEE WAITED UNTIL Otto and Smithers had disappeared into their rooms to make her call. She quickly discovered she had no cell signal in her room. She slipped outside and leaned against the railing with her phone pressed to her ear. The predawn air felt humid and heavy, promising another scorching July day.

When he answered, she said, "Theresa Lee. Sorry for the ungodly hour."

"No problem. Glad you called. I was up anyway," Senator Sansom replied. "What's the situation?"

Lee kept her voice low. "We're in Leland, North Carolina. We've got solid evidence Reacher was here two nights ago."

Sansom seemed surprised. "What kind of evidence?"

"Eyewitnesses and CCTV footage. It was definitely Reacher," Lee replied emphatically. "He approached a local woman asking about someone named Melissa. When her ex-boyfriend showed up and tried to manhandle her, Reacher beat the hell out of him."

"Good for Reacher. I've never understood why men think they should be able to beat women into submission," Sansom said with approval. "Any idea who this Melissa is or why Reacher is looking for her?"

"Nothing firm yet. It's our first lead to follow up on today."

"Good work. Keep me posted," Sansom replied. Then he added, "I've got some news for you, too."

Lee straightened. "What is it?"

"The Atlanta airport debacle is officially classified as domestic terrorism now," he said flatly.

"Damn," Lee muttered. "That's a big escalation."

"You've got that right. Hundreds of agents are working on it. They're tracking Hawkins and Docherty's actions in depth," Sansom reported. "So far, nothing useful for our purposes has come to light."

Lee frowned. "Why haven't we seen any of this on the news?"

"Information's been tightly controlled and contained. Until we have solid results, we don't want to spook the perpetrators," Sansom said. "We've got several leads, including a potential ecoterrorism angle."

"Ecoterrorism? Docherty didn't believe in anything like that. He was a strictly peaceful guy," Lee replied. "How does that stuff fit?"

"Hawkins babbled the usual catch phrases about economic justice during her initial police interview. Save the planet, defend the earth, corporate greed, and so forth." Sansom paused a moment. "The connection is not confirmed yet, but it could explain the seemingly random nature of the Hawkins and Docherty murders."

Lee raised her eyebrows. "Is that the official word now? That Hawkins didn't commit suicide, and Docherty didn't die in a car crash?"

"Not officially, no. But that's what we all believe. And it's the angle we're pursuing at the moment," Sansom said quietly.

"That actually makes a disturbing amount of sense," Lee replied. "Maybe we can get some additional resources now."

"Not likely. All the effort is going into finding the source of Daisy Hawkins's radicalization. We're still on our own here," Sansom replied.

"I'll poke around. See if I can locate any local environmental groups or organizations," Lee said.

"But be discreet about it. The connection is still speculative. We don't want any wild guesses getting out there or panicked crowds during the holiday madness," Sansom warned.

"Understood. I'll start digging."

"Keep this between us for now," Sansom said. "Get some concrete evidence before you bring Otto and Smithers into the loop. And definitely leave my name out of it."

Lee hesitated briefly and then agreed. "I'll keep you updated."

"Stay in touch," Sansom said as he ended the call.

Lee stared out at the empty parking lot. The Fourth of July was coming up fast. Across America, people would wake to begin the days long celebration and nightly fireworks.

An ecoterrorism group could get exponentially more mileage out of attacks surrounding the nation's birthday celebrations.

More news coverage.

More exposure to crowds.

More damage to what ecojustice warriors viewed as the perpetrators of violence against the planet.

Which meant the agents working on the case would be run ragged. They couldn't cover every inch of the country on days like that.

At least one attack was likely to succeed simply because of the overwhelming number of possible targets.

Lee unlocked her room and stepped inside. The air-conditioning hit her like a wall of ice. She wanted to view the contents of the USB drive she got from Zoe Seltzer, but her laptop didn't have a USB drive. She'd need to find an internet café or a USB reader first.

She booted up her laptop and began her search for local environmental groups instead. She found several almost instantly. How could she narrow them down?

She frowned at her laptop screen. The ecoterrorism angle gnawed at her. She dialed Sansom's number again. When he picked up she said, "Do you have any data on environmental justice groups in remote areas of western North Carolina? It's your state. Any on the radar for terrorism?"

"Why western NC?" he asked.

"A lead from Penny Wheeler, the woman Reacher defended in the bar. She mentioned she met Daisy Hawkins at a retreat for abused spouses held in that area," Lee explained.

"I'll see what I can find. Give me a few minutes."

Lee paced the small motel room for another thirty minutes until her phone buzzed. She picked up. "Theresa Lee."

"I've got something promising," Sansom said as if he were preoccupied. "A small group in western NC called EcoGuard Coalition for Environmental Justice. No known criminal activity, but they could fit the profile if we had more intel. For now, they're on the back burner while we dig into the more likely suspects. I've sent you what we have."

When he disconnected, Lee found the data he'd sent and examined it closely.

The group's online presence was minimal. A bare bones website and a sparse social media account. Recent posts mentioned protests against local mining operations. The phrase "environmental justice" appeared a few times in EcoGuard's mission statement.

She glanced at her watch. 6:30 a.m. Otto and Smithers would be ready for debrief and breakfast soon.

Lee grabbed her bags and scrawled a quick note, which she left on her bed knowing they'd come looking for her. *Following a lead. I'll join you later.*

She hurried to the parking lot where she checked several vehicles until she found an unlocked sedan. Quickly, Lee stuffed her bags inside, started the car and pulled out of the motel parking lot.

How long it would take the owner to report the car missing? With luck, he'd be sleeping for hours yet. She'd dump the car as soon as possible and find something else.

She merged onto the highway heading west toward EcoGuard's public interest meeting which was scheduled in a small town near the Blue Ridge Mountains.

CHAPTER 31

Leland, North Carolina

AFTER TOO LITTLE SLEEP, Kim awoke with a start. The room's tacky décor for the upcoming Independence Day celebrations exacerbated her pounding headache. She checked her phone. Three missed calls from Smithers.

She returned his call, moving before her brain fully engaged. Clothes on. Gun checked. Badge pocketed.

Smithers's voice was terse and brittle. "Lee's not here."

The words didn't register at first. "What do you mean she's not here?"

"I knocked on her door for breakfast. No answer," Smithers replied. "She left a note. *Following a lead. I'll join you later.*"

"What kind of lead? Something that will help us locate Reacher?"

"The note doesn't say."

"On my way," Kim said as she collected her bags. She'd paid the bill with cash last night. She left a tip for the maid and arrived at Lee's room five minutes later.

Smithers loomed by the window while Kim looked around the deserted room for herself.

"No signs of foul play. No indication where she's headed or what the lead is. She even took her bags with her," he said.

"Any idea how long she's been gone?" Kim asked.

"Her bed hasn't been slept in. There's no indication that she showered, either." Smithers shook his head. "If I had to guess, I'd say she left shortly after we checked in."

"We can't wait here for her. We don't know when or if she'll come back." Kim turned from the window. "Every second we hesitate gives Reacher another advantage."

Smithers leaned his back against the wall. "And what about Lee? We're really going to proceed without her?"

"I'd rather not. But she made the decision when she took off without us," Kim said. "I don't like it any more than you do, but we won't find Reacher while we're sitting around here watching fireworks."

"Copy that," Smithers replied seriously. "But we can't find him if we don't know where to look next, either."

Kim swiped her face with her palm, willing her headache to resolve itself. No luck. "I need coffee."

"Yeah. Eggs and bacon and toast to go with it would be good, too."

"Let's stash our bags and find a diner," Kim suggested.

"And then what?" Smithers said as he closed the door to Lee's room and followed Kim to the SUV in the parking lot.

The summer heat was already stifling. Kim couldn't shake the feeling that they were several moves behind Lee.

Still, she was closer to finding Reacher right now than she'd ever been. She didn't intend to lose what little advantage she'd managed to gain.

Kim stowed her bags and took the passenger seat. She placed her alligator clamp at the retractor. While Smithers drove west along the county road, she dialed Lee's number.

The call went straight to voicemail. She left her name and a call back request, which was all she could do.

"Nothing," Kim reported. "We're on our own."

They traveled in silence until Smithers spied a diner at a country crossroads six miles west of the motel. There were about ten vehicles in the gravel parking lot, suggesting the place was popular with the locals.

Smithers pulled into a parking space at the far end of the lot. Kim slid out of the SUV and landed on the gravel with both feet. Smithers engaged the alarm and followed her into the Leland Diner.

Kim opened the door and went inside. The layout was the same as a hundred diners in a hundred other small towns across America.

In the middle of the diner, an open serving shelf separated the kitchen from an open corridor where waitresses collected the food and prepared drinks.

A long counter stretched on the other side of the service station. Round stools were permanently affixed to the floor at the counter.

Several booths lined the exterior walls and tables filled the spaces between the counter service and the booths.

Kim spied an empty booth in the far corner and walked in that direction. Smithers, the giant-sized Black man, and Kim, the tiny Asian-American woman, drew curious looks from the local patrons as they passed.

Smithers slid into the booth with his back to the wall, giving him a clear sight line of the entire diner. He'd see trouble first, when there might still be time to deal with the threats before they became impossible to avoid.

That was the seat Kim preferred, too. Short of asking Smithers to move, she had no alternative but to sit across the table.

Which meant she was immediately uneasy.

The feeling wouldn't resolve itself. She knew from past experience. She spent no further time trying to settle her thrashing stomach.

The lone waitress arrived quickly with two plastic coffee mugs and a thermos of black coffee.

"I'll be back to take your orders in a minute," she promised after she poured the coffee and scurried off.

Kim swigged the hot, black coffee like she was desperate. Which she was. After a few gulps of the high-octane caffeine, her headache began to subside, allowing her to think clearly.

The waitress returned and they placed their orders. Smithers requested eggs and pancakes and bacon and hashbrowns. Kim ordered dry toast to calm her queasy stomach.

"So, now what?" Smithers asked while they waited for their food. "Time to call Cooper? Report in. Get some direction. He's got connections. He might be able to locate Theresa Lee. Save us some time."

Kim said nothing. Calling Cooper was never her first choice. Cooper was her boss, but he'd proven to be a lying, cheating snake. She didn't trust him. Not even a little bit.

But Smithers was too new on this assignment to know all of her rules. She didn't hold it against him. He'd catch up quickly enough.

She'd been reading him in as needed, but he'd only been her official partner for two weeks. Bringing him up to speed would take a bit longer.

"I can't call from here." Kim took another gulp of coffee and then slid out of the booth. "I'll be back."

CHAPTER 32

Madison, North Carolina

TWO HOURS LATER, LEE parked on a side street near the nondescript community center. She'd arrived an hour early thinking she'd have time to look around undisturbed, but several vehicles were already parked in the front lot.

The growing audience was mixed, reflecting EcoGuard's broad appeal.

Young hippie types wearing tie-dye, jeans, and sandals mixed with older professionals dressed in upscale casual golf shirts, khakis, and two-thousand-dollar sneakers. Vehicles ranged from old pickup trucks to pricey sports cars and decked out Harleys.

Somewhat surprisingly, EcoGuard was expecting a large enough crowd to require armed security. Lee's expertise identified them easily enough.

A fit, burly man in a dark jacket wearing an earpiece for comms stood near the entrance, scanning each arrival carefully before admittance.

Another burly man patrolled the perimeter, his hand near enough to his hip to grab a weapon concealed there, should the need arise.

They were the only two guards Lee could see from her vantage point, but there were likely to be more strategically stationed amid the crowd.

"Tight security for peaceful environmentalists," she muttered as she pulled out her phone to update Sansom.

She stopped the text without sending it and returned her phone to her pocket. She'd acquire more intel first so she could send a more complete report.

Lee left her car and approached the community center. Outside, firecrackers popped in the distance, an oddly festive backdrop to the shadows that seemed to grow around this investigation with each passing hour.

She smiled at the man at the door.

"Here for the meeting?" His voice was as rough as gravel in a blender.

Lee nodded. "Yeah, first time. Heard you folks were doing good work."

He stared at her for a long moment. Lee resisted the urge to shove him out of the way. Finally, he grunted and stepped aside.

Perfunctorily, he said, "Meeting starts in an hour. Refreshments inside."

Lee thanked him and crossed the threshold. She found a seat near the back with an unobstructed view as people continued to enter the room in a steady stream.

The atmosphere crackled with edgy anticipation that made her twitchy.

She identified the exits and the shortest route to each, realizing that she should have brought Otto and Smithers along. Too late to correct that mistake now because the meeting was about to begin.

A well dressed woman stepped up to the podium at the front of the room. She seemed relaxed and comfortable in front of the crowd.

"Friends," she began, her tone filled with intensity. "Today, we take the next step in our fight for true environmental justice. Come in, come in. Take your seats quickly. We have much to talk about."

The woman leaned left to speak privately with one of the security staff. Then she turned her head to look briefly at Lee.

The woman's angry glare raised the small hairs on the back of Lee's neck. Her gut said the two were talking about her and not positively. Lee raised her guard, sitting on the edge of her seat just in case she needed to dash out.

The woman said one last thing to the guard and moved on to talk to another man seated on the stage. The guard stepped off the stage and strode quickly toward Lee, maneuvering around the newcomers filling the center aisle between the folding chairs.

Lee stood and attempted to hurry outside, but she was pushing upstream of the flowing crowd all the way from the community center's entrance.

Eventually, she reached the exit and hurried down the stairs.

Where the mammoth security guard blocked her path.

"ID," he demanded, palm out.

"What?" she asked, as if she didn't understand the question.

"Show me your ID," he said in the same demanding tone.

"Why? You're not checking ID. Why did you single me out?"

He kept his hand out, waiting.

Lee shrugged and fumbled for her fake credentials.

The guard examined them and tossed them on the ground. "Nice try, former NYPD Detective Theresa Lee."

Which was when she knew for certain that she was in trouble.

Her hand moved rapidly toward her weapon.

Before she could reach it, a sharp pain exploded in her lower back.

She stumbled and her legs gave out, dropping her to the ground.

Two of the burly men grabbed her arms.

Lee struggled, but her limbs felt like lead. The world tilted and blurred.

She tried to call out, but her voice was a weak mumble.

Rough hands searched her, removing her phone and gun. The big guard smirked. "Looks like we caught ourselves a nosy Nelly, boys."

Lee's vision darkened at the edges. She fought to stay conscious, to memorize faces and details. But the drug coursing through her system was too strong.

The last thing she saw was the big man's sneering face before darkness took her.

CHAPTER 33

Leland, North Carolina

SELF-PRESERVATION DICTATED THAT KIM wouldn't call Cooper. But Finlay was an option. Her thumb hovered over the number for a moment before she inhaled deeply and pressed the call button.

The phone rang three times before he answered.

"Good morning," he said, as if he'd been waiting.

Which he probably had.

He seemed to be everywhere and know everything, all the time. Just like Cooper.

Kim tried not to wonder how they made that happen. She was already a confirmed skeptic. If she allowed full-fledged paranoia to sneak into her head, she'd never get anywhere.

In some weird, peculiar way, knowing Finlay was always aware of her actions didn't make her nervous. But the same behavior from Cooper felt threatening. She'd spent more than a few hours analyzing her reactions to the two men but had reached no final conclusions.

Gaspar, the one she trusted absolutely and at all times, repeatedly advised her to steer clear of both men. Advice that she'd refused to heed. Instead, she chose to make the least bad choice.

She took a deep breath. "We need intel."

Finlay paused for a long moment. "What's your current status?"

She gave him a brief report, focusing on the Docherty murder and the Reacher sightings, and ending with Lee's abrupt departure last night.

"I see. And you want what from me, exactly," he said, preoccupied.

"We need to know where Lee is. She left a note saying she was following a lead."

"What kind of lead? Reacher or Docherty's killer?"

Kim smiled. "So you don't think they're one and the same?"

"Not likely. Docherty was Lee's NYPD partner, as you know, during the old subway suicide bomber case. Which placed both Lee and Docherty squarely on Reacher's team," Finlay said.

"Meaning what?"

"Reacher wouldn't kill either of them without a damned good reason," Finlay said.

"You think not?"

"I'm serious," Finlay said. "For Reacher, that wouldn't be the right thing to do. Pursuant to Reacher's rules of ethics."

"Many people would say Reacher doesn't live by rules of ethics," Kim replied, cocking her head.

"Cooper, you mean? That's where you're wrong. He knows Reacher's rules as well as anyone," Finlay warned. "Don't make the mistake of thinking otherwise."

"Help me out, then. We believe Reacher has been investigating something. He's had at least two bar fights in the past few days that I know about. Both times in some Podunk town defending an abused woman," Kim said.

"Sounds like Reacher. He might have done that just because he wanted to, you know. He's no longer law enforcement. He doesn't actually need a reason to wipe the floor with jerks," Finlay replied. "Reacher figures teaching scumbags a lesson when he has the chance is the right thing to do."

"But that's not what's happening here, is it?" Kim challenged.

After a pause, Finlay asked, "What do you think he's doing?"

"He's looking for someone. Or some thing," Kim replied. "He's making no effort to hide himself or his actions. We've found CCTV video and still photos. Lee positively identified Reacher on both. Not that we needed confirmation. It's obviously him."

Finlay was quiet for a long time. When he finally spoke, he changed the subject. "We've identified several possible environmental groups that might be radicalizing. They're impatient with what they see as too little progress over too much time. Two of those groups are headquartered near your present location."

"Names? Locations? Contact information?" Kim asked.

"One is holding a public information meeting this morning. The group's name is EcoGuard Coalition for Environmental Justice," Finlay said. "You can find them online. They're making no secret of their goals and demands. So far, they seem disjointed, unorganized, and nonviolent. But they are moving in that direction."

Kim memorized the address. "And the other one?"

"They call themselves WRATH. Which is an acronym for Warriors Radically Avenging the Heartland. We don't have much on it yet," Finlay said. "I'll send you what we have. Along with the autopsy report on Daisy Hawkins, which you'll also find interesting."

"What does all of this have to do with Reacher? Or Docherty, for that matter?" Kim asked. She heard someone speaking in the background.

"I've got to go," Finlay said. "Look at the files."

Just like that, she was holding dead air.

She downloaded and flipped through Finlay's files quickly on her phone and then dropped it into her pocket.

CHAPTER 34

Madison, North Carolina

MARCUS MOLINA'S FINGERS TWITCHED as he approached the door. Muffled sounds from the silly EcoGuard meeting filtered through the thick walls. He had set up EcoGuard as a feeder system for WRATH.

So many wannabe eco justice warriors were nuts, flakes, or simply unstable. None of these were suitable candidates for WRATH.

EcoGuard opened its doors to everyone, which made it easier for WRATH to separate the real warriors from the dilettantes. Today's crowd was mostly tourists with the day off work. Waste of his time.

Molina paused a moment to listen. Silence awaited him on the other side of the door. He turned the handle and stepped inside.

The room was dimly lit by a single desk lamp, casting long shadows across the three men who stood waiting. At their feet lay an unconscious woman. Her straight, dark hair splayed across the worn carpet.

Molina's gaze locked onto her. He'd never seen her before.

"Report," he demanded, low and taut.

Decker, the tallest of the three men and a broad-shouldered ex-Marine, stepped forward with a noticeable limp. "Extraction was smooth. Slipped the sedative into her easily. She was out cold before she hit the floor."

Molina nodded, his eyes never leaving the woman. "Any complications?"

"None," Decker replied. "A couple of people asked, and we said she had a panic attack. They bought it hook, line, and sinker."

A thin smile creased Molina's face. "Good. What about her stuff?"

The second man, Cruz, was shorter and stockier with a long, full beard. He held up a small purse, a smartphone, and a Glock pistol.

"Got everything here. Haven't had a chance to go through it yet," he said with a shrug.

"Then what are you waiting for?" Molina snapped. "Search her. I want to know exactly who she is and why she's here."

Cruz nodded quickly and knelt beside the unconscious woman. His hands moved efficiently, patting down pockets and unzipping compartments.

He pulled out a flat leather wallet and flipped it open.

"Well?" Molina demanded.

Cruz's eyes widened as he read the ID. "She was NYPD. A detective, no less. Retired. Name's Theresa Lee."

The air in the room seemed to thicken. Molina's pulse quickened as recognition flashed across his face.

"Detective Theresa Lee. From the old New York City subway case," he murmured.

The third man, Ramos, was long and wiry and seemed wrapped a bit too tight for Molina's taste. He gulped and asked, "Subway case? What subway case?"

"The case that got my brother killed." Molina's eyes narrowed. "The case that should have had nothing to do with him. 'Wrong place, wrong time,' cops said. Lowlifes killed him. Didn't even have the decency to return his body. They left him rotting somewhere in a landfill, they said. My father never recovered."

Molina strode across the room, snatching the wallet from Cruz's hand. There it was in black and white: Theresa Lee's badge, marked "Retired," and her ID. Business cards listed her current employment. Senior Security, Office of Senator John Sansom.

Sansom. The name conjured images of public hearings and newspaper headlines in Molina's head. The rookie senator who'd rocketed to prominence, now Chair of the Senate Armed Services Committee.

Like Ed Docherty and Theresa Lee, Sansom had been involved in that damned subway case, too. The one that killed his brother and, ultimately, Molina's father, unable to cope with the loss of his first-born son.

"What else did you find?" Molina demanded angrily, his blood already boiling and the intel on Lee stoked the fire.

Cruz held up Lee's phone. "It's locked, but we can crack it."

"Do it," Molina ordered. "I want to know everything she's been up to. What she knows, who she's been talking to. Why she's here. All of it."

As Cruz set to work on the phone, Molina turned to Decker. "Before you grabbed her, was she talking to anyone? Taking notes?"

Decker shrugged. "She was sitting near the back. Looked like she was taking notes on her phone. Might have snapped a few pictures too, I guess."

Molina cursed. If Lee had managed to send any intel before they'd grabbed her, the entire operation could be compromised. He began to pace, churning through possibilities and contingencies.

Ramos eventually ventured, "What do you want us to do with her?"

Molina stopped pacing and stared down at Theresa Lee. Part of him wanted to kill her, terminate this threat right here, right now.

As a hostage, Lee was worth far more alive than dead. At the moment, anyway. He might very well need a bargaining chip if his grand plan went south.

"She's our insurance policy now," Molina said. "If anyone comes sniffing around, we've got leverage."

He paused to give each of the three an opportunity to agree, which they signaled without hesitation.

Molina continued. "Decker, you're in charge of getting her secured. No one goes in or out without my express permission, understood?"

Decker gave him a surly nod.

"Cruz, I want that phone cracked yesterday. And when she wakes up, you're going to have a little chat with her. Find out what she knows, who sent her, and what they're after."

Cruz's thin lips curled into a cruel smile. "With pleasure."

"Ramos, you're driving and you're on cleanup. Make sure there's no trace of what happened here. Understood?" Molina waited for Ramos to agree, and then continued. "Put her into the van and get on the road. It'll take a while to get there. And keep your eyes open. If anyone's asking questions about Lee or anything else related to this EcoGuard meeting, I want to know about it."

"What about her vehicle? It's parked on the side street. Our cameras caught her leaving the vehicle," Decker said. "A sedan with Virginia plates."

Cruz replied, "I'll leave it around the back of the Walmart on the outskirts of town. Take the plates off. No one will notice it for a few days, at least."

"Get a head start." Decker nodded his agreement. "We'll pick you up there."

As the men absorbed their orders, Molina's gaze drifted back to Theresa Lee.

An unexpected gift delivered right into his hands. Was finding her a stroke of luck or a distracting complication?

"One more thing," Molina added, his voice low and dangerous. "If any of you breathe a word of this to anyone, I'll make sure you end up like my brother. Flayed alive. Are we clear?"

A chorus of nervous "Yesses" echoed in the small room.

Molina nodded, satisfied. "Good. Now get her out of here. I need to get back before they notice I'm gone."

As Decker and Cruz moved to lift Lee, Molina held up a hand. "Wait. Give me a moment alone with her."

His men exchanged glances but complied, filing out of the room silently. As the door clicked shut behind them, Molina crouched down beside her.

"Well, well, Detective Lee," he murmured, studying her face for a good long time as if she were a priceless gift. Which she was.

His father had met with her, back in New York, back when his brother was murdered. She'd been long on sympathy and short on solutions back then. Same with her new boss, John Sansom. And her damned partner, Docherty, too.

Of course, there was plenty of blame to go around and most of it could be piled on Jack Reacher.

Molina realized his view was skewed. He'd been young when Peter, his older brother, football star, and all-around good guy was murdered.

Reacher had pushed Peter's mother past her limits, and she'd killed herself.

Sure, Reacher eventually found Peter's killers and stopped them cold.

Too little, too late. Peter was already dead by then.

The two deaths, his beloved son and his ex-wife, were too much for Molina's father. He couldn't take it. Less than a year later, he'd killed himself.

"You have no idea what you've stumbled into, do you, Detective Lee? But don't worry." Molina pushed a lock of hair away from her face. "You'll have plenty of time to think about it where you're going. We'll talk again. Very soon."

He stood, straightening his jacket. It was time to return to the EcoGuard meeting, to play the role of the concerned citizen.

But as he reached for the door handle, a soft groan froze him in place.

Molina whirled around to stare.

Theresa Lee's eyelids fluttered.

CHAPTER 35

Leland, North Carolina

KIM SLIPPED THE PHONE into her pocket and returned to Smithers inside the diner. He had consumed half his breakfast already. She slid into the booth, poured a second cup of coffee, and bit off a piece of cold dry toast which she had to wash down with a generous swig of coffee.

"You called Cooper?" Smithers asked after he'd swallowed, wiping the egg yolk from his mouth with a napkin.

"I called Finlay," she explained. "He gave me a name and location to check out. He thinks Lee might be there."

"Name of what?"

"An environmental group that Daisy Hawkins might have been involved with. EcoGuard Coalition for Environmental Justice. The thinking now is that she was an inexperienced ecoterrorism warrior," Kim said as she choked down more of the toast. "Finlay said they found a stylized tattoo during her autopsy suggesting she was intense about protecting the environment by violent means."

"Got a photo of the tattoo? Could help," Smithers asked.

"Not yet," Kim shook her head. "It's on the way, Finlay said."

"How long do we need to wait?"

Kim shrugged.

Smither's raised his eyebrows. "All this ratchets up the tension, doesn't it? Homeland is involved, I hope?"

"Yeah. The tattoo isn't in the databases, so they're trying to track it down," Kim nodded, still working on the dry toast. "Finlay says all hands are on deck working on the case. Hundreds of agents in the field. But they're also working to suppress the story and keep it out of the media for now."

"Good luck with that. I've never met a reporter who could resist a domestic terrorism exclusive," Smithers snorted, pushing his empty plate aside and refilling his coffee. "How does all of this impact us?"

"There's an EcoGuard meeting today. He thinks Lee might have headed there."

"How would Lee know about the ecoterrorism angle when we didn't know about it?" Smithers asked.

"Inside baseball would be my guess. She works for Senator Sansom, Chairman of the Armed Services Committee. He'd know about a credible terrorist threat," Kim replied.

"Sounds like we're falling behind and need to get going," Smithers said, pulling out his wallet and dropping two twenties on the table. "I'll stop in the head and meet you outside."

Kim swallowed her final bite and gulped the last of her coffee. She hurried to the restroom and then joined Smithers in the SUV.

She barely had her shoulder harness fastened when he pulled out onto the county road, driving faster than before.

She opened her laptop and searched quickly for EcoGuard Coalition for Environmental Justice. As Finlay had suggested, she found dozens of pages of content on the website and several articles from major news organizations about the group. But no physical address or telephone number. No contact information at all.

Most of the press reports posted on the site were pure puffery. All about the altruism of the group with no harsh critiques of their radical means and methods.

Not only that, there was no mention of Daisy Hawkins at all that Kim could find. If she was a martyr to the cause, most groups would have featured her prominently.

Hawkins's absence could mean the group was exactly as altruistic as it presented itself and Daisy wasn't part of EcoGuard. Or there could be a dozen other reasons for ignoring her, including her failure to complete her mission.

On the fifth page, Kim located a calendar of upcoming events. Today's public information meeting was prominent along with the time and address.

She punched the address into the SUV's navigation system and the route popped up on the screen.

"Almost two hours from here," Smithers said. "We'd better get a wiggle on."

Kim kept flipping through the pages to see what she could find that might have prompted Lee to rush out that morning. Nothing jumped off the screen and after a while, she closed the laptop.

"No luck?" Smithers asked. Kim shook her head.

"Then tell me about Reacher. I've read the official files, which are all old. No reports in the FBI files on your search for him, of course," Smithers said with a grin. "Tell me what I need to know that's not in the files that will keep me alive. I've got a wife and I'm too young to die."

Kim smiled. His request was more than reasonable. But she wasn't sure what to say.

Her knowledge of Reacher was severely limited. She'd thoroughly digested the same facts from the old files that Smithers had already reviewed. She had also reached several unsubstantiated conclusions after her experiences with Reacher's impact on people and situations.

Otherwise, she had very little progress to show for months of work.

Certain feelings about Reacher had developed and evolved over the past eight months, too.

Early on, Kim had believed her boss when Cooper had warned her that Reacher was a stone-cold killer. One of the best Uncle Sam had ever trained. Cooper had provided terrifying examples of Reacher's activities to bolster his warnings which kept Kim constantly looking over her shoulder.

But over the course of the past few weeks she'd become convinced that Reacher was not her enemy.

Which didn't mean he was likely to be a friend, exactly.

Just that he wouldn't come after her in the dark without warning or provocation.

Maybe.

While she was running all this through her head, Smithers tired of waiting. He suggested, "Start with Reacher's habits. Where he might go, what he might do."

"He's not an easy man to pin down, but he does have certain tendencies," Kim replied easily. "First thing to remember is that trouble is drawn to Reacher like iron to a magnet."

"What kind of trouble are we talking about?" Smithers asked.

"Usually small towns with outsized problems. Places where the local law enforcement might be compromised or overwhelmed," Kim said. "When Reacher sticks his nose in where it doesn't belong, the powers that be and their enemies don't generally like it that much. Chaos reigns and Reacher always wins."

Smithers raised an eyebrow at Kim. "What about his travel patterns?"

"He hitchhikes, which is impossible to trace. Occasionally, he'll acquire a plane ticket. Otherwise, bus stations are key," Kim replied. "Reacher travels light. Carries nothing but the clothes on his back and very few items in his pockets. He's always on the move."

"That complicates things."

"He likes diners, especially ones that serve cheap coffee. He drinks it by the gallon."

"More gallons than you, you mean?" Smithers teased with a grin.

"Maybe not," Kim acknowledged. "When I find him, I'll ask."

"Anything else I should know?"

"Dozens of things," Kim replied. "Don't forget his military background. He uses old contacts when he needs to. It often helps to check army bases near our search areas."

"I was a Marine, so I understand those close combat brothers-in-arms connections," Smithers said. "Reacher was Army, Military police for thirteen years. Which means he's had a lot of the same training I've had."

"Right."

"Small towns with corruption issues near military bases." Smithers's forehead creased in thought as he processed the details. "That doesn't exactly narrow things down much, does it?"

"We can sometimes cross-reference the location with bus routes," Kim said, sharing how she'd worked on the problem. "We watch his ATM activity. He withdraws money from time to time. But it's a short and infrequent occurrence. He doesn't stick around long enough afterward to allow us to find him."

Smithers nodded slowly. "What about the diner angle?"

"No luck yet." Kim shook her head. "And we can't afford to waste time checking every coffee shop we see."

They drove in silence for a few minutes.

"We should leave another message for Lee," Smithers said eventually, breaking the quiet.

Kim's expression tightened almost imperceptibly, but she picked up the phone and made the call. When Lee's voicemail picked up, she said, "We're headed your way. Call me back."

"I don't like this." Smithers's frown deepened. "If EcoGuard is engaged in terrorism, she's at risk. Hell, she could be dead already. Did you tell Finlay that?"

"Finlay knows," she replied.

As the drive wore on, they pulled into a bustling truck stop. While Smithers filled the vehicle with gas, Kim stepped out to stretch her legs, scanning the busy parking lot for anything unusual out of habit.

"Ready to hit the road?" Smithers asked as he finished up at the pump.

Kim took another look at the horizon stretching out before them. "Ready as I'm gonna get."

Half an hour later, Smithers slowed and pulled into the Bluebird Diner. The neon sign flickered weakly, casting an eerie blue glow over the nearly empty parking lot.

"Why are we stopping here?" Kim asked.

"Fits Reacher's profile. Small town, off the beaten path. And look at that coffee pot in the window. Bet it never runs dry," Smithers said. "Worth five minutes to check it out."

They left the SUV and walked to the Bluebird. The door chimed as they entered, drawing the attention of the lone waitress behind the counter.

"Sit anywhere you like," she said without looking up while she was filling the ketchup bottles.

Kim approached with her photo of Reacher ready. "We're looking for a big man who probably came through here recently. Drinks a lot of coffee. Do you recognize him?"

The waitress looked at the photo and her eyes widened slightly. She nodded. "Yeah, he was here earlier today. Left a few hours ago."

Smithers and Kim exchanged a look. So close.

"Did he say where he was headed?" Smithers asked.

The waitress shook her head. "He was in a hurry. Left some cash on the table and practically ran out."

"Mind if we take a look around?" Kim asked, skeptical of her intel. Reacher generally didn't run anywhere, in her experience.

The waitress nodded reluctantly, and Kim began to search the diner. It didn't take long to spot the anomalies.

In the far corner booth, remnants of a shattered coffee mug lay on the floor. The table was askew, as if it had been shoved hastily.

Smithers stepped forward from a corridor near the restrooms. "You need to see this."

Kim walked back there, immediately noticing a smear of dried blood on the wall, partially wiped away but still visible.

"Think this is related to Reacher?" Smithers said quietly.

Kim knelt, examining the floor. She reached into her pocket for a glove and then carefully picked up a small, brass object.

"Shell casing," she said, holding it up. "9mm."

The waitress appeared behind them, wringing her hands. "I didn't want to say anything. I was scared."

Kim turned to her, keeping her voice calm. "What happened here?"

"Two men came in right after your guy. They talked for a bit. I was busy. Couldn't hear the conversation," she paused for a deep breath. "Then all hell broke loose. It happened so fast. By the time I came out from behind the counter, they were all gone."

Smithers asked, "Did you call the police?"

The waitress looked surprised. "Why would I do that? They were already gone. No harm done."

Kim pointed to the broken mug. "Was that Reacher's cup?"

The waitress shook her head and shrugged. "Can't say. It's one of ours. We have dozens just like that one."

Kim pulled out her phone and took photos. She used a small blade to scrape the dried blood into an evidence bag, sealed it, and dropped it into her pocket.

She'd never come this close to getting a sample of Reacher's DNA, and not for lack of trying.

Reacher's DNA should have been in government databases somewhere, for a lot of reasons. He was active military when the Army began routinely collecting DNA. Somehow, those records no longer existed.

He'd been military police for thirteen years. At a bare minimum, exclusion samples of his fingerprints and DNA would have been used in crime scene analysis. Those records, too, were now missing.

Reacher's old files had been scrubbed as clean as a hospital operating room. Absolutely nothing about Reacher existed in any of the databases she'd been allowed to check from his active military days.

It seemed no fingerprints, DNA, ear prints, medical records, photos, or other evidence related to Reacher or his exploits while on active duty or afterward still existed.

If this was his blood, the lab at Quantico could extract DNA from it. The profile might match something unidentified in the existing databases. If not now, then soon.

She collected the broken mug and dropped the pieces into another evidence bag. The shell casing went into a third bag.

Just in case the long shot might have a chance to work out at some point.

Kim stood back and took a last look around, visualizing the scene and committing it to memory. The waitress said Reacher had been here. For sure. A confirmed sighting.

Kim was finally on the right track. She could feel it.

Now he was in the wind again, possibly injured, definitely involved in something.

She had nothing but a cold trail and a handful of trace evidence to show for her efforts. So far. Which was more than she'd ever had before.

Smithers said quietly for Kim's ears only. "Want me to call this in?"

She shook her head. "No reason to get stuck here for hours while they process and investigate. Reacher's gone. No bodies to pick up. We need to get going."

Kim thanked the waitress, and they stepped outside.

"Where are you, Reacher?" she said aloud. "And what the hell have you gotten yourself into?"

CHAPTER 36

Madison, North Carolina

SMITHERS SLOWED AS HE maneuvered the SUV through the outskirts of Madison, North Carolina. Kim checked her phone again.

"Still nothing new from her?" Smithers asked, his eyes on the road.

Kim shook her head. "She should have checked in by now."

As they approached the town, Kim spotted the sign for the community center and pointed. "There. Pull in."

Smithers guided the SUV into the parking lot. A mix of vehicles filled the lot, suggesting the meeting was still in progress.

"Lee's ride should be here somewhere," Kim said, scanning the vehicles as they slowly drove through the lot, but she didn't see it.

"I've got a bad feeling about this," Smithers muttered as they approached the main entrance on foot.

Kim nodded, her expression tense. "Let's find out what's going on inside."

She pulled the door open, and they stepped into the lobby. A sign directed them to the EcoGuard Meeting in the auditorium.

They made their way down the hallway. Muffled voices grew louder as they neared the auditorium doors.

Kim glanced at Smithers. "Ready?"

He nodded and she pushed the door open, revealing a packed auditorium. A speaker at the podium droned on about conservation efforts. Rows of attentive listeners filled the seats.

Kim scanned the crowd searching for any sign of Theresa Lee. She leaned close to Smithers, keeping her voice low. "No sign of her."

Smithers nodded, his gaze still sweeping the room. "Let's work the perimeter. You go left, I'll go right."

They split up, moving along the edges of the auditorium. Kim studied each face, looking for Lee or Reacher or anyone who seemed out of place. The speaker's voice faded into background noise as she focused on the task.

Halfway around the room, Kim spotted a side door, slightly ajar.

As she neared the door, a man in a dark jacket stepped out. He tensed when he saw Kim, then quickly melted into the crowd.

Kim's hand moved instinctively toward her weapon. She caught Smithers's gaze across the room and signaled toward the door.

He began making his way over, but the dense crowd slowed his progress.

Kim reached the door and eased it open. A narrow hallway, poorly lit and unoccupied, stretched ahead. At the far end, a man disappeared around a corner.

Kim slipped through the door and into the hallway, her footsteps quick but quiet on the worn carpet, as she hurried to reach the man.

She moved swiftly, senses on high alert. All noise faded behind her. As she approached the corner, she slowed, listening for any sound ahead.

Silence.

She peered around the corner. Another empty corridor stretched ahead. This one ended at a fire exit. The door was slightly open, and a sliver of daylight was visible.

Kim advanced halfway down the hall.

A door to her right burst open.

The man in the dark jacket lunged at her aiming for her gun hand.

She pivoted, avoiding his grasp.

Her sharp elbow, deftly deployed, connected solidly with his ribs. He grunted but didn't slow, driving her back against the wall.

Kim brought her knee up hard into his solar plexus. The man doubled over. She shoved him aside and sprinted for the fire exit.

She burst through the door, away from the air-conditioning into the hot and humid outdoors. A van's engine roared to life in the parking lot. Kim caught a glimpse of Theresa Lee, slumped over and probably unconscious, already loaded inside.

"Stop! Stop!" Kim shouted, but the effort was useless.

The van's tires squealed as it accelerated away. She was tempted to fire at the rear tires, but there were people milling around.

Behind her, the fire door banged open again. Kim spun, weapon ready, only to see Smithers.

"What happened?" he demanded, slightly out of breath.

"They've got Lee," Kim said, holstering her gun. "Dark van, headed east. Let's go."

Smithers hustled toward the SUV while Kim surveyed the nearly empty parking lot. Her jaw clenched. They'd been so close. Now Lee was gone.

Smithers slid behind the wheel, engine already rumbling to life as Kim buckled in.

"Which way?" Smithers asked, hands gripping the wheel.

"East on Main," Kim replied, eyes scanning the road ahead. "Couldn't make out the plates."

Smithers gunned it, tires squealing as they peeled out of the parking lot. The SUV roared down Main Street, weaving through sparse traffic.

"There," Kim pointed.

A black van was just visible, turning onto the highway on-ramp.

Smithers pressed harder on the accelerator to close the distance. The van driver had spotted them. The van swerved, cutting off a sedan as the van accelerated.

"Damn," Smithers muttered, hands tight on the wheel. He maneuvered around the disrupted traffic, but it was slow going.

Kim's phone buzzed. She glanced at the screen, then looked sharply at Smithers. "It's from Lee's phone."

She opened the message. Her expression hardened as she read aloud: "Back off or she dies. Final warning."

"Back off?" Smithers's jaw clenched. "Your call, Otto."

Kim stared at the van ahead, now weaving dangerously through traffic. She thought of Lee, Reacher, Docherty, and the larger mission at stake.

"Your call," Smithers repeated, tension evident in his voice.

CHAPTER 37

Rural North Carolina

SMITHERS DROVE THE SUV in pursuit of the black van while Kim punched Gaspar's speed dial on her phone. The line crackled to life.

"Chico, we need eyes on a black van. Heading northwest toward Boone."

"On it," Gaspar's voice came through, all business. "Any other details?"

"Late model. Tinted windows. Moving fast on state roads."

Smithers navigated the winding mountain highway, scanning for any sign of their quarry.

"You're driving through no-man's land, Suzie Wong. Mostly private or government-owned property in every direction. Very little to work with out there," Gaspar said, as if he were catching her up on the realities. "To the extent there are any, accessing traffic cams and local CCTV feeds now."

Kim's free hand gripped the armrest. "How long will it take you to get eyes on him?"

"Give me a minute," Gaspar said softly as his keyboard clacked in the background. "Got it. Black van, matches your description. License plate coming up. It's stolen. Reported missing two days ago in Knoxville."

"Where's the van now?" Smithers called out.

Kim relayed the question.

"About three miles ahead of you," Gaspar answered. "Just passed through Blowing Rock, heading toward Boone."

"Guide us in," Kim requested.

"Will do. Want backup? Local sheriff's departments can set up checkpoints."

"Not yet," Kim replied. "We've also got a lead on Reacher. He could be headed to the same area."

"Want me to prioritize that?"

"Not yet," Kim said, her voice tight. "Focus on the van."

"Understood. There's a stretch of straightaway coming up in about a mile. You might be able to close the gap there."

Smithers said, "Got it."

Kim ended the call and turned her attention to the immediate problem.

"We're gaining," Smithers said, accelerating as the road straightened out.

Kim braced herself. "Let's end this chase and get Lee back."

The mountain scenery blurred past them, but the stolen van was now visible in the distance.

Smithers accelerated, closing the gap. Until the van swerved up ahead, taking a sharp turn onto a narrow two-track through the forest.

"Dammit," Smithers said under his breath as he followed the turn. "They're trying to lose us in the woods."

The road narrowed. Tree branches scraped the sides of the SUV.

Kim's phone buzzed. "Gaspar, what've you got?"

"Bad news. That road dead-ends at an old logging camp. Neutralizing them won't be easy. They've got a strong defensive position."

A deafening crack split the air. Half a moment later, the SUV lurched violently.

"Shots fired!" Kim yelled, ducking low in her seat.

Smithers swerved, barely avoiding a tree, and continued moving forward.

Another shot rang out and hit the SUV. The windshield spiderwebbed on impact. Smithers stopped the SUV.

"We're sitting ducks here," Kim growled. "We need to move."

A flash of movement caught her eye. A man bolted from the van and dashed into the dense forest.

"There! He's making a run for it!"

Smithers slammed on the brakes. Otto was out of the SUV before it fully stopped, sprinting after the fleeing kidnapper.

"Otto, wait!" Smithers called out.

"Check the van!" She shouted over her shoulder as she plunged deeper into the forest, keeping the suspect in her sights. Branches whipped her face as she ran. The suspect was just ahead, crashing through the underbrush.

Kim's chest burned as she gulped air into her lungs. Her foot caught a root that sent her sprawling. She scrambled up, gun drawn, listening.

Silence.

Then, a twig snapped behind her.

She whipped around and her eyes locked on the fleeing kidnapper.

Without hesitation, she sprinted after him, crashing through the underbrush.

The lanky kidnapper darted between trees, desperate to lose her. Kim's lungs burned, but she pushed on, closing the gap.

Suddenly, the man stumbled.

Kim seized her chance, leaping forward and tackling him to the ground.

They grappled, rolling over leaves and twigs, for more than a minute. He was young and wiry, but strong as an ox.

Finally, Kim pinned him with her knee on his back.

"Don't move," she growled, pulling his hands behind him and securing them with a plastic tie.

The forest fell silent except for their heavy breathing. Kim hauled the suspect to his feet, marching him back toward the road.

"What's your name?" Kim demanded.

The kidnapper growled, "Superman."

"Okay, Superman. Get moving," she said, giving him a strong push in the center of his back to propel him in the right direction.

Smithers emerged from the trees, wearing a bleak expression. "We've got a problem."

Kim's stomach roiled. "What is it?"

Smithers reached them, eyeing the captured kidnapper. "She's not in the van."

Kim's grip on the suspect's biceps tightened. "She's not there? We saw them take her."

"The van's clean. No sign of her."

The kidnapper chuckled, a dark sound that sent a chill down Kim's spine.

"You're too late," he sneered. "She's long gone."

Kim spun him around, facing him. "Where is she?"

The man's eyes glittered with malice. "You'll never find her. And even if you do, it'll be too late."

Kim resisted the urge to punch him in the face. She tossed him to the ground on his belly. She ordered him not to move.

"What now?" Smithers asked.

Kim's jaw clenched. They were back to square one. She gave the kidnapper a sharp kick to the kidneys. "I asked you a question."

The man sneered. "I've got nothing to say to you."

"Listen to me." Smithers growled as he stepped closer in a menacing way and grabbed the kidnapper's shirt, hauling him to his feet and pulling his face inches from Smithers's own. "We can do this the easy way or the hard way."

A twig snapped in the distance. Kim's head whipped around, scanning the dark forest for threats. Her instincts pushed her to run.

"We need to move," she said.

Smithers nodded, still holding the suspect. "Back to the SUV?"

Shaking her head, Kim replied, "They'll be watching it. We need to find another way out."

As if on cue, a distant engine roared to life. Headlights cut through the trees, coming their way.

"Move!" Kim hissed, pushing Smithers and the suspect deeper into the woods.

CHAPTER 38

Rural North Carolina

THEY SCRAMBLED THROUGH THE underbrush, the sound of approaching vehicles growing louder.

The kidnapper gasped as he stumbled and nearly fell. "They'll kill me if they find me with you."

Kim grabbed his arm, hauling him forward. "Then start talking. Who are they? Where's the woman?"

A gunshot cracked in the distance.

Bark exploded from a tree near Kim's head.

"Down!" Smithers yelled, pushing the suspect to the ground when he swiveled his head wildly, terrified.

Bullets whizzed overhead, thudding into trees and kicking up dirt around them. Kim crawled behind a fallen log, dragging the kidnapper with her. Smithers took cover behind a large oak.

"We need to go," Smithers shouted over the gunfire.

Limited cover, unknown number of assailants, one hostile captive. Not good.

Kim caught Smithers's eye and signaled with her hand. He nodded, understanding.

"On three," Kim mouthed.

One. She grabbed the kidnapper and tightened her grip.

Two. Smithers tensed, ready to move.

Three.

They burst from their cover. Kim pulled the suspect in front of her as a shield while Smithers returned fire.

"What the hell are you doing?" the kidnapper yelled, his eyes wide and terrified.

"You're Superman, right? Those bullets will bounce right off your chest," Kim replied sarcastically with another strong shove to move him along.

Then they ran, zigzagging between trees. Shouts echoed behind them.

"There!" Smithers pointed to a rocky outcropping ahead.

Kim scrambled up the slope, loose stones clattering beneath her feet. The kidnapper stumbled. She hauled him roughly to his feet and gave him a hard shove forward. He landed on his face and struggled to stand up again.

Finally, Kim reached the top of the hill, still hauling the kidnapper, chest heaving. Below, flashlight beams cut through the shadows.

"Now what?" Smithers asked, reloading his weapon.

Kim peered over the edge of the hill. A very steep drop on the other side was likely to result in broken limbs at the very least. Which wasn't the whole problem.

"Water," she said. "I hear running water down there. A river."

The kidnapper's eyes widened. "You're crazy. We'll never survive that jump."

Kim met Smithers's gaze. He nodded mirthlessly.

"We don't have a choice," she said.

The flashlights came closer. It was now or never.

Kim gripped the kidnapper's arm. "You first, Superman. Just spread your cape and fly."

"No way in Hell." He shook his head violently and began to protest.

She snapped the plastic tie from his wrists to free his hands and then shoved him, hard.

He toppled over the edge with a scream that echoed off the rocks.

After a sickeningly long time, Kim heard the splash when he hit the water.

"Go!" Kim yelled to Smithers.

He leapt without hesitation.

Kim followed, pushing herself off the ledge and jumping into empty air.

The fall seemed to last forever.

Wind rushed past her ears.

The thick trees covered everything she saw.

Dappled sunlight dotted the leaves and the rocks below.

Until finally she hit the water, feet first.

The impact jarred her entire body.

She plummeted down deeper into the river.

Cold water enveloped her, shocking the breath from her lungs.

The current grabbed her instantly, tumbling her downstream.

Kim gasped and fought to the surface.

When she opened her eyes, dangerous rocks loomed along the riverbanks. She twisted, narrowly avoiding a collision with a particularly sharp boulder as the river carried her farther downstream.

"Smithers!" she shouted between breaths.

A spluttering cough answered nearby. "Here!"

She caught a glimpse of him, clinging to a fallen tree jutting into the river. Kim swam hard, reaching for his outstretched hand.

Their fingers brushed, then locked. Smithers pulled her in.

"The suspect?" he asked as they clung to the makeshift raft.

Kim scanned the churning water. No sign of him.

A gunshot cracked above them.

The bullet splashed inches from Kim's head.

"Come on," she said.

They kicked off from the tree, letting the current carry them farther away from the hunters. The shouts faded as the raging river put more distance between them.

After what felt like hours, the river widened and slowed. Kim and Smithers dragged themselves onto a muddy bank, collapsing on solid ground.

For a long moment, they just lay there, chests heaving, exhaustion threatening to overwhelm them.

Finally, Smithers propped himself up on an elbow. "Think we lost them?"

Kim nodded, too wrung out for words.

"So," Smithers said between breaths, "no van, no suspect, no Theresa Lee. Hell of a day."

Kim sat up, wincing. She felt like she'd spent a couple of hours in a rock crusher. Everything hurt.

"We're missing something," she said, ignoring the bruises and glad she'd suffered nothing worse. "Why take Lee, then abandon the van? Who were those men back there?"

Smithers sighed. "And let's not get distracted. How does Reacher fit into all this?"

Kim stood grimacing as she wrung water from her clothes. "I don't know. But I'm damned well going to find out."

She offered Smithers a hand up. "Come on. We've got work to do."

"What about Superman?" Smithers asked.

"He'll turn up," Kim replied as they stumbled away from the river, shoes squelching with each step while she regained her balance and her footing.

After a few minutes of silent trudging, Smithers spoke up. "Any idea where we are?"

Kim squinted at the sky, trying to get her bearings. "Not exactly. But if we keep heading west, we should hit a road eventually."

A twig snapped nearby. They both froze.

"Too heavy for anything friendly." Kim shook her head, her hand moving to her weapon.

She crouched low, scanning the shadows.

A man emerged from behind a tree, hands raised.

"Don't shoot," his familiar voice called out. "It's me."

Kim's eyes widened in disbelief. "Russell?"

"Copy that." Travis Russell stepped into a patch of light.

"How the hell did you find us?" Smithers asked.

Russell tapped his ear and shrugged. "Your comms are waterproof. Gaspar's been tracking your signal since you went off-grid. He called me for an extraction."

"Gotta love Gaspar," Smithers said with a wide grin.

Kim holstered her weapon, shaking her head, bemused. Gaspar had called Finlay's righthand man. Normally, Gaspar would rather chew glass than ask Finlay for help. He must have been more worried than he let on.

"You came alone?" Kim asked.

"Seemed like the best plan in the moment," Russell replied. "Didn't have enough time to round up the entire calvary."

Kim's hand instinctively moved back to her soaking wet holster. Her weapon was there, but even after being submersed in water for her ride downstream, she had no choice but to rely on it.

The Glock was designed to be fired in harsh conditions. The polymer frame and internal mechanisms were resistant to rust and corrosion. There could still be potential issues like water in the barrel or the firing pen channel which could affect performance.

But the pistol should still fire.

And even an unreliable Glock was way better than no weapon at all.

Smithers asked, "What about Theresa Lee? Any news?"

Russell shook his head. "Nothing concrete. But there's been some strange activity reported near Devil's Hollow. Might be worth checking out."

Kim's eyes narrowed. "Devil's Hollow?"

"It's an old mining town," Russell explained. "Abandoned for decades. Lots of tunnels, easy to hide things and people."

Kim nodded. "How far?"

"About ten miles north," Russell said.

"What's the play?" Smithers looked at Kim before he said, "Let's go. Gaspar can keep us connected and under the radar."

"All right." Kim replied. "Come on. Every second counts."

Russell led them through the forest along another fire trail.

Devil's Hollow. Kim had never heard of the place. What would they find there?

They trudged fifty yards along the rough trail when Russell approached a waiting off-road vehicle and settled into the driver's seat. The sound of the engine rumbling to life was beyond welcome.

Kim jumped into the passenger seat and Smithers took the backseat moments before Russell pressed the accelerator and they set off.

CHAPTER 33

Rural North Carolina

THERESA LEE'S HEAD THROBBED as consciousness slowly returned. She blinked, trying to focus in the dim light. Cold, damp earth pressed against her cheek. The musty scent of soil and decay filled her nostrils.

Where am I? How'd I get here? The questions echoed in her foggy mind.

She tried to move, but her wrists were bound tightly behind her back. Plastic zip ties, if she had to guess. She'd had training in how to bust out of the restraints and she'd done it before. But not yet. If the kidnappers were around, they'd simply bind her hands again and they might do a better job of it next time.

Panic threatened as fragmented memories flashed across her vision like a collage. The EcoGuard meeting. A sharp pain in her back. Then nothing.

What did they drug me with? How long have I been unconscious? Where the hell am I?

Lee forced herself to breathe slowly, stay calm, and assess the situation.

The space around her gradually came into clearer focus as full consciousness returned. She saw rough stone walls curved high overhead. Cold earth everywhere.

A giant tunnel?

The only light came from a battery-powered lantern several feet away, casting long shadows dancing on the uneven surfaces like a badly lit horror movie.

She kept her head still, feigning unconsciousness while she observed through barely open eyes.

Two men stood near the lantern. One was tall with a noticeable limp. The other, shorter and stockier, sported a thick beard.

"How long's she gonna be out?" the bearded one asked.

The tall one shrugged. "The drug's pretty strong. Could be a while yet."

Who were these men? Where had they taken her? And why?

Was this related to Daisy Hawkins? Ed Docherty?

Jack Reacher?

Where were Otto and Smithers?

Lee had many questions and no answers. She listened intently, gathering every scrap of available intel.

The bearded one left, his footsteps echoing down the tunnel. The one with the limp stayed closer, occasionally checking on her.

Time passed, though Lee couldn't tell how much. Her body ached from lying on the hard ground, but she forced herself to remain still. Knowledge was her only weapon now.

Eventually, the sound of approaching footsteps echoed through the tunnel. A new voice, authoritative and cold, spoke from the shadows.

"Any change?"

"Nothing yet," the limping man replied. "Still out cold."

"Good. Get her ready for transport."

Whatever they had planned, Lee knew she was running out of time. Quickly, she considered the options.

Sansom wouldn't come looking for her because she'd specifically asked him to give her a wide berth. "I'll call you when I need you," she'd said at the time, and he'd agreed.

Otto and Smithers might find her eventually. Were they actually looking?

She could rely on Reacher, but only if he somehow learned that she needed him. No clue how that might happen since Otto hadn't found him in more than eight months of looking. Maybe they'd get lucky, but Lee didn't expect Reacher to just show up with candy and flowers.

As the three kidnappers huddled together, discussing logistics in hushed tones, Lee still had no idea where she was or who had taken her. Her body hummed with the certainty that she was in grave danger, and she needed to act fast.

But what could she do?

The one that seemed to be the leader turned toward her, and she quickly closed her eyes, evening out her breathing. She felt his gaze and tried not to attract more attention.

"One way or another," he said, his voice laced with malice, "Detective Lee is going to give us what we need."

"Perimeter's clear," the tall one reported. "No sign of anyone sniffing around."

Lee filed away the information, already working on potential scenarios and escape routes. They knew her name and they seemed to know more about her than they should.

"Should we wake her?" the bearded one asked, closer this time.

"Not yet," the leader ordered. "Check her restraints. We move in twenty."

Footsteps approached. Lee kept her breathing steady as rough hands checked the zip ties around her wrists and ankles. He felt for weaknesses in the plastic, which she'd already done. He didn't find any.

The footsteps retreated. Lee cracked her eyes open a fraction, taking in as much as she could see.

Her gaze darted around, searching. Her fingers brushed against something small and hard in her back pocket. Key fob for the sedan she'd left parked near the community center a lifetime ago. Whoever owned the car had left the fob in plain sight in the cup holder. Crazy thing to do in most cities, but not at all uncommon in rural areas.

They hadn't been thorough when they searched her. One lucky break. So far.

As the three men turned away, engrossed in conversation, Lee slowly maneuvered the key fob from her pocket. She worked the key to sever the zip tie, carefully silent.

The plastic began to give way just as he turned back toward her.

"Time's up, Detective Lee," he announced. "Your vacation is over."

Lee kept her expression neutral when they hauled her to her feet. Her wrists were still bound, but the zip tie was weakened. She stumbled deliberately, using the movement to scrape her shoe against the wall, leaving a faint but distinct mark.

If Otto came here, she'd see it. Otto was like that. She never missed anything. Reacher would appreciate that about her, if the two ever met in person.

As her captors marched Lee along the rough, dirty, damp tunnel, she paid careful attention, analyzing every detail.

The pieces didn't fit yet, but they would. After she'd acquired all the pieces. Which might take too long, but it was the best she could do.

She had nothing but her wits to defend against their plans. Whatever came next, safer to assume she was on her own. No rescue, no backup.

His hand clamped down on her shoulder as they emerged into the fading daylight. His voice was laced with menace. "Suck it up. We've got a long night ahead of us."

"What do you want with me?" she asked.

"You'll know soon enough. Until then you can stay quiet, or we'll find a better way to silence you," he said gruffly, landing a quick, hard shove to her sternum to emphasize his point.

Lee fell to the cold dirt floor. She landed painfully on her left shoulder before landing on her ass. Before she had a chance to register the damage, he reached down and yanked her to her feet.

"Watch where you're walking. You'll hurt yourself," he said snidely with a nasty grin, giving her another harsh shove to move her forward.

CHAPTER 40

Rural North Carolina

THE ORV LURCHED TO a halt at the edge of a dense thicket. Russell killed the engine and turned to face Kim and Smithers.

"This is as far as I go," Russell said. "Devil's Hollow is a quarter mile east through those trees. We left your SUV in a clearing on the other side. You should be able to drive out of the fire from there."

"Just to be clear, you're dumping us here?" Smithers squinted at the forest. "In the middle of nowhere? With no backup or transportation?"

"Orders. We're up to our ears in alligators at the moment. All hell is breaking loose. You're lucky I could do as much as I have," Russell said, his face impassive. "You'll find supplies in the back and in your SUV. Good luck."

Smithers grabbed the duffel bag from behind the seat and climbed out.

"Thanks for the extraction, Russell. See you when I see you," Kim said and then followed Smithers.

The ORV's tires spun in the loose dirt as Russell sped away. Smithers shouldered the bag and peered into the woods.

"Shall we?" he said.

They pushed through the undergrowth, branches whipping their faces. The air grew thick and hazy. An acrid stench stung Kim's nostrils.

"You smell that?" Kim said.

"We need to hurry, while we can still get in and out," Smithers nodded. "Forest fire. Heat. Smoke. It's all deadly."

They quickened their pace and kept moving. The trees thinned, opening onto a precipice. Below, a sea of flame seemed to devour the valley like hungry kids eating jellybeans.

A fireball erupted from the inferno, billowing skyward.

"Holy crap," Kim whispered, involuntarily flinching.

A distant explosion cut off conversation for a few moments.

"Look," Smithers grabbed Kim's arm and pointed.

Across the valley, a plume of black smoke rose from a clearing. It stood out against the orange haze as unnatural and probably deliberate.

"That's not part of the forest fire," Kim said.

"No," Smithers agreed. "But I'd bet my pension it's where we'll find Theresa Lee."

"How the hell do we get there?" Kim replied rhetorically. She squinted at the heavy smoke, then at the raging fire which was growing and consuming the forest at a terrifying pace.

A distant crack echoed through the valley.

Across the gorge, massive pines toppled, consumed by flames.

Kim pointed to a narrow path snaking down the cliff face. "We'd better start climbing down."

"You're insane," Smithers said.

"Got a better idea?" Kim said as she started down the treacherous trail.

Smithers shrugged and, without another word, followed Kim into the abyss.

Kim's boots slid on loose gravel as she navigated the precarious path. Heat seared her face, and ash stung her eyes. The roar of the inferno below drowned out everything but her ragged breathing.

She struggled to maintain her footing on the crumbling ledge.

Without warning, an unexpected gust of superheated air slammed into them.

Kim stumbled, her hand scraping against jagged rock as she caught herself. Blood welled from her palm, but she gritted her teeth and pressed ahead once the blast had moved on.

"How much farther?" Smithers shouted over the cacophony of destruction.

Kim scanned the hellscape below. "Another hundred yards, then we hit the valley floor."

The path narrowed, forcing them to inch along sideways, backs pressed against the cliff face. Sweat trickled down Kim's spine, her shirt clinging to her skin.

A thunderous crack split the air.

Kim's head snapped up. Above them, a massive boulder teetered on the edge of the cliff.

"Look out!" Kim yelled, shoving Smithers backward.

They scrambled along the ledge out of the path of the boulder crashing down, missing them by inches, careening past Kim and taking a chunk of the path they wanted to travel along with it.

Smithers stared at the gap the big boulder had left behind, chest heaving. "Now what?"

Kim assessed the break, seeing no alternatives. "We jump."

"You can't be serious."

Kim peered over the edge. "It's that or turn back."

The drop was steep, but not impossible.

She took a deep breath, ignoring the scorching air that filled her lungs.

"Ladies first," Smithers said with a wry smile.

Kim shot him a glare, then backed up a few paces. She sprinted forward and leapt across the gap. Her feet hit solid ground, momentum carrying her forward. She rolled, absorbing the impact.

Smithers repeated the process and landed beside her a moment later.

"Nice form," he said, offering a hand up.

Kim pushed herself to her feet. "Let's keep moving."

They descended the rest of the way in silence, saving oxygen. The fire's heat grew more intense with each step. At the base of the cliff, Kim paused to assess.

The smoke was thicker here, reducing visibility to mere yards. Flames licked at the edges of her vision, devouring everything in her path.

"There," Smithers said, pointing right.

Through the haze, Kim spotted a faint trail leading away from the main blaze. Without a word, they set off, staying low to avoid the worst of the smoke. Smithers led the way.

The path wound through a maze of charred trees and smoldering underbrush. Kim's lungs burned, each breath a struggle. She focused on putting one foot in front of the other, trusting Smithers to navigate.

After what felt like hours, the smoke began to thin. They emerged into a small clearing, relatively untouched by the fire.

So far.

A jagged rock formation jutted from the scorched earth, its surface blackened by smoke.

Kim scanned the area. "I don't see anyone."

Smithers pointed to a narrow crevice at the base of the rocks. "There. That could be an entrance."

They approached cautiously, senses on high alert. The crevice widened into a low opening, barely large enough for a person to squeeze through.

Kim crouched down, peering into the darkness. A cool draft whispered against her face, carrying the scent of damp stone. She pulled out her phone and turned on the flashlight. The beam revealed rough-hewn steps descending into the earth.

"Underground cave system," Smithers murmured. "Perfect place to hide."

Kim agreed and holstered her weapon to navigate the tight entrance. "I'll go first. Watch our six."

She eased into the opening, wincing as sharp rock scraped her back. The steps were slick with moisture, forcing her to move slowly. Smithers struggled to shove his much larger body through the narrow cave opening and then followed close behind, his breathing echoing in the confined space.

The damp, dark passage leveled out, opening into a larger chamber.

Kim's flashlight beam swept across uneven walls, catching glimpses of crude markings and old mining equipment.

A muffled sound reached her ears. She strained to hear a human voice, laced with pain or fear. Or something worse.

Kim held up a hand, signaling Smithers to stop. They listened intently, trying to pinpoint the source.

Another cry, clearer this time, emitting from deeper in the cave.

They advanced cautiously, alert for any sign of Reacher or whoever was behind this.

The main tunnel branched off in several directions. Kim paused at each intersection, straining to hear.

A flicker of light caught her attention. She gestured to Smithers, pointing down a narrow side passage.

As they drew closer, the flickering resolved into the warm glow of lantern light. Voices drifted toward them, along with a man's low growl, followed by a woman's whimper.

Kim pressed herself against the wall, inching forward until she could peer around the corner.

The passage opened into a small cavern. A figure huddled on the ground, illuminated by a battery-powered lantern.

It was Theresa Lee. Her wrists were bound, and a dark bruise mottled her cheek. A man loomed over her, his back to Kim.

Kim caught Smithers's eye, nodding once. They had found their target.

Kim and Smithers crept into the cavern, weapons drawn. The man looming over Theresa spun at the sound of their footsteps.

"Step away from her," Kim ordered, her voice low and commanding.

The man lunged for a weapon. Smithers rushed him, attempting to grapple. They crashed to the ground, trading blows.

The attacker landed a vicious elbow, stunning Smithers.

Then he scrambled up, eyes wild, and charged toward Theresa.

"Stop!" Kim shouted. "Last warning!"

He didn't slow. Kim fired one shot, which was all she needed from this short distance. The noise echoed off the cave walls, which was far from ideal. But she'd had no real alternative.

The man stumbled, then crumpled to the ground.

Kim rushed to Lee, cutting her bonds. "Can you walk?"

Theresa nodded weakly. Kim helped her up as Smithers regained his feet, nursing the bruised jaw and injured dignity. "That guy had a wicked elbow."

"Come on. Help me with her," Kim said, and Smithers was quick to oblige.

They half-carried Theresa through the winding tunnels, eventually emerging into a smoke-filled clearing. The forest around and above them was ablaze.

Kim pointed to a barely visible trail. "That way. Russell left our transport there."

They stumbled along the path, ducking falling debris. Lee's strength gave out. Smithers hoisted her onto his back.

"Just hold on," he grunted, but Lee didn't seem to hear him.

The trail opened onto a dirt road. The SUV waited nearby as Russell had promised.

They piled in, Smithers taking the wheel. Tires spun as he floored it. The heavy SUV fishtailed before shooting forward just ahead of the wall of flame that engulfed the spot they'd vacated seconds before.

Smithers navigated the winding road, the SUV jolting beneath them. In the rearview, the inferno receded, replaced by thick smoke.

Theresa slumped in her seat, barely conscious.

CHAPTER 41

Wednesday, July 3
Rural North Carolina

EVENTUALLY, AN OLD LOGGING camp materialized out of the haze. Smithers idled the SUV's engine and scanned the dilapidated structures. Smoke hung thick in the air, carrying the acrid scent of burning pine. The forest fire crackled in the distance, but it was coming their way fast.

"We're cutting it close," Smithers muttered, eyes fixed on the orange glow on the horizon.

Kim nodded. "Closer than I'd like."

She pointed to a weathered building with peeling paint. "That's our best bet for the main lodge."

They moved silently through the camp. Kim in front, Smithers behind, and Theresa Lee stumbling along as best she could in the middle.

Kim's entire body was on high alert, cataloging every shadow and sound. A twig snapped in the distance. She froze.

A man darted between two cabins in the distance. Kim's pulse quickened.

"Reacher," she murmured.

She signaled to Smithers, pointing out Reacher's direction.

Smithers raised an eyebrow, silently asking if they should make contact.

Kim shook her head. "Not yet. Let's finish our recon. We need to know what we're up against here."

The main lodge loomed ahead, windows dark and uninviting. Kim and Smithers approached the front entrance. The wooden steps creaked under their weight, setting Kim's nerves on edge.

Inside, the air was stale and thick with dust. Shafts of fading daylight cut through gaps in the boarded-up windows, revealing overturned furniture and general debris.

Kim's eyes adjusted to the gloom, picking out details.

A discarded cigarette butt, still smoldering.

Fresh scuff marks on the floor.

"They've been here," she whispered.

A muffled thump from upstairs confirmed her suspicion. Kim shared a look with Smithers. They moved toward the staircase, weapons drawn.

Each step was an exercise in precision, avoiding the spots most likely to creak. Halfway up, a floorboard groaned despite Kim's caution.

She froze, straining to hear any reaction from above.

Nothing.

They reached the second-floor landing. A narrow hallway lined with closed doors.

Kim motioned for Lee to stay put and Smithers to take the left side while she covered the right.

The first two rooms yielded nothing but cobwebs and abandoned furniture.

As they approached the third door, Kim heard voices.

She pressed her ear against the weathered wood, deciphering fragments of conversation.

"Running out of time," a woman said, her voice tight with frustration.

"The buyer's on the way," a male responded.

"And what about Theresa Lee?" the woman again, dripping with disdain.

Lee gasped when she heard her name.

Kim's grip tightened on her weapon.

She caught Smithers's eye and nodded.

Kim kicked the door open, weapon raised. "Stop! Hands where I can see them!"

The room erupted into chaos.

Marcus Molina lunged for a gun on a nearby table.

Melissa Black grabbed Theresa Lee, using her as a human shield.

Kim assessed threats and calculated risks in a fraction of a second.

As swiftly as she'd moved, she'd also waited too long.

Molina fired the first shot.

The bullet whizzed past Kim's ear, embedding itself in the doorframe.

Smithers returned fire, forcing Molina to dive for cover behind an overturned desk.

"Drop your weapons!" Kim commanded, her voice steady despite the adrenaline coursing through her body.

Black sneered, pressing a knife against Lee's throat. "You drop yours, or she dies."

"Don't do it, Agent Otto!" Lee's angry gaze met Kim's determined one.

Kim's finger tensed on the gun, seeking a clear shot that wouldn't take out the hostage.

A crash from downstairs shattered the standoff.

All heads turned toward the sound.

In that distracted split second, Lee made her move.

She drove her elbow into Black's solar plexus, breaking free from her grasp.

Kim seized the opportunity.

She fired once. The bullet grazed Black's shoulder.

Black's knife clattered to the floor as she stumbled backward, clutching her wound. She managed to stay on her feet. She turned and ran.

Molina used the distractions to make a break for it, shoving past Smithers and bolting down the hallway.

Smithers gave chase, leaving Kim to deal with Black and Lee.

"You okay?" Kim asked, quickly checking Lee for injuries.

Lee nodded, her breath coming in short gasps. "I'm fine. Go after her."

Kim hesitated, torn between pursuing Black and ensuring Lee's safety. The decision was made for her as the building shook, accompanied by the ominous sound of creaking timber.

"The fire," Lee said reflexively. "It's reached us."

Smoke began to seep through the floorboards, filling the room with an acrid haze. Kim grabbed Lee's arm, guiding her toward the exit. "We need to move."

As they reached the door, a tremor rocked the building. The floor beneath them groaned, timbers weakened by heat and age finally giving way.

Kim felt the world tilt as the floorboards collapsed.

She reached for Lee, desperate to protect her, but gravity had other plans.

They plummeted through a shower of splintered wood and choking dust, the ground floor rising up to meet them with brutal indifference.

Both women slammed onto the floor below.

The impact drove the air from Kim's lungs.

For a moment, she lay stunned, struggling to breathe through the thickening smoke.

Her ears rang, muffling the sounds of crackling flames and creaking wood.

She blinked, forcing herself to focus.

She scanned the room looking for Theresa Lee.

Coughing on the heavy smoke, Lee emerged from a pile of debris, bruised but mobile.

Kim's quick wave of relief was quickly replaced by renewed urgency.

"Smithers?" she called out, scanning the room for her partner.

No response.

A heavy wood ceiling beam crashed down nearby, showering them with embers. Kim and Lee dashed away from the beam's destruction.

The heat was becoming unbearable, the smoke so thick it was hard to see more than a few feet in any direction.

From experience, Kim knew the worst thing to do was stay one moment too long. Smoke inhalation was deadly. In a fire like this, smoke was filled with toxins that could drop a human faster than a speeding bullet.

But in this instance, there was precious little they could do to avoid breathing the toxic smoke.

Kim made the decision. "We need to find Smithers and get out. Now."

Before they could leave, Melissa Black emerged from the heavy smoke like a magic show. Her face was contorted with rage and pain.

"You're done," Black snarled, gun raised and aimed squarely at Kim's chest.

CHAPTER 42

Rural North Carolina

TIME SEEMED TO SLOW. Kim was in that moment where she saw with the absolute clarity of an eagle and heard every small sound with a bat's precision and crispness.

She saw the shift in Black's stance and the subtle tightening of her hand on the pistol's grip.

Kim was an excellent marksman, but even she couldn't draw her weapon fast enough to shoot before Black squeezed the trigger.

Kim rapidly weighed the very few alternatives open to her.

Before she had a chance to implement any sort of plan, a massive section of the ceiling gave way.

Several tons of burning timber plummeted down from directly overhead.

Kim felt herself being yanked backward off her feet as a strong grip pulled her clear of the collapse. Smithers? She wasn't sure. But who else could it have been?

Melissa Black's scream was cut short as the falling debris forced her to turn and run before it erupted in a mountain of flame and splintered wood.

From an assured clear distance, Kim stared at the burning pile for a long, hard minute.

No way could Black possibly have pushed through it. She must have found another way out.

No time to waste. The entire structure was falling down around them.

Kim grabbed Lee's arm and pulled her along as they carved a terrified path through the inferno.

She shoved Lee ahead and they burst through the front door, gulping in precious, clean air as they stumbled down the damaged outdoor steps to the ground.

The night sky glowed orange. Kim saw the forest fire had reached the edge of the logging camp. Sirens wailed in the far distance.

Too late for rescue.

The fire surrounded them now on all sides.

Kim scanned the chaos, desperate for any sign of Smithers. In the thick smoke, she couldn't see more than five feet away.

The noise of the fire was deafening. It raged at decibels even a hard metal rock band would envy.

"Otto!" Smithers's voice cut through the roar of the flames. He emerged from behind a battered pickup truck, limping slightly.

"Status?" Kim barked.

"Molina's in the wind, but he won't get far. I tagged him before he slipped away."

Kim nodded, already formulating her next move. Her phone buzzed in her pocket. A message from Gaspar flashed across the screen: "Backup 2 minutes out. Helo evac."

As fire trucks screeched to a stop and emergency responders swarmed the area, Kim allowed herself a moment to breathe.

They had Theresa Lee.

Black was in the wind.

Molina was wounded and on the run.

She turned to Smithers, her voice barely audible over the chaos around them.

"What the hell do we do now?" Kim's question was punctuated by the crackle of flames and distant sirens.

Smithers wiped soot from his face. His eyes scanned the chaotic scene.

Lee stumbled toward them, nearly collapsing.

Kim caught her arm, steadying her. "First, we get you to a medic."

A black SUV skidded to a stop nearby, kicking up gravel. Two agents in tactical gear leapt out, weapons at the ready.

"Special Agent Otto?" one called out.

Kim nodded, relief washing over her. "This woman needs immediate medical attention."

As they whisked Lee away, Kim's phone buzzed again. Gaspar's voice came through the speaker. "Satellite imagery shows a vehicle leaving the camp ten minutes ago, heading east on Forest Road 27. Could be Molina or Black or someone else entirely."

"Roger that," Kim said as she turned to Smithers. "You up for a chase?"

Smithers checked his weapon, a flinty smile on his face. "Always."

They sprinted to the SUV, tires spinning as Smithers floored the accelerator. The forest was a blur of orange and black and gray smoke reducing visibility to mere yards.

Smithers started to warn her, but Kim had already seen it.

A fallen tree blocked half the narrow road. He swerved and the SUV fishtailed dangerously close to the edge of a two-hundred-foot drop-off, knuckles white on the steering wheel.

The road curved sharply. As they rounded the bend, headlights pierced the gloom ahead. The battered pickup truck swerved erratically, smoke pouring from its engine.

"There!" Kim shouted.

Smithers pushed the accelerator to the floor, closing the gap rapidly.

Suddenly, the pickup's rear window exploded outward, front to back.

Glass shattered across the SUV's windshield all the way across as bullets pummeled the hood.

"Down!" Smithers yelled, ducking low behind the steering wheel.

Kim returned fire, emptying her gun at the fleeing vehicle.

The pickup's tires blew, sending it into a wild spin. It careened off the road, flipping once before coming to rest on its side in a deep ravine.

Smithers slammed on the brakes, bringing the SUV to a screeching halt.

Kim and Smithers burst out, weapons trained down the cliff and on the wreckage.

"Come out with your hands up!" Kim shouted.

For a long moment, only the crackling of the spreading fire filled the air.

Then, slowly, a man, bloodied and dazed, covered in soot, crawled from the twisted metal, hands raised in surrender.

As Smithers moved down the embankment to cuff him and haul him back up, Kim's instincts screamed a warning.

A branch snapped in the underbrush behind her. She spun, weapon raised.

A shadowy figure lunged from the smoke, arm outstretched.

A gunshot echoed through the forest. The shadowy figure stumbled, then crumpled to the ground. Kim approached cautiously, weapon still aimed.

"Don't move!"

No response. She inched closer, kicking away a pistol that had fallen from the attacker's grasp.

As the smoke cleared, Kim's breath caught in her throat. She didn't recognize the face staring back at her, eyes wide and lifeless. In one hand, he held a gun. In the other, a radio.

"Smithers! We've got another player here," she called out.

Smithers appeared at her side once the driver was securely cuffed. "Who the hell is that?"

"No idea," Kim said, crouching to search the body.

Her fingers found a wallet. Inside, a badge gleamed in the firelight. Kim's blood ran cold as she read the ID.

"Homeland Security," she whispered.

Finlay had told her they'd deployed hundreds of agents on the domestic terrorism investigation following the Atlanta bomb scare. Was this guy one of those agents?

Smithers cursed. "What the hell? Who is he?"

A crackle of static from the man's radio interrupted. "Agent Otto. We've got a situation at the evac point."

Kim grabbed the radio and pressed the transmit button. "Go ahead."

"It's Theresa Lee. She's gone."

CHAPTER 43

Rural North Carolina

KIM'S HEAD SNAPPED UP, meeting Smithers's shocked gaze. "What do you mean, gone?"

"She overpowered the medic and stole a vehicle. We're in pursuit, but she's far out ahead of us and seems to know exactly where she's going."

The rest of the transmission was lost as a deafening roar filled the air. The forest canopy above them bent and swayed as a black helicopter swooped low, spotlight cutting through the smoky haze.

"This is a restricted area!" a voice boomed from a loudspeaker. "Stand down and prepare for extraction!"

Lee's escape. The Homeland Security operative. The sudden appearance of a second helicopter that definitely wasn't part of their backup plan.

What the hell was going on here?

She grabbed the unknown driver by the collar and shook him, hard. "Talk. Now."

His eyes darted between Kim and the hovering helicopter. Fear and desperation warred on his face.

Finally, he spoke, barely audible over the roar of the rotors.

He shook his head and gave her a sorrowful look, as if it pained him to point out the obvious. "You have no idea what you've stumbled into, do you?"

Before she had a chance to reply, she heard a single gunshot fired in the distance.

The driver's head snapped back, a dark red stain spreading across his chest.

Kim dove for cover, dragging Smithers down with her.

"Sniper!" she yelled.

More shots peppered the ground around them.

The helicopter's spotlight swept the trees, searching for the hidden shooter.

Kim crawled on her belly to the SUV, using it as cover. She checked her weapon, acutely aware of how few rounds she had left.

Smithers crouched beside her.

"Now what?" he asked, voice tense.

Kim quickly assessed the options. The forest fire was closing in. An unknown sniper had them pinned down. The operative lay dead at their feet.

And Theresa Lee had disappeared again.

Kim met Smithers's gaze. "We find Lee. You take the SUV, I'll go with the helicopter team. We'll cover more ground that way."

Smithers nodded. "You sure about splitting up?"

She was as far from sure as she could get, but no way would she tell Smithers that. She hated flying and hated helicopters. Helos were inherently unstable. They crashed way too often to suit Kim.

Flying in a helo in a forest fire right here and now seemed the absolute height of lunacy.

When there's only one choice, it's the right choice, her mother's voice admonished in her head.

Another bullet pinged off the SUV's frame, as if to punctuate the danger.

Kim's jaw set and she gave Smithers the order. "Go!"

As Smithers peeled away in the SUV, Kim made a dash for the helicopter. She said a little prayer along the way, for insurance.

Bullets kicked up dirt at her heels. She leapt, fingers grasping the helicopter's landing skid as it began to lift off.

A hand reached down, hauling her inside. Kim found herself face-to-face with a stern-looking man in tactical gear.

"Agent Kim Otto?" he shouted over the engine noise. "I'm Agent Larry Donovan, Homeland Security. We need to talk."

A moment later, a massive explosion rocked the helicopter. Alarms blared as the craft lurched sickeningly to one side.

"We're hit." the pilot yelled. "Losing altitude."

CHAPTER 44

Rural North Carolina

KIM BRACED HERSELF AS the ground rushed up to meet them. Trees whipped past the open door, branches shattering against the fuselage. The pilot fought the controls, trying to level their descent.

The helo clipped the top of a tall pine.

The impact spun the big bird violently.

Metal screamed as the tail section sheared off.

Kim's world turned upside down as the helicopter rolled.

With a bone-jarring crash, they slammed into the forest floor. The rotor blades dug into the earth, snapping off and cartwheeling into the darkness. Sparks showered the cabin as they skidded to a stop.

Silence fell, broken only by the hiss of ruptured fuel lines and the crackle of the approaching fire. Which was the last thing she heard.

Consciousness returned in fragments. The acrid smell of burning fuel. Sharp pain in her left arm. Distant shouting.

Kim forced her eyes open. The helicopter lay on its side, smoke pouring from the engine. Donovan lay motionless nearby, blood trickling from a gash on his forehead.

Kim dragged herself from the wreckage, every movement agony. Her eyes scanned the chaos around her, trying to make sense of the situation.

A twig snapped behind her. Kim spun, raising her gun despite the protest of her injured arm.

Theresa Lee emerged from the smoke, hands raised. "Don't shoot, Kim. I can explain."

Kim's finger hovered over the trigger. "You've got thirty seconds."

Lee's eyes darted to the burning helicopter, then back to Kim. "I stumbled onto something that involves people in high places. I had to get that information before they could bury it."

"Who's 'they'?" Kim demanded.

A bullet whizzed between them, kicking up dirt. Both women dove for cover.

"I don't know the details," Lee replied, voice tight. "But I've been a government employee, one way or another, for a long time. Twenty years with NYPD and now working for Senator Sansom. Corruption permeates every government everywhere. All the way to the top."

"The entire government is out to get you? The Evil Empire has run amok and you're the one person who can save it?" Kim asked sarcastically, raising both eyebrows. "Sounds grandiose and more than a bit paranoid, doesn't it?"

"Yes. Which is what I thought, too," Lee replied. "I was wrong. And so are you."

"I've been FBI quite a while now. Shouldn't I have run across this endemic corruption somewhere along the line?" Kim asked, still skeptical. "I'll need proof, and a lot of it, before I can agree."

"You haven't spent enough time in DC. The whole town is corrupt," Lee said emphatically. "I've been collecting evidence for more than a year. You'd be shocked."

Another shot fired, closer this time. "Tell me later. Right now, we've got to get away from here."

They plunged into the smoke-filled forest with the sounds of pursuit close behind. Kim tried to piece together Lee's corruption allegations with what she already knew.

"This evidence," Kim said between breaths. "What is it? Where is it?"

Lee vaulted over a fallen log. "Safe. But we need to get to it before they do."

An armed man loomed suddenly out of the smoke. Kim raised her weapon, but Lee was faster. She tackled the man, sending them both crashing to the forest floor.

Kim recognized him. He was one of the men from the evac point.

His eyes were wild, filled with a desperate fury as he grappled with Lee.

"Otto," Lee shouted when she briefly gained the advantage. "Run."

The rest of her words were lost as the man broke free and slammed Lee's head against a rock.

Kim didn't hesitate. She leveled her gun and fired twice, center mass, taking him down.

Lee stumbled to her feet, blood streaming from a gash on her head.

"Thanks," she gasped, pressing her forearm against the wound to slow the bleeding.

"Don't thank me yet," Kim said, grabbing Lee's arm. "Start talking. What is this evidence that's worth risking our lives for?"

Before Lee could answer, the woods around them erupted in gunfire.

Kim dragged Lee behind a thick tree trunk, bullets splintering bark off the trees inches from their heads.

"How many of them?" Lee asked, removing her forearm from her bleeding head.

Kim risked a quick glance. Muzzle flashes lit up the smoky darkness. "At least three. Maybe more."

"We're outnumbered and outgunned," Lee said. "There's a cave system half a mile east. We can lose them there."

Kim's eyes narrowed. "How do you know that?"

"Because that's where I first hid the evidence before I had to move it. I didn't want them to find it on me if they search me again," Lee admitted. "We need to get it out before they kill us to keep it quiet. That's our only chance, Kim. Believe me, if there were another way, I'd have found it already."

A bullet struck dangerously close, showering them with wood chips. Kim made her decision. "Lead the way. But so help me, Lee, if this is a trap."

"Come on," Lee insisted and took off running. Kim followed close on her heels.

They crashed through underbrush, pursuers never far behind. The forest fire cast an eerie orange glow through the trees, smoke stinging their eyes.

Lee stumbled and Kim caught her arm, half-dragging her forward.

"There." Lee pointed to a rocky outcropping ahead.

As they approached, Kim saw the dark mouth of a cave opening. They dove inside just as another volley of bullets peppered the rocks in every direction.

They ran until darkness enveloped them and Kim fumbled for her phone. She activated the flashlight.

"Now what?" she demanded.

Lee leaned against the cave wall, breathing heavily. The blood gushing from her scalp wound had slowed but continued to run down her neck. "The cave system is like a maze. We can lose them if we go deeper."

"And the evidence? Where is it?"

"Downloaded to a zip drive." Lee met Kim's gaze. "Hidden so well they'll never find it. You need to see for yourself."

"What does any of this have to do with Ed Docherty?" Kim asked.

A shout echoed from the cave entrance. Pursuers were closing in.

"Come on," Lee said, ignoring the question and pushing deeper into the cave.

As they navigated the twisting passages, Kim was filled with questions. What had Lee uncovered? Who could they trust? How long would her phone battery power the flashlight? And how the hell were they going to get out of these caves alive?

Voices carried from somewhere and Kim's grip tightened on her weapon. The voices grew closer, echoing off the cave walls.

She turned to Lee and kept her voice low. "Options?"

Lee scanned the cavern. Her gaze settled on a narrow fissure in the rock wall. She pointed. "There. It might lead to another passage."

Kim nodded. "Go. I'll cover you."

Lee squeezed through the opening.

Kim backed up slowly, weapon trained on the approaching threats.

The strong beam of a flashlight swept across the cavern, followed by a rush of heavy footsteps.

"In here," a gruff voice called out.

Kim fired two shots, forcing the pursuers to take cover. She shut off her light and squeezed through the narrow fissure after Lee.

The passage was tighter than she'd realized. Rough stone scraped against her body as she inched forward. Ahead, Lee's labored breathing echoed in the confined space.

"How much farther?" Kim whispered.

Lee's reply was a stifled yelp.

Half a moment later, Kim felt the passage slope downward sharply.

She lost her footing, sliding uncontrollably.

Struggling to regain her balance, Kim suddenly stumbled out of the fissure and landed with a hard thud onto the rocky floor.

CHAPTER 45

Rural North Carolina

GROANING, KIM PUSHED HERSELF up from the hard ground. They were in a larger chamber, dimly lit by phosphorescent fungi on the walls. Lee was already on her feet, scanning their surroundings.

"We need to keep moving," Lee urged.

Kim grabbed her arm. "Not until you tell me what's going on. All of it."

Lee's eyes darted to the fissure, realizing the men were still coming as fast as they could move. "Fine. But quickly."

She moved a medium-sized rock away from the wall and reached inside. She pulled out a small, protected case. Inside was a USB drive. She held it up to show Kim.

"This contains evidence," Lee said.

"Evidence of what?"

"I haven't had a chance to examine it personally," Lee explained as she slipped the small drive into her bra. "The witness who gave it to me said it's solid evidence of serious crimes to keep the courts busy for decades. Heads should roll, the witness said."

"If you don't know what the evidence is, how can you agree with that?" Kim blinked.

Whatever she'd expected Lee to say, a plan to take on the entire government wasn't it. Nor was she willing to get distracted from finding Reacher. Not when she was so close to victory.

Unless and until she obtained better intel, she had no interest in joining Lee's vendetta.

"They'll kill to keep the evidence on this zip drive quiet. Make no mistake," Lee said emphatically.

"Is that so?" Kim replied, preoccupied with staying alive and out of the line of fire.

"Politicians have protected their pals and their operations from public scrutiny for years," Lee said. "You never noticed how they come into government service broke and with zero experience, but they leave millionaires and billionaires?"

"Uh, huh," Kim replied, continuing to scan.

"It's always the same story. No one keeps track of the bodies as long as the guys at the top of the pyramid stay unsullied," Lee continued breathlessly. "You think all those leaders in office for decades, stay in office forever because they're just so damned good at their jobs?"

A shower of pebbles fell from the fissure above. Someone was walking around up there, looking for a way to continue the chase.

"This way," Lee urged, moving farther into the darkness. "When I was here before, I spotted another passage on the far side of this chamber."

Kim nodded, feeling along the cave's rock wall. "Lead the way."

They moved as quickly as possible across the chamber where the uneven ground was treacherous in the dim light.

As they reached the far side of the chamber, a shot was fired. The bullet ricocheted off the rock wall near Kim's head.

"Down," she yelled, pulling Lee behind a large boulder as more shots came toward them.

Each shot echoed deafeningly in the enclosed space.

Kim aimed as close as she could to the brief muzzle flash at the origin of the shots and returned fire.

After she loosed the third round, she heard a pain-filled cry followed by a clatter she hoped was his weapon hitting the rocks.

"Move," Kim ordered, pushing Lee toward the passage.

As they entered the new tunnel, a deep rumble shook the cave and small rocks rushed down toward them.

"What was that?" Lee's fear was evident.

"Either an earthquake or natural shifting of the rocks or the gunfire and activity has jarred things loose," Kim responded with a shrug. "Or they're trying to bring the cave down on us."

"Swell," Lee replied flatly.

The tunnel shook again, more violently this time. Larger chunks of rock crashed down around them.

"Run!" Kim shouted.

They sprinted through the narrow passage, ducking and weaving to avoid the falling debris. The sounds of foot pursuit faded, replaced by the ominous rumble of shifting earth.

Suddenly, the ground beneath Kim's feet gave way.

She stumbled to regain her balance, nearly falling into a widening fissure. Lee grabbed her arm, hauling her back to the cold stone floor.

"Thanks," Kim gasped.

"Don't thank me yet," Lee replied, her eyes fixed on something ahead. "Look."

The passage opened into a vast cavern. Shafts of daylight streamed down from cracks in the rock ceiling high above.

On the far side, Kim could make out what looked like an old mining tunnel.

"That's our way out," Lee said, pointing.

They started across the cavern floor, picking their way through a maze of stalagmites. The ground continued to shake, dust and rocks raining down from above.

A deafening crack split the air.

Kim looked up to see a massive section of the ceiling breaking free.

"Hurry!" she yelled and shoved Lee forward.

They sprinted for the tunnel exit as the cavern collapsed in big sections behind them just as they cleared each section.

Kim felt the rush of air like a typhoon as the final tons of rock crashed down mere feet from her heels.

Coughing and covered in dust, they sprinted into the mining tunnel just before the rock roof's collapse sealed off the cavern behind them.

The collapse thwarted the posse chasing them, which was better than okay.

But it also meant they couldn't go back the way they came in, which was probably not okay.

"Can you keep going?" Kim gave her a glance as she scanned her own body for injuries.

Lee nodded, catching her breath. "Yeah. You?"

"I'll live." Kim's body ached in too many places to focus on any of them. She couldn't think about that now. She turned her attention to the tunnel ahead. "Any idea where this leads?"

"Out, hopefully," Lee said. "These old mines often have multiple exits for safety."

They moved forward cautiously. Kim's phone flashlight illuminated rusted tracks and rotting support beams.

After a while, she broke the tense silence. "Tell me more about your government corruption theories."

"Back when I first came on the job with NYPD, I learned that many of my heroes had feet of clay. The first things I discovered were small transgressions," Lee said between quick breaths caused by exertion. "A corrupt judge taking a bribe here, a senator doing favors for foreign governments there. But when they got away with it, they grew bolder, greedier."

"How many people are involved?" Kim asked, still making her way as carefully as possible.

"I don't know," Lee replied.

"And when the corrupt get caught?" Kim asked. "It seems like they're always accusing each other of criminal or unethical activity. Political enemies are not shy about taking each other down."

"Yeah, they offer a sacrificial lamb, circle the wagons, discard whatever and whoever they need to get rid of, and move on to scheme another day. Like Major League Baseball, this sort of thing has been going on for decades," Lee replied. "Public scandals erupt involving small-time players while the big guys just keep on keeping on. I'm from New York City. We know about corruption."

"Yeah, I hear you. I'm from Detroit. Plenty of corruption there, too," Kim replied as she trudged through the dark, dank tunnels trying to ignore the creepy creatures that were no doubt crawling over everything. "And you think Daisy Hawkins and Ed Docherty got mixed up with one of these corruption things?"

"Maybe not knowingly. But it makes sense. Daisy was part of whatever is going on here, for sure." Lee explained. "But Docherty wasn't involved with WRATH or terrorism of any kind. I know Ed. He was as honest as the day is long."

"So when Daisy got arrested, that's when they sent someone after her and Docherty, too," Kim said thoughtfully, trying out the idea in her head.

"Daisy Hawkins was the catalyst. But she's not the mastermind for whatever the hell this all is," Lee replied. "She just wasn't that smart. Or dedicated. Or deadly."

Kim said, "So what's your role?"

"Domestic ecoterrorists are not some new breed. They had quieted down and we got complacent. We took our eye off the ball while we worked on other things." Lee's eyes met Kim's in the dim light. "I'm not a cop anymore. It's not my job to hunt down criminals these days. But Docherty paid the price for those failures."

Another faint rumble echoed through the tunnel. Kim tensed, raising her weapon.

"Aftershock?" Lee whispered.

Kim shook her head. "No. Listen."

The rumble grew louder. A beam of light appeared around a bend in the tunnel ahead.

"Company," Kim said wearily.

Kim grabbed Lee's arm, pulling her behind a rusted mine cart. They crouched low, weapons ready.

The rumble intensified. An ATV rounded the corner, a single headlight cutting through the gloom.

Kim squinted to see only one man alone in the front seat.

She flattened her back against the cave hiding amid the shadows and signaled Lee to let the ATV pass. But as it drew closer, the driver suddenly cut the engine.

"Otto, Lee? Are you there?" Smithers called out.

Kim's tension eased slightly once she could see him clearly.

Smithers said, "Come on. While we can."

Kim met Lee's uncertain gaze.

Was Smithers alone?

Kim approached the ATV cautiously.

Smithers's relief was evident. "We've got trouble coming."

"What kind of trouble?" Kim asked as she climbed into the ATV's front seat, leaving Lee to take the back.

"EcoGuard's men are out there," Smithers explained. "We intercepted their communications."

Lee's eyes widened. "How did they find us?"

"I don't know," Smithers said. "Right now, we need to get out of here."

Kim's personal threat meter had been on high alert and still was. "Who's with you?"

Before he could answer, shouts and rapid footsteps echoed from the tunnel headed toward them.

CHAPTER 46

Rural North Carolina

"WE'LL TALK LATER. LET'S go," Smithers urged.

"You two go." Kim stepped out of the ATV. "I'll hold them off, buy you some time."

"No way," Lee protested. "Going forward, we stick together. There's too many of them and not enough of us."

The footsteps grew louder. Kim could see flashlight beams bouncing off the tunnel walls.

"This isn't a discussion," Kim said firmly. "Smithers, go. Find a place to wait for me. I'll be right behind you."

Smithers nodded, understanding both the chain of command and the gravity of the situation. "There's an exit for the old mine about half a mile ahead. That's how I came in here. We'll wait for you there."

As Lee and Smithers sped away on the ATV, Kim took cover behind the mine cart, weapon ready.

The first man rounded the corner. A powerful flashlight beam swept across the tunnel illuminating Kim's position. She held her nerve.

A man's voice called out, "I know you're there, Agent Otto. Let's not make this messier than it needs to be."

Briefly, Kim wondered how he knew her name, but she recognized the voice instantly. It was the leader again.

"Funny," Kim replied, her voice echoing in the tunnel. "I was about to say the same thing to you."

He chuckled without humor. "Only one of you, Otto. Be smart about this."

Kim quickly assessed her options. She needed to buy time, keep them talking.

"How about you be smart. You really think you can get away with killing an FBI agent?" Kim scoffed. "Touch one hair on my head and the FBI will hunt you down if it takes forever."

"Get away with what?" His voice was closer now. "I'm just doing my job. Like you."

Kim shifted her position slightly, trying to get a better angle. "Your job? Is that what you call murder these days?"

"Casualties happen in our line of work. You know that."

A pebble skittered across the ground to Kim's left. Someone was trying to flank her.

"We're nothing alike," Kim said, raising her voice to cover the sound of her movements.

She slid to the right, still behind the mine cart.

His voice hardened. "You have no idea what's really going on here, Otto. You're in over your head."

"Then enlighten me," Kim challenged.

He paused briefly. "Sorry, but that's need-to-know. And you don't."

Kim heard the subtle click of a safety being disengaged. She tensed, ready to move.

"Last chance, Otto," he called out. "Surrender now."

Kim didn't wait to hear the rest. She spun out from behind the cart, firing twice at the flashlight beam. The light shattered, plunging the tunnel into darkness.

Confused shouts erupted. Followed by a burst of gunfire.

Kim rolled away from the bullets that peppered the spot she'd barely vacated.

Which told her they knew exactly where she was. How? Night vision? A tracker of some sort?

Using the chaos to her advantage, Kim sprinted deeper into the tunnel. Behind her, she heard him barking orders.

"Don't let her get away!"

Kim's breath came in short gasps as she ran. She was a daily runner and betting he was not.

She couldn't outrun a speeding bullet, but she could run far enough and fast enough to reach the exit where she'd join Lee and Smithers.

Pounding footsteps grew fainter behind her as she pushed forward. Just when she thought she might have lost them, a brief glimmer of light appeared ahead.

The exit. She was almost there.

A small grin lifted the corners of her mouth as she continued to run.

Suddenly, the tunnel floor tilted sharply beneath her feet.

Once again, Kim felt herself sliding and then falling and tumbling into the darkness.

She landed hard and the impact knocked the wind from her lungs.

Pain shot through her left ankle.

Gravel and dirt rained down from above, showering her with grit.

She lay still, fighting to catch her breath, taking inventory of her body.

The fall had been short, but disorienting, and the landing as hard as the rocks she'd slammed into.

As her eyes adjusted to the gloom, she realized she was now in some kind of lower passage.

Voices echoed from the tunnel above.

"Where'd she go?"

"Check down there."

Kim forced herself to move, ignoring her throbbing ankle, which seemed to be the worst of her injuries so far.

She crawled behind a pile of fallen rocks, just as another powerful flashlight beam swept across the cave.

"See anything?"

"Nah, it's too dark. She couldn't have survived that fall anyway."

"We need the body to prove she's dead. Go get it."

Kim pressed herself against the cold stone. The light lingered for a moment, then retreated.

"I'm not jumping into that hole. Forget it," he said roughly. "Let's check further along. Even if she survived, she can't have gone far."

The voices faded as they moved away. Kim allowed herself a small sigh of relief, then assessed her status.

Her ankle was swollen, possibly sprained. Her gun was still in her hand, but she'd lost her phone in the fall. Without the phone's light, the passage ahead was pitch black.

She had two choices.

Try to climb back up to the main tunnel and risk running into the EcoGuard men again. Their attempts to kill her would eventually succeed if she gave them more chances.

Or press on through the unknown passage and hope it led to an exit.

Neither option was ideal.

Kim gritted her teeth and stood, testing her weight on the injured ankle. It hurt, but it would hold. She'd had worse injuries.

Using the wall for support, she began to move forward, one hand outstretched to feel her way. She tried not to think of the creatures crawling among the rocks.

The passage was narrow and rough. The thick cloying smell of damp earth permeated everything.

After a few moments, a faint sound reached her ears. She listened until she identified it.

Running water.

The passage was sloping downward, leading her deeper underground. The sound grew louder as she continued, which helped to silence her footsteps.

Suddenly, her outstretched hand met empty air.

The passage opened into a larger space.

Now, the water's roar was deafening.

A faint glow caught her eye. More phosphorescent fungi clung to the walls of a vast cavern.

In the eerie light, Kim could make out the source of the noise. An underground river, churning and frothing as it cut through the rock.

She'd come the wrong way. This was a dead end. She turned to retrace her steps.

"Otto. Over here," a deep voice called out softly, barely audible over the roar of the water.

Kim spun toward the voice, her hand instinctively tightening on her weapon. Through the dim phosphorescent light, she spotted Smithers waving from the far side of the cavern.

"Smithers?" she called back, hustling toward him. "How did you get here?"

"There's another passage," he said. "Come on. They're closing in."

Kim hesitated. The cavern was wide, the underground river swift and treacherous between them.

"There's no way across," she yelled.

Smithers pointed urgently to his left. "There's a narrow ledge. It's your only shot."

Kim saw it now. A thin strip of rock hugging the cavern wall, barely wide enough for a slightly built person to inch along.

The ledge disappeared into the spray of the river at one point but seemed to continue on the other side.

The sound of voices echoed from the passage behind her. EcoGuard's men, getting closer. They would find her soon.

Frozen by indecision, Kim hugged the wall, hoping for a better option to reveal itself.

EcoGuard's warriors approached relentlessly, without faltering or committing any unforced errors she might use to her advantage.

They were jogging toward her. Perhaps they'd heard the river, too.

Which was when she realized she'd waited too long.

Now, she only had one choice.

CHAPTER 47

Rural North Carolina

THERESA LEE INCHED HER way through the underground passage with Smithers following, footsteps barely audible on the damp stone floor. The scent of moss and mineral-rich water permeated everything. Eerie shadows danced on the rough-hewn walls, creating a claustrophobic atmosphere that set her nerves on edge.

"We need to reach the surface access point," Lee whispered, her voice barely above a breath. She kept her eyes forward, scanning the darkness ahead for any sign of movement.

Smithers nodded, his usually placid face set in grim determination. "It's risky, but—"

A sudden strike of rapid footsteps cut him off mid-sentence.

Lee's hand shot out, gripping Smithers's arm with an urgency that needed no words. Her eyes, now accustomed to the gloom, allowed her gaze to dart around the narrow passage. She spotted a jagged rock formation jutting from the cave wall, creating a small alcove.

Lee pointed silently, and Smithers nodded. They moved as one, sliding into the shadows behind the rocks just as voices drifted closer. Lee pressed her back against the cold stone, willing her breathing to slow. Beside her, she could feel Smithers's tension, coiled like a spring.

The voices grew louder, accompanied by the rhythmic thud of boots on stone. Lee risked a glance around the edge of their hiding spot.

A group of heavily armed figures emerged from the shadows, weapons at the ready. But it was the man at their head that caught Lee's attention.

Even in the low light, Eugene Cannon was unmistakable. His broad shoulders and confident stride exuded the command-and-control attitudes appropriate for WRATH's COO. His résumé was long and his successes impressive.

Although she'd seen photos, Lee had never met Cannon in person, but she recognized him from photographs. He'd been high up in the CIA at one point, based in New York City when she was a rookie with NYPD. His reputation for tactical brilliance was the stuff of legends and nightmares among his enemies.

As Lee watched the WRATH agents sweep the area, a flicker of light caught her eye. The cave's dim emergency lights, which had been steadily glowing, now pulsed in an odd, rhythmic pattern. At first, she thought it was a malfunction, but as the pattern repeated, she realized what it was.

Short, short, short. Long, long, long. Short, short, short. Morse code. S.O.S.

"Reacher?" she breathed, the name barely a whisper on her lips.

Smithers gave her a questioning look across the gap, his brow furrowed in confusion. Lee shook her head slightly while she considered the options.

Reacher had gained access to WRATH's systems. He was manipulating the infrastructure. They were no longer overwhelmed underdogs. Which was more than fine with her.

Lee's attention snapped back to their immediate surroundings as Cannon's deep voice resonated through the passage.

"Sweep every inch," he commanded. "They can't have gone far."

WRATH agents spread out, flashlights cutting through the gloom. Lee held her breath as a beam of light passed dangerously close to her hiding spot. She could feel Smithers tense beside her, hand inching toward his weapon.

In that moment of heightened tension, a small pebble was dislodged by Smithers's shifting weight and skittered across the cave floor. The slight scrape echoed in the confined space.

Cannon's head snapped toward the sound and their hiding spot. "There!"

In an instant, the cave erupted into chaos.

Gunfire shattered the silence. Bullets peppered the rocks around Lee and Smithers. Stone chips flew through the air as they returned fire.

Lee assessed the options. They were pinned down, outgunned, and rapidly running out of time. She needed a plan, and fast.

A series of sparks suddenly erupted from WRATH's equipment. Radios squealed with ear-piercing feedback while several handheld tactical lights flickered and died.

Lee's grim smile stole its way onto her face. Reacher's handiwork, no doubt.

Pointing forward, she gave Smithers quick directions over the din of gunfire.

But they were still massively outnumbered. Cannon was already rallying his forces, barking orders to compensate for WRATH's malfunctioning gear. Lee's eyes darted around frantically, seeking any possible escape route.

Which was when she spied a narrow passage concealed by the shadows. She hesitated for a split second, thoughts flashing to Reacher. What would he do in this situation?

The moment of reflection sharpened her focus, as if Reacher's analytical mind had briefly merged with her own.

Details she hadn't noticed before suddenly jumped out at her. Faint scuff marks on the floor near the passage entrance.

A barely perceptible draft of fresher air. This was an escape route after all. And it was their best shot.

"Smithers!" Lee shouted, her voice cutting through the chaos. "This way!"

Without waiting for a response, Lee sprinted for the passage, trusting Smithers to follow. Her legs burned with the effort. Adrenaline surged through her veins as bullets whizzed past.

She had barely made it ten feet into the narrow tunnel when a thunderous crack split the air.

Her heart leapt into her throat as she realized what was happening.

The cave was collapsing.

"Hurry!" she screamed, pushing herself to run faster.

Lee felt a strong shove from behind, propelling her forward just as a wall of debris crashed down between her and Smithers.

Coughing in the dust-filled air, Lee spun around. The passage behind her was completely blocked by fallen rocks.

"Smithers!" she yelled, her voice raw with panic. "Smithers, can you hear me?"

For a heart-stopping moment, there was only silence. Then, muffled but unmistakable, came Smithers's voice through the rubble.

"I'm okay!" he called. "The rocks have cut me off. I can't get through!"

Lee quickly weighed options that all seemed equally impossible.

"I'll find another way out," Smithers continued, his voice strained but determined. "You keep moving. Go!"

Every instinct in Lee's body screamed at her to stay, to find a way to get Smithers out, too. But rationally, the part of Lee trained for situations exactly like this, knew Smithers was right.

Staying would get them both captured or killed.

She had to go now and save Smithers later.

Lee turned and pushed deeper into the twisting tunnels.

WRATH warriors echoed behind her as they moved the rocks to escape the cave-in.

Lee relied on memory and instinct, feeling her way along, praying that her internal compass wouldn't fail her.

In the near total darkness, the cave passages seemed to blur together, each turn indistinguishable from the last. Lee's lungs burned and her legs ached, but she pushed on.

The sound of footsteps behind her grew louder, more urgent. Carefully, she sped up as fast as she dared.

She rounded a corner and skidded to a halt.

A massive steel door sealed the cave at the end of the passage. This was it. End of the line. She was trapped.

But then the door hissed and began to slide open.

"Thanks, Reacher," Lee muttered, a mixture of relief and gratitude washing over her as she charged through a narrow opening as soon as it appeared.

The door opened abruptly into a vast cavern, so large that the beam of Lee's flashlight couldn't reach the far walls. Multiple exits beckoned from different points around the perimeter, each one a potential escape route or a deadly trap.

Lee paused, every sense on high alert. This was too easy. The hairs on the back of her neck stood up, warning her of unseen danger.

Reacher's rules echoed in her mind, as clear as if he were standing beside her. Read the room. Trust your gut. Be the enemy.

She forced herself to take a deep breath and carefully observe her surroundings.

As her eyes adjusted to the gloom, details began to emerge. A flicker of movement, the barest shift of shadow near one of the exits, caught her attention. It could easily go unnoticed.

She dove into the shadows to her left just as Cannon stepped into view from behind a rocky outcropping. His weapon was already raised, and he squeezed the trigger.

The shot would have hit Lee if she'd waited even a nanosecond longer. Instead, it struck harmlessly against the cave wall.

"Impressive, Ms. Lee," Cannon said, his deep voice echoing in the cavernous space. "But you're done now. Nowhere else for you to run."

Lee assessed her situation. She was cornered, outgunned, with no clear escape path.

But then she noticed a subtle change in the air currents of the cavern. It was barely perceptible but unmistakable.

Reacher wasn't done yet. He was setting something up, some final play that only he would execute.

She needed to buy time.

Lee slowly rose to her feet, keeping a hard, steady gaze on Cannon. She shifted her weight, settling into a fighting stance that could quickly transition from defense to offense.

"You're right about one thing, Cannon," Lee said, her voice steady despite the pounding of her heart. "This ends now."

The tension in the cavern was like electricity crackling in the air. Lee and Cannon stood motionless, each waiting for the other to make the first mistake.

In the distance, Lee could hear the sound of more approaching WRATH agents. Time was running out.

But as she stared into Cannon's cold eyes, she felt a strange sense of calm settle over her. Whatever happened next, she was ready.

Reacher had shown her the way and now it was time to put those strategies to the test.

Lee's eyes narrowed as she faced Cannon in the dimly lit passage. His smug grin fueled her determination.

"End of the line, Cannon," Theresa called out, her voice echoing off the walls. "Why don't you make this easy on both of us and surrender?"

Cannon's laughter was cold and harsh. "Always the optimist."

She shrugged. "I try."

He cracked his knuckles menacingly. "I've got a better idea. How about I send you home in a body bag?"

"Your funeral," Theresa muttered, shifting into a fighting stance.

Cannon lunged forward with surprising speed, telegraphing a wild haymaker. "Too slow, sweetheart!"

Theresa ducked under his swing, feeling the air whistle above her head. The momentum of his missed punch left Cannon off-balance.

"My turn," she growled as she stood tall again.

Lee pivoted on her back foot, twisting her core to generate explosive power. Her dominant hand curled into a tight fist as she launched a vicious punch.

Time seemed to slow as her fist arced toward Cannon's face. She aimed her strong hook precisely for the mandibular angle, that vulnerable spot where the jawbone meets the ear.

The impact was thunderous.

Theresa felt the shock reverberate up her arm as her knuckles connected with Cannon's jaw.

The force of the blow whipped his head to the side, sending a violent jolt through his skull.

"Lights out," Theresa said, watching his eyes roll back.

Cannon's body went limp, collapsing in an unconscious heap. Theresa stood over her fallen foe, shaking out her hand.

"Jaw-dropping performance," she quipped, allowing a small smile as she reached into her pocket for a sturdy zip tie.

A slight movement caught her eye. Cannon's fingers twitched, then curled into a fist.

"Not bad," he groaned, eyes fluttering open. He pushed himself up, blood trickling from a split lip. He massaged his jaw. "But it'll take more than that to keep me down."

How was he still conscious? As Cannon staggered to his feet, she noticed something glinting in his hand. A radio or cell phone?

"You want to know the best part about abandoned caves?" Cannon sneered, his thumb hovering over a button. "No one notices when we rig them with explosives."

Lee's heart raced as she realized the danger.

Cannon's finger was already moving toward what could be a detonator.

Lee raised her weapon to fire, but Cannon was faster. He glanced behind her and upward. "About time you got here," he said, nodding toward Lee.

She whipped her head around to see behind her, but she wasn't fast enough.

The big man slid in behind her and grabbed her in a choke hold. She resisted and his grip tightened. She relaxed slightly in an attempt to stay alive, which made it easier for him.

"Take her back to the WRATH bunker," Cannon ordered. "I'll bring the other one."

A moment later, Lee lost consciousness.

CHAPTER 48

Rural North Carolina

KIM HOLSTERED HER WEAPON and started for the
ledge. The rock was slick, and every step sent jolts of pain
through her ankle. She pressed herself against the wall,
trying not to look down at the churning water below.

Halfway across, the ledge narrowed further. Kim had to
turn sideways, her cheek scraping against the rough stone as
she inched forward.

"There she is," a man shouted from behind.

A bullet ricocheted off the rock near her head.

Kim didn't dare turn to look. She'd stowed her gun to
free her hands. She couldn't shoot back.

She pushed forward, ignoring the pain in her ankle and
the fear twisting her gut as the spray off the river soaked her
clothes.

More shots fired. The sound was amplified in the cavern.

Kim felt the sting as a bullet barely grazed the arm of her jacket.

"Otto," Smithers yelled. "Jump."

She had inched forward until she'd reached the gap in the ledge. The river roared beneath her. The other side was tantalizingly close but way too far away.

Kim hesitated for a split second, then pushed off with all her strength.

Time seemed to slow.

She was airborne.

The spray of the river obscured her vision.

Then strong hands gripped her arms, yanking her to safety.

She collapsed against Smithers's big, broad chest gasping for breath.

"We've got to go before they figure out where we are," he urged as he pulled her to her feet.

They ran into another passage, the sound of frustrated shouts fading behind them. After a few minutes, Smithers slowed the pace.

"You okay?" he asked.

Kim nodded, still catching her breath. "What happened to Lee?"

Smithers's expression darkened. "We got separated. There was an ambush. Lee took off."

"If they find her first, they'll kill her."

"So we'll get there before they do," Smithers replied, tilting his head to the left. "I think I know a way out of here."

Before she could speak again, a low rumble shook the tunnel. Dust and small rocks rained down from above.

"Let's go," Kim said urgently. "This place is unstable. The whole thing could come down on us at any time. I don't know about you, but I've had enough rotting, collapsing structures for one day."

Kim and Smithers pushed forward, the tunnel gradually widening as they progressed. The rumbling intensified, small tremors causing loose rocks to clatter around their feet.

"What's causing this instability?" Kim asked.

Smithers shook his head. "Could be mining operations. Or worse."

She knew what he meant. Someone could be trying to bring the tunnels down. A stick or two of dynamite would do it easily enough.

The passage curved sharply to the left. As they rounded the bend, they came to an abrupt halt. The tunnel ahead had collapsed, leaving a wall of rubble blocking the path.

"Dammit," Smithers muttered.

Kim scanned the area, her eyes settling on a narrow opening in the rock wall. "There. It might lead to another passage."

They squeezed through the opening, finding themselves in a smaller, rougher tunnel. The air was stale, and the rumbling seemed more distant here.

"Any idea where this passage leads?" Kim asked.

Smithers shook his head. "Your guess is as good as mine. But it's away from EcoGuard, so I'll take it."

They pressed on, the passage twisting and turning. After what seemed like forever, but was likely only minutes, they emerged into a larger cavern. Faint daylight filtered through cracks in the ceiling far above.

"We must be close to the surface," Smithers said, hope creeping into his tone.

Before Kim could respond, a noise echoed through the cavern. Footsteps, coming from one of the other passages leading into the space.

They ducked behind a large boulder, weapons ready. Kim's heart raced as the footsteps grew closer.

A beam of light swept across the cavern floor.

"I know you're in here," the leader's gruff voice called out. "Come out now, and maybe we can talk this through."

Kim glanced at Smithers, who offered a stony nod. They were trapped and running out of options.

His footsteps drew nearer. "Last chance, Otto. Don't make this messier than it needs to be."

Kim took a deep breath, steeling herself for what came next. She stood slowly and raised her hands.

"Alright," she called out. "Let's talk."

He emerged from the shadows, his gun trained on Kim. Two armed men flanked him.

"Hands where I can see them," he ordered.

Kim complied because she needed to buy time to create an alternative.

"You're making a mistake," she said, keeping her voice steady.

His laugh was harsh. "The only mistake was letting you live this long."

"Who's pulling your strings?" Kim pressed.

A flicker of uncertainty crossed his face, but he quickly masked it.

"Enough talk," he snapped. "Where's the flash drive?"

Before Kim could respond, a gunshot cracked through the cavern. One of the men was hit. He dropped, clutching his chest as he breathed his last.

Chaos erupted.

Kim dove for cover as the leader and his remaining man opened fire.

Smithers, having circled around during the conversation, provided cover fire from his hidden position.

Kim scrambled behind a boulder. Her hand closed around a fist-sized rock.

"Otto," Smithers called. "East tunnel."

She spotted the opening Smithers indicated. About twenty feet away, partially hidden by stalagmites.

Kim took a deep breath, then sprinted from cover. Bullets peppered the ground at her heels. She zigzagged, using the cavern's terrain for protection.

Halfway to the tunnel, the leader stepped into her path, gun raised.

"It's over, Otto," he snarled.

Kim didn't hesitate. She hurled the rock with all her strength. The rock caught him squarely in the face, staggering him.

She closed the distance in two strides.

Blood streaming from his broken nose, he swung wildly.

Kim grabbed his wrist and ducked under his arm.

They grappled for the gun.

Another shot fired.

Kim felt the bullet's heat as it sailed past her ear. She'd been lucky. Again. But how long would her luck hold?

With a desperate surge of strength, she wrenched his arm down and away.

The gun fired again.

His eyes went wide.

He looked down at the spreading red blood on his belly, then back at Kim.

His legs buckled.

As he collapsed, Kim wrenched his gun from his grasp.

She spun, firing twice at EcoGuard's remaining man. He went down like a marionette with his strings cut.

Silence fell, broken only by Kim's ragged breathing. She stood over the last man, watching the life fade from his eyes.

"Otto." Smithers's voice snapped her back to reality. "Come on."

She bent down to search for ID. She found his wallet. Eugene Cannon. She didn't recognize the name.

Gaspar could chase Cannon's ID later. She slipped his wallet into her pocket.

Tucking Cannon's gun into her waistband, she sprinted for the east tunnel while the cavern rumbled ominously around them.

CHAPTER 49

Rural North Carolina

MARCUS MOLINA'S BOOTS CRUNCHED over the carpet of fallen leaves. The North Carolina forest loomed around him, the remaining trees standing tall in every direction.

Melissa Black followed, her footfalls nearly silent in comparison.

Men who believed themselves to be masters of the universe had ignored or depleted the earth's resources at alarming speed for far too long.

No more.

After July 4, people would understand exactly how serious the destruction of the planet could be. Millions would be without power for a good, long time when he was finished. Which served justice for all in his mind.

They passed a clearing where camouflaged solar panels peeked out from beneath a layer of strategically placed foliage and debris that demonstrated a veneer of environmental consciousness in a carefully constructed façade.

Molina's jaw clenched. Melissa understood what was going on. The events of the past weeks, months, years were competing for his headspace. Everything had led to this moment, this precipice.

He was so close now that he could almost taste the completion and success of his long-nurtured plans.

Abruptly, Molina stopped. He turned to flash Black with the experienced cold fire stare he regularly deployed to reduce lesser men to whimpering puddles, obsequiously following his whims.

But Melissa Black was not easily cowed. She met his gaze steadily wearing a perfect mask of attentive concern.

"The Atlanta airport attack was flawless," Molina said, low and sharp as a freshly honed blade. "Snaring Reacher's attention was the goal. It worked. He took the bait, hook, line, and sinker."

Black nodded, a slight tilt of her head encouraging him to continue. She knew her role in this dance all too well and it was way too early to reveal her own plans.

"Two years of hunting down whispers and rumors about some Army MP involved in the subway case. Then those Afghanistan vets gave me Reacher's name." He paused, savoring the memory. His lips curled into a mirthless smile.

"That was solid intel, for sure," Black said nodding.

"Docherty shouldn't have stopped Hawkins from completing her mission," Molina trailed off and his cold smile widened. "Well, accidents happen when the idiots attempt to thwart us, don't they?"

Black took a calculated step closer and spoke the kind of honey-sweet words he preferred. "I'm worried that the focus on Reacher might compromise our operations. We've worked so hard, planned for so long."

Molina's gaze, hard as granite, bored into hers. For a moment, the forest seemed to hold its breath. "Are you questioning my commitment, Melissa?"

"Never. You're the visionary here," she replied smoothly, laying a gentle hand on his arm. "I just worry that personal vendettas might cloud our judgment. We can't afford any missteps when we're so close."

Molina shrugged off her touch, turning to pace a tight circle in the small clearing. "Reacher was there when my brother died," he spat, years of pent-up rage coloring his words. "He was part of the system that failed us, that let a good kid die before he even had a chance to become a man. That makes Reacher just as guilty as the rest."

Black watched him carefully, gauging his mood. "And what about Theresa Lee?" she prodded gently. "She's just a cop doing her job."

"Collateral damage," Molina replied, chillingly matter-of-factly. "Theresa Lee's chosen to align herself with Reacher, she's made herself a target. It's that simple."

Black nodded slowly, as if carefully considering his words. "And you're certain this won't detract from our primary objectives?"

Molina whirled to give her a thunderous glare. "Ten coordinated attacks across the country. Maximum chaos, maximum impact. I wrote the plan. I know the plan."

"Of course," Black replied in the same tone a mother might use to soothe a toddler's tantrum. "I just don't want us to lose sight of the bigger picture."

Molina's jaw worked silently for a moment before he spoke again. "Reacher's death is part of the plan now. We'll make sure the world sees it as ecojustice. Reacher will be just another casualty in the war to save the planet."

Black nodded, a smile playing at the corners of her lips. An outside observer might have interpreted her expression as simple admiration.

His eyes took on a fanatical gleam. "Reacher's fate will be a warning to anyone who might stand in our way."

"Brilliant, as always," she said, but there was something colder, more calculating in the depths of her eyes. "Let's review the details of the operation once more to make sure every contingency is covered."

As Molina began to outline the intricacies of the planned attacks, Black listened with feigned attention. Carefully crafted expression of rapt admiration in place, she ignored him while she made her own plans.

Molina was at least partially aware of her manipulations and the dangerous game she played. His anger, his thirst for vengeance, made him predictable. And useful. For now.

Cannon was a bigger problem. He was cold, calculating, and a tactical genius.

She could manipulate Molina with sex, but Cannon was another matter.

Black noticed the sun continuing its slow descent. In this peaceful setting, surrounded by the quiet majesty of nature, three apex predators plotted destruction on an unimaginable scale. Each believed they held the upper hand, each confident in their ability to outmaneuver the other when the time came.

Molina's voice droned on, detailing explosive placements and timetables and personnel chosen for each target.

Black interjected occasionally with pertinent questions, playing her part to perfection. But soon a new tension began to build between them.

"There's one more thing we need to discuss," Black said, her tone carefully neutral. "The failsafe."

Molina's eyes narrowed. "What about it?"

"I think we need to move it," Black replied. "The current location at WRATH is too obvious. If anyone were to find it, we'd have a huge problem."

"The basement of the bunker is secure. I made sure of that personally," Molina snapped.

Black took a deep breath, as if steeling herself for confrontation. "I know how much this means to you. But we can't afford to take unnecessary risks. Not when we're this close."

For a long moment, Molina said nothing. The only sound was the whisper of wind through the trees and the faint call of a bird in the distance.

When he finally spoke, his voice was dangerously soft. "You're overstepping. The failsafe stays where it is. End of discussion."

Black opened her mouth to argue, then thought better of it. She nodded once, as if she were offering a terse acknowledgment of his authority. But she was already formulating contingencies and backup plans.

Molina and Black began the trek back to their hidden compound. The forest seemed to close in around them while branches reached out like grasping fingers in the growing darkness. The silence between them was charged with unspoken threats and barely concealed mistrust.

They emerged from the tree line to find the compound bustling with activity. Men and women loading equipment into vans and checking weapons with practiced efficiency.

Molina surveyed the scene with satisfaction, while Black's gaze darted from face to face, assessing potential allies and threats.

She was the human resources director for WRATH. She'd identified and recruited the patriots. She'd encouraged them to participate and volunteer for these dangerous and deadly projects. The patriots trusted her.

Without Black, Molina and Cannon would be left with a small fighting force which could be easily subdued. The patriots were the backbone of the entire plan and the one thing absolutely essential to the operation.

Everyone else was expendable.

Molina and Cannon could not successfully deploy the patriots without Black and she didn't expect them to try.

"It's really happening," Molina murmured with something like reverence, more to himself than to Black. "After all these years, all the planning and sacrifice. We're going to change the world."

"Yes, we are." She placed a hand on his shoulder, a light touch unmistakably possessive. "And nothing, not Jack Reacher, not the entire US government, can stop us."

"Get some rest," Molina nodded with cold, hard resolve. "Soon, we make history."

As she watched him stride away, barking orders to their assembled followers, a chill ran down her spine that had nothing to do with the cool air.

She had set this plan in motion, nudging Molina's grief and anger in the direction she'd wanted.

But now, as zero hour approached, she had doubts.

The forces she had unleashed would destroy segments of the world economy.

She shuddered.

Was she prepared to live with the blowback? Had Molina asked, she'd have said, "Absolutely."

Privately, she wasn't so sure.

In the shadows between two buildings, Black pulled out a burner phone and quickly typed out a message: "Packages secure. Awaiting final confirmation."

She hesitated for a moment, then added: "Subject becoming unstable. May need to accelerate timeline."

She hit send and immediately powered down the phone, slipping it back into her pocket.

Then she moved to join the others. One way or another, they were nearing the endgame. Many of her colleagues wouldn't survive and she was okay with that.

Sacrifices had to be made.

Melissa Black intended to be the one left standing when the dust settled.

In the compound below, the architects of the coming chaos made final preparations.

The stage was set.

The players were in motion.

As the clock ticked inexorably toward July 4th, the fate of countless lives hung in the balance.

Melissa Black lowered her head to hide the nearly constant smirk she couldn't wipe off her face even if she were to try.

Which, of course, she would not.

CHAPTER 50

Rural North Carolina

SMOKE CLAWED AT KIM'S lungs as she and Smithers emerged from the cave. The forest fire, a ravenous beast, devoured the landscape to their left. Ash rained down, coating everything in a ghostly shroud.

Kim's phone buzzed. She saw the one bar of signal strength as a lifeline in the wilderness. The text came from an unknown number.

"*Eagle's Nest. Evidence secure. Hurry.*" The signature was *T. Lee.*

"The old fire tower," Kim said, pocketing the phone. "Three miles northeast."

Smithers nodded curtly. "Our only shot. Let's move."

They plunged into the underbrush and the deafening roar of the inferno soon engulfed them. The forest was a maze of smoke and shadow, every path treacherous with fallen debris and hidden dangers.

An hour of slow, grueling progress brought them to the base of a steep ridge. The fire tower perched atop it like a sentinel.

"There," Smithers pointed, his voice hoarse from the smoke.

As they began their ascent, a new sound cut through the chaos.

Kim recognized it instantly. The rhythmic thump of helicopter rotors. "That doesn't sound like fire suppression equipment."

"Military," Smithers confirmed. "There's no base nearby. What's he doing out here?"

"Pick up the pace," Kim said, leading the way.

The climb to the tower became a desperate race. Hands bloodied from scrabbling over rocks, lungs burning with each smoky breath, Kim pushed on and Smithers followed.

The helicopter's searchlight swept the tree canopy, drawing ever closer. Was the helo friendly? No way to know.

Finally, they reached the tower's base. The ancient structure creaked ominously in the wind. Its metal skin was corroded by years of neglect.

"Lee!" Kim shouted, her voice swallowed by the inferno's roar.

No response.

They climbed the rickety stairs up the tower. Twice, the treads gave way and Kim dropped down to the lower step.

At the top, the observation deck offered a panoramic view of hell. From her vantage point, Kim saw fire stretched all the way to the horizon in every direction.

The decrepit fire tower swayed in the hot wind as Kim and Smithers ascended the final flight of stairs. Sweat trickled down her back.

Exertion and the oppressive heat from the approaching wildfire soaked through to her shirt.

The metal steps groaned under Smithers weight. Each creak set Kim's nerves further on edge.

"Watch yourself," Kim warned as they reached the observation deck. "This whole place could come down any minute."

Smithers nodded. "Let's find what we came for and get out."

The circular room at the top of the tower was cluttered with old equipment. A rusted desk, toppled filing cabinets, and broken chairs.

Layers of dust covered everything, disturbed only by Kim's footsteps and the ash floating in through the broken windows.

Her gaze scanned the room, searching for any sign of Lee or the zip drive containing the evidence Lee had promised. Where the hell was she?

"Lee?" Kim's voice was nearly lost in the fire's deafening roar.

No answer.

Smithers peered through the windows and out at the smoke-filled landscape. "The fire's coming this way from three directions. We don't have much time. If we're still here when the fire reaches us, we'll never get out alive."

Kim continued her search until her gaze fell on a section of a slightly askew floorboard. "Smithers, over here."

She knelt to pry up the loose board. Beneath it lay a small waterproof case. Inside the case was a USB drive and a hastily scrawled note.

"*Insurance policy activated. Trust no one. L*"

"Got it," Kim said as she pocketed the drive and replaced the floorboard. "Lee was here, but where is she now?"

A sudden creak from the ladder had both agents spinning, weapons drawn.

"Federal agents!" Smithers barked. "Show yourself!"

Melissa Black emerged from the shadows pointing a pistol at Kim. Black was disheveled and her eyes were wild with desperation and triumph.

"I'll be taking that zip drive now, Otto," Black said, her voice eerily calm.

Kim's grip tightened on her weapon. "Whatever game you're playing, you've already lost."

A humorless laugh escaped Black's lips. "You have no idea what you're involved in. Give me the zip drive. Otherwise I'll be forced to take it from your cold, dead hand."

Smithers demanded to know the truth. "Why kill Daisy Hawkins and Ed Docherty? What were they involved in?"

Black's eyes narrowed. "Loose ends. Docherty was foolish enough to step into the operation."

"Hawkins wanted a bigger cut of what?" Kim pressed to keep Black talking while she evaluated the options.

"Oh, come on, Otto. You're smarter than that," Black taunted, eyes glowing with a zealot's fervor. "Think bigger. Eco-terrorism is a means to an end. We're reshaping the entire energy landscape of this country and the world."

CHAPTER 51

Rural North Carolina

THE TOWER GROANED OMINOUSLY, punctuating Black's taunts. The fire was approaching rapidly. A blast of heat zapped a small tree nearby which seemed to explode, sparks flying in several directions.

"You said 'we are reshaping' the world's energy landscape. Who's we?" Kim insisted.

Black's smile was cold as she held out her palm. "The drive, Otto. You're out of time."

Kim quickly scanned the tower for alternatives. According to Theresa Lee, the evidence on the drive could blow the conspiracy wide open.

But why would Black care about that? Blackmail potential, maybe?

Suddenly, the tower lurched violently. Kim stumbled, momentarily losing her footing. Black seized the opportunity, lunging forward.

After that, several things happened at once.

Smithers moved to intercept Black, but the unstable floor shifted beneath him.

He staggered and fell into one of the old filing cabinets.

Kim regained her balance as she brought her weapon to bear on Black.

But Black was faster.

Black was stronger than she looked. She was also several inches taller and at least twenty pounds heavier than Kim.

Black closed the distance in two quick strides and grabbed Kim's right forearm, shoving her gun down and aside.

Kim felt the heat of the barrel against her ribs as they struggled.

"Give it up, Otto," Black hissed. "You're out of your depth."

Kim gritted her teeth, using every ounce of her strength to keep the gun from turning toward her. "Not a chance."

The sound of splintering wood overwhelmed the roaring fire.

A moment later, one of the support beams gave way.

The entire tower tilted precariously.

Which was when Kim made her move.

She drove her knee up, catching Black in the solar plexus.

Black's grip loosened as she doubled over from the blow.

Which allowed Kim to wrench the gun away.

She used all of her strength and leverage to shove Black backward through the door to the observation deck.

Black stumbled gasping for breath.

Her heel caught on a hole in the floor. She pin-wheeled her arms, trying to regain her balance.

Time seemed to slow as Black teetered on the edge of the observation deck. Her steely glare was a mixture of fury and fear.

Then she was gone.

As if she'd plummeted into the smoky abyss below.

But did she?

Kim stood frozen for a moment, the questions about what had just happened washed over her.

The tower shuddered again, groaning, swaying in the hot air, which snapped her back to the present.

"Smithers!" she called out, scanning for her partner.

A groan answered her. Smithers pulled himself up, using the overturned filing cabinet for support. A gash on his forehead bled freely.

"I'm okay," he said, though his grimace suggested otherwise. "Let's get out of here."

Kim nodded, moving to help him. "Can you make it down the stairs?"

Before Smithers could answer, a deafening crack split the air. The floor beneath them buckled, timbers splintering under the strain.

"Move!" Kim shouted, pushing Smithers toward the stairwell.

They half-ran, half-stumbled down the twisting metal stairs. Each step threatened to give way beneath them. The rails were too hot to touch.

The oppressive heat surrounded everything. Thick smoke became worse with every passing second.

Halfway down, a burning timber crashed through the ladder above. A shower of embers and debris attacked.

Kim felt the stairs give way beneath her feet.

She reached for the side rail. Her fingers just barely grazed the blistering hot metal as she fell.

She landed flat on her back on the landing below. The impact drove the air from her lungs.

She lay dazed for a moment, struggling to breathe through the thick smoke.

"Otto!" Smithers's voice seemed distant. "Answer me!"

Kim coughed, forcing herself to focus.

She was sprawled on what remained of the second-floor landing. Above her, the stairwell was a twisted mess of metal and flame.

"I'm here," she called back, her voice hoarse. "You okay?"

"Yeah," Smithers replied. "But the stairs are gone. There's no way down to you."

Kim assessed her situation. The fire was spreading rapidly, consuming the dry wood of the tower's interior now like a kid eating popcorn.

Unbearable heat enveloped everything around her.

"There's a window," she shouted up to Smithers. "I'll jump."

"It's too high!" Smithers protested.

Kim moved to the window, peering out. It was a long drop, but she spotted a pile of old tarps and equipment at the base of the tower. It wasn't ideal, but it was her only shot.

Melissa Black had fallen from the same side of the tower. She might have landed safely on the tarps, too.

She wasn't there now. Where did she go?

Kim told Smithers, "Get yourself out. I'll meet you on the ground."

Before Smithers could argue further, Kim took a deep breath and launched herself through the small opening.

The world spun as she fell, causing disorientation in the heavy smoke.

She hit the pile of tarps hard.

The impact knocked the wind out of her for the second time in as many minutes.

But she was alive.

Kim rolled off the makeshift landing pad, every muscle screaming in protest.

She looked around swiftly to see Smithers emerging from the tower's ground entrance, coughing and stumbling.

She rushed to his side, supporting him as they moved away from the collapsing structure.

Behind them, the fire tower gave one final groan before collapsing in on itself. The structure landed on the pile of tarps, sending a plume of embers into the night sky.

They didn't stop moving until they reached a significant distance where Kim finally allowed herself a moment to rest.

"That was too close," Smithers wheezed, leaning against a tree trunk.

Kim nodded, her hand instinctively going to her pocket. The USB drive was still hidden there. One small victory in the chaos.

"We need to find cover," she said, scanning the smoky forest. "Treat your wounds and figure out our next move."

Smithers straightened up, wincing slightly. "What about Lee? And the rest of Molina's crew?"

Kim's expression hardened. "Lee's in the wind. As for Molina's people, they're still out there. But right now, our priority is getting out of here alive."

As if on cue, the distant sound of engines reached their ears. Headlights appeared on the forest road below, multiple vehicles approaching fast.

"Looks like our night isn't over yet," Smithers said flatly.

Kim drew her weapon, checking the magazine. "You up for this?"

Smithers managed a wry smile despite his injuries. "Do I have a choice?"

"No," Kim replied, drawing her weapon.

The vehicles were getting closer now, headlights cutting through the smoky darkness. Kim could make out at least three SUVs, engines growling as they navigated the rough terrain.

"On my mark," Kim whispered, tensing as the lead vehicle approached their position. "We take the first one, use it as cover."

"Got it," Smithers nodded.

Kim took a deep breath, adrenaline coursing through her veins.

"Now!" she shouted, bursting from her hiding spot, running to intercept the first SUV.

She jumped onto the running board on the driver's side. Before the driver realized what had happened, she slid toward the rear of the running board and jerked the handle to open the driver's door.

He held the steering wheel in both hands, struggling to keep the SUV moving in the right direction over the potholed dirt trail.

Kim seized the moment to grab him by the neck with her right arm while aiming her weapon at his head.

"Raise your hands," Kim yelled into his left ear.

He did.

The moment he released the wheel, Kim's leverage pulled his torso aside. He was bigger, stronger, and way more freaked out than she was. He flailed and twisted and struggled to get free of her grasp.

Briefly, he lifted his foot off the accelerator, causing the SUV to slow while changing his center of gravity and throwing Kim off balance. She hung onto his head with the crook of her arm and stuffed her weapon under his chin.

"One shot and you're done," she said harshly. "Dead or alive, you're coming out of that seat."

His eyes widened and his mouth opened to scream. Before he had the chance, Kim fired her weapon into the cabin.

The bullet whizzed past his face.

Instantly, he leaned his body left. A brief moment before his momentum carried him through the open door, Kim moved out of his path.

He fell out onto the charred ground and rolled into the underbrush.

Kim slid into the driver's seat and braked to a hard stop. She unlocked the passenger door to allow Smithers to jump aboard while she fastened her seatbelt.

The moment he closed the passenger door, she stomped on the gas. The SUV jumped ahead into the fire.

CHAPTER 52

Rural North Carolina

KIM'S KNUCKLES WHITENED AS she gripped the steering wheel. The hijacked SUV lurched forward, tires spinning on ash-covered ground. Acrid smoke filled her nostrils, stinging her eyes.

Beside her, Smithers braced himself against the dashboard as they sped away from the collapsing fire tower.

The forest around them crackled and popped, an inferno devouring everything in its path. Flames licked at the edges of the narrow road, casting an otherworldly orange glow across the landscape.

Heat radiated through the vehicle, turning the interior into a mobile sauna.

"There!" Smithers pointed through the smoke-blind windshield, his voice hoarse from the thick air.

A black sedan weaved between burning trees ahead, barely visible through the haze. Kim squinted, trying to make out details. A flash of blond hair in the passenger seat caught her attention.

"It's Melissa Black," Kim said, certain. "She's not alone."

The SUV's engine roared as Kim kept the accelerator pressed to the floor. Embers swirled behind them in a deadly dance of fire and ash.

The sedan disappeared around a bend.

A massive pine behind the sedan, trunk engulfed in flames, creaked and groaned ahead.

Kim realized the tree's likely trajectory.

"Hold on!" she shouted as she mashed the accelerator while willing the SUV to speed faster. "Come on, come on, come on."

Half a moment later, the SUV passed the burning tree as it fell and crashed across the road behind them. Kim checked the rearview mirror, watching as the escape route vanished behind a wall of flame.

"No going back now," Smithers muttered.

Kim cranked the wheel hard left as the main road became impassable. The SUV careened onto a narrow fire trail, barely wide enough for the vehicle.

Branches whipped against the windows, leaving scratches in the glass. The undercarriage scraped against exposed rocks, each impact jarring their teeth.

"We're gonna lose them," Smithers said, gripping the handle above his door as he peered into the smoke seeking the sedan ahead.

"Not a chance." Kim's jaw was set with determination.

The trail widened slightly, offering a brief respite from the claustrophobic tunnel of smoldering and flaming vegetation.

She spotted the sedan again, fishtailing on the curved road ahead.

She accelerated to close the gap.

The sedan's brake lights flared red through the haze.

Kim swerved to avoid rear-ending the sedan and the SUV's tires skidded on the ash-covered gravel road.

The two vehicles raced side-by-side down the mountain trail in a deadly game of cat and mouse as each tried to move in front of the other.

A wall of orange flame erupted to Kim's right. A crowning fire leapt from treetop to treetop.

Kim flinched as intense heat battered the SUV.

She fought to keep the wheels straight although the steering wheel was slick with sweat beneath her palms.

The sedan veered left, kicking up a spray of pebbles and debris.

Kim cursed when the volley peppered the SUV's windshield and a web of cracks spidered across the glass, obscuring her vision.

"I can't see," she said, leaning forward in her seat.

Smithers mirrored her posture, squinting through the fractured windshield. "Slow down!"

Kim tapped the brakes. The SUV fishtailed. The back end slid ominously toward the drop-off on the right.

Kim overcorrected, sending the SUV toward a stand of burning trees on the left.

Screeching tires echoed ahead. The sedan spun sideways, momentarily blocking the road.

Kim caught a glimpse of Black's face. Her features were contorted by a mix of fear and anger.

"Who is driving?" Smithers said, peering through the gloom.

The man behind the sedan's wheel was unfamiliar. His expression was hidden behind dark sunglasses and smoky conditions.

"Hold on!" Kim shouted.

She cranked the wheel hard right.

The SUV plowed through dense underbrush, leaving the relative safety of the road. Branches snapped against the hood and roof. Kim's teeth rattled as they bounced over exposed roots and rocks.

The SUV burst from the tree line into a small clearing.

A sheer drop yawned ahead. The bottom was obscured by billowing smoke.

The valley below was a sea of flame. Entire sections of forest had been reduced to skeletal, burning husks.

Kim stood onto the brake pedal with both feet.

The SUV skidded, tires scrabbling for purchase on the loose soil.

The vehicle slid sideways, momentum carrying the SUV toward the cliff's sharp edge. Kim's heart pounded faster as time seemed to slow while the SUV skidded forward.

Finally, the SUV shuddered to a stop, front tires mere inches from fiery oblivion.

Pebbles and dirt tumbled over the edge, disappearing into the smoky abyss below.

For a moment, the only sound was the fire's distant roar and their own ragged breathing.

Smithers exhaled sharply, his face pale beneath a layer of soot. "That was too close."

Kim nodded, hands trembling slightly as she released her death grip on the steering wheel. She took a deep breath to calm her racing pulse.

CHAPTER 53

Rural North Carolina

KIM THREW THE SUV into reverse. The tires spun briefly before finding traction and peeling away from the cliff's edge.

She completed a quick turn and slammed the transmission into drive.

Headlights cut through the smoke behind the SUV, the sedan growing larger in the rearview mirror by the second.

"He's gaining on us," Smithers said, twisting in his seat to keep an eye on the sedan.

Kim gritted her teeth, focusing on the treacherous road ahead. The SUV bounced and jolted as she navigated around burning debris and fallen branches. The cracked windshield made it nearly impossible to see more than a few yards ahead.

A burning tree limb crashed onto the road. Kim swerved too late. The SUV tilted dangerously on two wheels before slamming back down on all four. Smithers grunted as his head knocked against the side window.

"You okay?" Kim shot a quick glance toward her partner.

Smithers nodded, rubbing his temple. "Just keep driving."

The road curved sharply to the left. As they rounded the bend, Kim spotted the black sedan again. It was moving erratically, weaving back and forth across the narrow mountain road.

"What are they doing?" Smithers muttered.

As if in answer, the sedan's passenger window rolled down. Black's arm emerged, a metallic object glinting in her hand.

"Get down!" Kim shouted.

Black fired off several rounds, punctuating the roaring engines and crackling flames.

The SUV's right-side mirror exploded in a shower of glass and plastic.

Kim hunched low over the steering wheel, trying to present as small a target as possible while maintaining control of the vehicle.

Smithers fumbled for his weapon, cursing as another bullet pinged off the hood. "I can't get a clean shot."

Kim's mind raced, assessing their options. The road ahead split, one path continuing to wind down the mountain while the other branched off to the right.

"Hold on," she said.

She wrenched the steering wheel to the right branch of the road. The SUV's tires squealed in protest as it drifted around the turn.

In the rearview mirror, Kim saw the sedan overshoot the turn, forced to continue straight.

"We've in the lead," Smithers said, a note of triumph in his voice. "But we don't know where this road goes."

"Sometimes you have to gamble."

The new road was even narrower than the last, barely more than a hiking trail widened for vehicular use. Trees pressed in on both sides, trunks blackened by the advancing fire. Smoke grew thicker, reducing visibility to near zero.

An orange glow intensified to their left.

"The fire's jumping the gap," Kim said. "We need to find a way out of here, fast."

Smithers pulled out a map, squinting to read in the dim light. "There should be a fire break about a mile ahead. If we can reach it."

His words were cut off by a deafening crack.

A massive tree, base eaten away by flames, toppled across the road directly in front of the SUV ten feet ahead.

Kim stomped on the brakes, but it was too late. The heavy vehicle simply couldn't stop.

The SUV plowed into the fallen trunk.

The impact threw them forward against the seatbelts.

Steam hissed from the crumpled hood as the airbags deployed and deflated in microseconds.

For a moment, everything was still.

Then Kim became aware of a new sound.

Creaking and popping wood gave way to roaring flames.

"Let's go," she said quietly, as if any additional sound might tip the balance against them.

They unbuckled seatbelts and forced the doors open.

As they stumbled from the wrecked SUV, the full magnitude of the situation became clear.

Outside, Kim noticed a leak as gasoline puddled around the gas cap. She pointed toward the fuel and yelled over the roar of the fire. "Let's get out of here!"

The forest was an inferno. A ravenous beast closing in from all sides.

Smithers gestured toward an opening in the trees ahead on the left. "There. A fire break."

Kim nodded, coughing when she inhaled a lungful of smoke. "Let's go."

They ran with the heat at their backs spurring them on.

A moment later, the fuel leaking from the SUV's tank ignited and the vehicle soon disappeared in a ball of flame.

Kim and Smithers kept running.

CHAPTER 54

Rural North Carolina

"THAT WAS TOO CLOSE," Smithers muttered, wiping soot from his face as they stopped to rest.

Kim's gaze was fixed on the raging fire they'd narrowly escaped.

Before she could utter any response, a gunshot cracked from afar, splintering bark inches from Kim's head. She dove for cover as bullets from the same direction pinged off around her.

"Persistent bastard." Smithers growled, drawing his weapon and firing back.

Kim peered through the thickening smoke, catching glimpses of men moving through the trees. The heat from the approaching wildfire pressed against her back like an implacable force.

"There." She pointed to a barely visible trail snaking away from the clearing. "Old forest service road. It's our only option."

Smithers agreed. "On three. One... two..."

They ran from their cover, zigzagging through the hail of gunfire.

The chase was a nightmarish blur of smoke and shadows. Branches whipped at her face as she stumbled down the overgrown path, pursuers never far behind.

Suddenly, a battered sedan burst from the tree line, fishtailing as it careened toward her. Smithers shoved Kim clear a moment before the vehicle roared past.

The driver's window rolled down, revealing a face twisted with desperation and hate. The same man they'd been chasing earlier. Melissa Black's driver.

"Who is that guy?" Smithers asked.

Kim shrugged and kept running. They scrambled for what little cover the scrub brush provided.

The sedan had turned and sped toward them again, crashing through the undergrowth.

Kim and Smithers ran through the thinning trees and pulled up short when they reached a sheer drop-off.

Far below, the inferno raged, a sea of hungry flames devouring everything in its path.

Kim skidded to a halt at the cliff's edge, turning to face her partner.

With a screech of tortured metal, the sedan slammed into a boulder. The vehicle flipped, rolling to a stop mere yards from where Kim and Smithers stood.

The driver crawled from the wreckage, bloodied but still clutching his weapon. He staggered to his feet, gun wavering between his two cornered targets.

"It's over," Kim's weapon was trained steadily on the man's chest. "Drop it."

For a long moment, only the roar of the approaching fire filled the air. The driver's eyes darted from Kim to Smithers to the precipice behind them several times, as if he were making a tough decision.

"Like hell," he spat. A mirthless laugh bubbled from his throat.

He spun his entire body and sprinted for the cliff edge. Without hesitation, he hurled himself into the abyss and was quickly swallowed by the inferno below.

Kim and Smithers stood in stunned silence, the heat of the fire pressing ever closer.

"We need to go while we still can," Smithers said quietly, still breathing hard.

Kim cast one last glance at the spot where the driver, whoever he was, had disappeared. Another piece of the puzzle gone, consumed by the flames that threatened to engulf them all.

CHAPTER 55

Rural North Carolina

KIM'S LUNGS BURNED WITH each ragged breath. Smoke choked the air, stinging her eyes and coating her throat. Flames seemed close enough to lick hungrily at her heels as she and Smithers stumbled through the inferno.

The forest around her had become a hellscape of orange and red, trees transformed into towering torches that crashed to the ground in showers of sparks. Embers rained from above, singeing her clothes and peppering her skin with tiny, searing pinpricks.

"There!" Smithers's hoarse shout barely carried over the roar of the fire. He pointed to a stream twenty yards away.

They splashed into the shallow stream. The cool relief lasted mere seconds before steam hissed from Kim's superheated clothes. The water barely reached her calves, but it was enough.

Kim followed the water downstream, with Smithers close behind.

They sloshed through the stream, feet slipping on algae-slick rocks. Low-hanging branches whipped her face leaving stinging welts. The relentless roar of the fire pursued like a hungry beast unwilling to relinquish its prey.

Kim's legs burned with fatigue. Her muscles screamed for rest. Her throat felt as raw as if she'd swallowed shards of glass. Sweat and soot-streaked Smithers's face in grotesque war paint. Her face was probably worse.

Smithers stumbled on a slippery rock. His knee buckled. Kim hauled him up with strength fueled by pure adrenaline.

She didn't need to tell him to keep moving.

The trees began to thin, offering a tantalizing glimpse of open sky. Suddenly, they left the forest's edge.

Air seemed to rush into Kim's starved lungs. She and Smithers collapsed on a grassy slope, chests heaving as they gulped down sweet, almost smoke-free breaths.

With trembling hands, Kim splashed fresh water from the stream to soothe her stinging eyes. Her clothes were now a patchwork of singes and holes.

Smithers looked no better. His salt-and-pepper hair was streaked with ash, his face smeared with soot and scratches. The injury to his forearm was oozing soot.

"We made it," Smithers wheezed, his voice barely above a whisper.

Kim nodded, unable to speak for a moment. The gravity of the situation settled with cold dread in the pit of her stomach.

Smithers broke the somber quiet. "What now?"

"Same as ever. We find Reacher." Kim's determination overrode her exhaustion even if she wasn't immediately able to execute any sort of real plan.

A glint of metal caught her eye, out of place in the natural landscape. Kim tensed, every instinct screaming danger. "Smithers, don't move."

"Excellent advice," a cold voice cut through the air like a knife.

Hostiles melted from the shadows, emerging from behind rocks and trees with practiced stealth. Kim quickly counted six. All heavily armed.

Melissa Black, eyes steely, stepped forward, radiating confidence and menace. "How kind of you to deliver yourself to us."

Kim assessed the options in fractions of seconds. The odds were overwhelmingly against them. Yet giving up was not an option.

She locked her gaze on Smithers. He gave an imperceptible nod, ready to follow her lead.

Kim launched herself at the nearest hostile. Her fist connected with his jaw in a satisfying crunch. He staggered back, caught off guard by her ferocity.

Gunshots cracked quickly in response.

Kim felt a searing sting in her shoulder where a bullet tore her jacket and grazed her skin. She stumbled but did not fall.

Smithers yelled a primal sound of defiance. He raised his weapon and aimed at a second assailant. The bullet struck true. The target dropped to his knees at the edge of the stream, eyes open but lifeless.

Smithers small victory was short-lived. Two more men rushed forward and tackled him to the ground, pinning him with brutal efficiency.

Rough hands seized Kim from behind. She thrashed and kicked, landing a couple of solid blows. Painful grunts rewarded her efforts, but did not neutralize her attackers.

A fist slammed into Kim's stomach with crushing force. She doubled over, gasping for air that wouldn't come.

Melissa Black approached, steps measured and calm. She smiled coldly. "Did you really think you could simply escape?"

Kim glared defiantly, refusing to give Black any sort of satisfaction.

Smithers continued to struggle against his captors, but his efforts were growing weaker by the second.

Black's smile widened, savoring her triumph like the predator she was. "Search them. Thoroughly."

Rough hands patted Kim down, probing every pocket and seam. Weapons, phones, and gear were tossed aside, leaving her feeling naked and vulnerable.

"Into the van," Black ordered, gesturing to the vehicle that had appeared as if by magic.

Kim and Smithers were unceremoniously shoved into the cargo area. Doors were slammed shut. The van's engine rumbled to life. She felt the vibrations thrumming through the metal floor.

Kim assessed the situation and searched for an advantage. She caught Smithers's eye in the dim interior. He gave her a grin sending a tiny spark of hope to flicker in her chest. They weren't beaten yet.

"Where are you taking us?" Kim demanded, injecting as much bravado into her voice as she could muster.

Black smirked. "You'll find our accommodations are quite secure."

The van wound through backroads and Kim paid close attention to the route. The landscape gradually changed. Hills gave way to steeper terrain, eventually transforming into mountains that loomed ominously against the sky.

Kim's muscles cramped from the confined space and lingering exhaustion. Her shoulder throbbed where the bullet had grazed her skin.

She ignored it all.

Suddenly, the van tilted downward at a steep angle. Kim's ears popped as they rapidly lost elevation while descending.

Bright light flooded a wide interior tunnel. As her eyes adjusted, Kim realized they'd entered some kind of massive underground hideaway.

Finally, the van came to a stop with a sudden, almost deafening, silence.

"Out," Black barked.

Kim blinked rapidly, taking in her surroundings as they were yanked from the vehicle. They stood in an enormous underground garage, easily large enough to house two dozen vehicles. More armed guards waited, weapons trained on the new arrivals.

Melissa Black prodded them forward. "Welcome to WRATH headquarters."

They were marched through a maze of sterile white corridors, each indistinguishable from the last. Kim caught glimpses through partially open doors of laboratories filled with equipment she didn't recognize, armories stocked with weaponry, and rooms humming with banks of sophisticated computers.

This was a fortress, a seat of power for an organization with terrifying resources.

Black led them into a vast central chamber. Massive screens covered the walls, displaying a dizzying array of data feeds and surveillance footage. A hive of activity surrounded a raised central platform where dozens of people worked at computer stations.

"Impressive, isn't it?" Black gloated, her voice dripping with smug satisfaction. "WRATH's impenetrable fortress. The culmination of planning and resources."

Kim's gaze swept the room.

"Don't get too comfortable. Your stay will be eventful, but very short." Black's gaze glittered with malice. "Lock them in a cell. We'll deal with them later."

CHAPTER 56

Rural North Carolina

KIM'S MUSCLES SCREAMED IN protest as she shifted her weight on the cold metal floor of her cell. Her back was pressed against the unyielding concrete wall.

Black's smug face as she'd ordered them locked away continued to fuel Kim's quiet rage.

Harsh fluorescent lights buzzed incessantly overhead, casting no shadows in the open cell. Kim's gaze swept over the sparse furnishings for the hundredth time, but nothing had changed.

A narrow cot with a thin, worn mattress promised no comfort, and a stainless-steel toilet gleamed dully in the corner. Nothing else broke the monotony of the stark walls.

With a soft grunt, Kim pushed herself to her feet. Her joints popped as she stretched, working out the kinks from hours of inactivity. She resumed her silent count of the ceiling tiles, a mental exercise to keep her mind sharp and focused on escape.

The sudden click of the door lock shattered the silence. Kim's body tensed, spine straightening and shoulders squaring.

A guard's face appeared in the small opening of the door. His expression was a mixture of boredom and disdain as he shoved a tray through the slot. The contents were an unidentifiable mush reminiscent of soggy cardboard.

"Dinner's served," the guard announced, his voice dripping with sarcasm. "Don't expect a mint on your pillow."

Kim met his gaze with a steely glare of her own.

"Where did you take Smithers?" she demanded, her voice low and controlled.

The guard's smirk faltered for a moment and a flicker of uncertainty passed across his features. Without answering, he slammed the food slot shut with more force than necessary.

His retreating footsteps echoed down the corridor, leaving Kim's question hanging in the air.

Ignoring the unappetizing meal, she returned to her methodical count of the ceiling tiles. Quickly, she pieced together fragments of information, searching for any weakness in security that she could exploit.

A muffled thud from the corridor interrupted her concentration.

Kim froze, senses on high alert.

Footsteps approached, different from the heavy tread of the guard who'd delivered her meal. Quicker. Purposeful.

The lock disengaged with a soft beep that seemed to reverberate through the cell. The door swung open, revealing a familiar face.

Smithers stood in the doorway, his appearance a far cry from his usual polished self. A fresh white bandage wrapped around his forearm, stark against his dark skin. An ugly bruise settled above his left eye. He offered Kim a weak grin.

"Your chariot awaits," Smithers said, his voice barely above a whisper.

Relief flooded through Kim, though she allowed only the slightest nod to betray her emotions.

"About damned time. Chariots are so damned unreliable these days," she replied with a reassuring grin, laying a comforting hand on his arm as she slipped past him into the dimly lit hallway.

The corridor stretched ahead. A maze of identical white walls and fluorescent lights. On the floor near her cell, the unconscious guard Smithers had shoved aside lay propped against the wall.

Smithers knelt beside the guard, quickly and efficiently searching the man's pockets.

He held up a small plastic card with the WRATH logo emblazoned across one side. "Access badge. They all have one. Should open most doors in this section, at least."

Kim took the card and examined it closely. "How much time do we have?"

Smithers glanced at his watch, his brow furrowing. "Patrol changes in eight minutes."

They set off down the corridor, footsteps eerily muffled on the polished floor. Each intersection looked identical to the last, probably a deliberate design meant to disorient and confuse. Kim's internal compass struggled to maintain a sense of direction.

"How'd you escape your cell, anyway?" she asked. "I couldn't find a way out. Believe me, I looked."

Smithers grinned. "Reacher."

"What?" Kim whipped her head around, astonished.

"He overpowered the guard. He had a key. He used it to open my cell and then gave it to me so I could use it to open yours," Smithers explained.

"Where is he now?"

Smithers shrugged. "Said he had more to do and he'd be in touch."

Kim would have demanded a more thorough explanation, but as they approached the next bend, Smithers held up a hand, signaling Kim to stop. He cocked his head, listening intently before pointing to the left.

"I overheard some chatter about a high-value prisoner down this way," he whispered.

Smithers led them deeper into the heart of the facility. They were deep underground, surrounded by hostiles willing to kill, with no clear exit strategy.

Kim accepted that she might never see daylight again. She shrugged. At least she wasn't claustrophobic, she thought, which made her grin wryly.

At the end of the new corridor, a heavily reinforced door blocked the path. Unlike the others they'd encountered, this door boasted an advanced security panel.

Kim swiped the stolen badge along the key card reader, holding her breath.

A red light flashed. Access denied.

Smithers leaned in, studying the panel intently. "It needs a biometric scan. Fingerprint, probably."

Kim considered the options. Without a word, she turned and retraced her steps to where she'd left the unconscious guard. Grabbing his arms, she began to drag him toward the secured door.

Smithers raised an eyebrow but quickly moved to assist. Together, they maneuvered the limp body in front of the scanner. Kim lifted the guard's hand, pressing it firmly against the glowing panel.

For a heart-stopping moment, nothing happened. Then, with a soft beep, the door lock disengaged. The heavy barrier slid open with a pneumatic hiss, revealing the cell beyond.

Inside, a woman they knew sat on a metal chair, hands bound behind her back. Theresa Lee's eyes narrowed as a mix of relief and wariness played across her features.

"Took you long enough," Lee said, her voice low and steady despite her position.

"Vacation's over. Time to clock in." Kim smiled, simply glad to know Lee was still alive, as she worked to free her restraints.

As her bindings fell away, Lee rolled her shoulders, working the feeling back into her arms.

"What's our exit strategy?" she asked, rubbing her wrists where the restraints had damaged her skin.

Smithers checked his watch again, his expression terse. "We improvise. Fast."

They stepped back into the corridor, alert for any sign of approaching guards. Kim caught a flicker of movement at the far end of the hallway and raised a finger to her lips in warning.

They pressed themselves against the wall out of sight as a guard passed by, speaking into a radio. "The package is prepped for transport," he said.

Wondering what package he meant and where and how it would be transported, Kim held her breath until his footsteps faded into silence. After he'd passed, the three continued.

The narrow corridors eventually opened into a cavernous room that took Kim's breath away.

Rows of gleaming metal vats lined the walls, each easily twice the height of a man. A pungent, organic smell permeated the air, sharp enough to make Kim's eyes water. Banks of computers and control panels filled the center of the room. Screens displayed a dizzying array of data.

Lee's eyes narrowed as she surveyed the scene. "This looks like some kind of bioengineering lab."

Smithers moved closer to one of the vats, peering at a label affixed to the side.

"Genetically modified algae," he reported, his voice tight. "Designed to rapidly consume petroleum products."

"An oil-eating super-organism," Kim said. "Released into the oceans, this stuff could destabilize the global oil industry in a matter of weeks."

"These people are supposed to be ecowarriors. How the hell is this stuff respectful of the planet?" Smithers shook his head in disbelief. "They could devastate entire ecosystems. The environmental impact would be catastrophic."

Before Kim could respond, multiple alarms shattered the silence. Red lights began to pulse overhead, bathing the room in an eerie, blood-red glow.

Smithers's voice cut through the mind-numbing noise. "They must have found our empty cells. We're out of time."

A door at the far end of the room burst open. Armed guards flooded in, weapons raised and ready.

But they didn't fire.

Which probably meant the vats were filled with substances toxic to humans.

Kim dove behind the nearest vat, dragging Lee down with her. Smithers grabbed the unconscious guard's weapon and provided covering fire in controlled bursts.

The guards didn't fire back, which confirmed Kim's assessment of the contents of the big vats, at least in her head.

More guards poured into the room, shouts barely audible over the din of battle.

Smithers must have reached the same conclusions about the guards' reluctance to shoot because he slowed down his rate of fire. After a few moments of unsettling silence, Smithers aimed and fired twice, taking out two of the guards.

Kim scrambled toward one of the dead guards and snatched his weapon.

"The vats," Lee shouted. "Flood them out!"

Kim took careful aim at the nearest vat, focusing on what looked like a potential weak point in the reinforced glass.

She fired several times. The noise was lost in the general chaos, but she saw fissures spreading across the glass surface.

Smithers caught on quickly, redirecting his fire to another vat. His well-placed shots shattered the thick glass, releasing a torrent of viscous green liquid. The noxious odor intensified as the genetically modified algae culture spread across the floor.

Chaos consumed the WRATH forces as they scrambled to contain the rapidly expanding spill. Several guards lost their footing on the slick surface. Weapons clattered across the floor and slid out of reach.

"Exit!" Smithers shouted over the din. He pointed to a doorway on the east side of the room previously hidden behind equipment.

They made a break for it, carefully skirting the edges of the expanding puddle of algae. Kim sprinted, half-carrying Lee.

The hallway beyond the lab stood mercifully empty while the facility's resources were dealing with the breach. Kim pushed herself to maintain the pace, counting every second.

After what felt like an eternity, they rounded a final corner to find themselves face-to-face with a massive blast door designed to seal off this section of the facility in case of emergency, such as a toxic spill, probably.

Smithers attacked the control panel, fingers flying over the keypad as he attempted to override the security protocols.

Precious seconds ticked by as Kim and Lee stood guard.

Finally, agonizingly slowly, the blast door began to inch open. The gap widened slightly, revealing a tantalizing glimpse of the world beyond.

Shouts echoed down the corridor behind them. The guards had regrouped and were closing in fast.

"Hurry!" Kim urged, as Smithers put his shoulder to the door, using all of his strength to force it wider.

Cool night air rushed in as they stumbled outside, filling Kim's lungs with the sweet scent of freedom. The star-filled sky stretched endlessly above.

A WRATH transport vehicle sat unattended with its engine idling. Smithers slid behind the wheel and Lee took the passenger seat. Kim climbed into the back, scanning constantly for signs of pursuit.

Smithers threw the vehicle into gear. Tires squealed on pavement as he peeled away, bouncing down the rough access road at breakneck speed.

Kim watched guards spill out of the open blast door, weapons raised. Bullets peppered the back of the vehicle and pierced the rear window and continued through to shatter the front windshield.

"Head east." Kim shouted over the din, leaning forward between the seats.

Smithers gripped the steering wheel as he swerved onto a main road. In the passenger seat, Lee checked her weapon, prepared to return fire if necessary.

The WRATH compound slowly disappeared behind them into the darkness.

After several miles, Smithers was the one to break the tense silence. "So, where to now?"

"I got a text from Gaspar. He said WRATH has operations in an abandoned fracking operation," Kim said. "The location is nearby. We can start there."

CHAPTER 57

Rural North Carolina

THE NIGHT SKY SHIMMERED now with an otherworldly brilliance. Countless stars pierced the inky darkness like diamond dust scattered across black velvet.

Tomorrow, fireworks would be lighting up the skies across the country. Crowds, awed by the spectacle, would be gathered to watch, clueless about WRATH's threats.

Kim crouched behind the sprawling fracking equipment. The distant pumps and generators worked with mechanical rhythms in the otherwise untouched landscape.

"I'm in position," she said quietly into her comms.

"Copy that," Smithers's voice crackled in her ear. "Any sign of Black or Molina?"

"Negative," she replied, her tone cautious as she scanned the shadows. "But she's here."

"Stay sharp," Lee's voice chimed in. "Black's not your average opponent."

"Tell me something I don't know," Kim muttered.

"We'll get her this time," Smithers said. "She can't outrun us forever."

"Looking for me, Agent Otto?"

Kim whirled around, her hand instinctively reaching for her weapon. Melissa Black seemed to materialize from the darkness like a specter. Her eyes glinted with the predatory gleam of an eagle diving for the final kill.

"I'm flattered by your persistence," Black continued, words dripping with sarcasm. "It's almost admirable how you refuse to give up, even when you're so hopelessly outmatched."

Kim's jaw clenched and she tightened the grip on her weapon. "Yeah? I guess you'll demonstrate for me. Can't wait to see it."

Black's laugh was cold and mirthless. Her eyes narrowed to dangerous slits. "You have no idea what's coming, do you?"

"Why don't you enlighten me?" Kim challenged.

"Now where's the fun in that?" Black's lips curled into a sneer. "I prefer to watch you squirm, trying to piece it all together."

"You do like to play games," Kim retorted, her eyes never leaving Black's face.

"Games?" Black scoffed with disdain. "You think those killers out there deserve to live? They're destroying our planet, Otto. It's them or us. Even you should understand that much."

Kim's eyes flashed with anger. "You're not God, Black."

"No," Black agreed, her voice eerily calm. "I'm something far more effective."

Without warning, Black lunged forward with a hard left, cutting through the air with deadly precision.

Kim barely had time to dodge, feeling the rush of air as Black's knuckles passed mere inches from her face.

"Too slow, Otto," Black taunted, pressing her advantage. "Age catching up with you?"

Kim countered with a quick jab to Black's ribs, but her fist connected with solid muscle and practically bounced off.

"I'll take you down," Kim grunted, ignoring the pain shooting through her hand.

She heard Lee call urgently on the comms. "Smithers, what's your position?"

"Basement level, southeast corner," came Smithers terse reply, punctuated by the sound of more gunfire. "I've got eyes on something that looks very much like a bomb, but Molina's blocking my access."

"A what?" Kim asked, not sure she'd heard correctly. "Get the hell out of there."

"Otto, what's your status?" Lee asked through the comms, already moving toward the facility entrance.

"Little busy here," Kim's strained response reflected her struggle with Black. "Black's not going down without a fight."

Before Lee responded, a WRATH operative appeared from around a corner, gun raised and ready to fire.

"Freeze!" Kim heard the operative shout. It wasn't hard to visualize his weapon trained on Lee's chest.

"I don't think so," Lee said, breathing heavily as if she were moving fast to close the distance between them.

"Last chance," the WRATH operative warned, his finger tightening on the trigger. "Stand down."

His words were cut off as Kim heard Lee moving with swift, brutal efficiency.

His gun clattered to the ground when Lee flipped him over her hip, and he hit the concrete with sufficient impact to drive the air from his lungs.

"Sorry," Lee said, not sounding sorry at all. "I don't stand down."

As Lee telegraphed her victory over the limp body, the sounds of fighting continued to echo around Kim.

The gunfire from inside the facility had intensified, punctuated by the occasional explosion. And from the other direction, she could hear the unmistakable sounds of both Lee and Smithers engaged in their own battles.

"Otto, Smithers, I'm on my way," Lee said, her voice tight with tension. "Who needs backup more urgently?"

There was a moment of silence, filled only by the sounds of combat. Then Kim said, "Lee, get to Smithers. If what he's got eyes on is really a bomb, that's the priority."

Lee began to object, but Kim cut her off. "Go there. I'll join you shortly."

"Copy that," Lee acknowledged reluctantly.

Kim's world had narrowed to the space between her and Black. Every move, every breath, could mean the difference between victory and defeat. The rest of the world had fallen away, leaving only this deadly dance which was almost finished.

"Always such a righteous hypocrite," Black sneered as she pressed her advantage with a sharp jab that narrowly missed Kim's jaw. "You're just as dirty as the rest."

Kim ducked under a wild swing, feeling it sail past her head. She countered with a swift kick to Black's midsection.

Black absorbed the blow, barely flinching.

"No?" Black taunted, gleaming with malice. "We both kill. We both deceive. The only difference is, I'm on the right side of history. You're still serving a corrupt system."

"We're nothing alike," Kim growled, blocking a vicious jab and throwing a better punch to Black's gut. "I protect and you destroy. World of difference there."

"Protect?" Black's laugh was harsh and mocking. "You're a lapdog for corruption. Nothing more and nothing less."

Using Black's momentum against her, Kim swept her legs away. She sent Black crashing to the ground with a satisfying thud. A couple of her bones cracked when she hit the hard rock bed.

Half a moment passed followed by Black's ear-splitting howl.

"You're wrong." Kim growled while she pressed her advantage with another swift kick to Black's kidneys.

But Black rolled with the fall, coming up with a handful of dirt that she flung into Kim's eyes.

Kim staggered back, momentarily blinded, eyes burning as she blinked furiously to clear her vision.

Black circled Kim and moved in for the kill. "Look around you, Otto. Look at what your kind have done to this place. The greed, the destruction. WRATH will remove this blight from the planet. We'll return to less destructive times."

"You don't get to make that choice." Kim's vision was slowly clearing. She could sense Black closing in, could almost feel the malevolent glee radiating from her.

"Someone has to be vigilant," Black retorted, her voice cold. "The world is dying, Otto. We're saving the planet while your kind is killing it."

Molina emerged from behind a tangle of pipes like a spider from its web. A twisted, maniacal glee burst from his lips as if the hysteria could not be contained. "Took you long enough, old man. I was beginning to think you wouldn't show."

"Molina." Smithers's eyes narrowed and his body tensed for action. "I should have known you'd be here."

"Couldn't miss the party," Molina sneered, his hand hovering near his weapon. "Especially when the guests of honor finally arrived."

"Hate to disappoint you," Smithers said, his voice deceptively calm, "but I'm here to crash this party."

Molina's grin widened, revealing teeth that seemed too sharp in the dim light. "Oh, I'm counting on it. It wouldn't be any fun if you didn't put up a fight."

"Fun?" Smithers's voice was cold. "You think this is a game?"

"Life is a game, old man," Molina replied, his eyes glinting dangerously. "And I'm about to win. Which makes you the loser."

Without another word, Molina raised his weapon and opened fire.

Smithers dove for cover.

Molina's deafening gunshots exploded in the enclosed space. Bullets ricocheted off metal surfaces, sending sparks flying and adding to the chaos.

"We've got a situation," Smithers spoke into his comms as he returned fire. "Molina's here, and he's not playing nice."

"Lee, status report," Kim said into her comms while keeping her gaze firmly fixed on Black.

Lee didn't respond, but Smithers's reply was punctuated by the sound of gunfire. "Molina's got me pinned down."

His voice cut off abruptly, replaced by static.

"Sounds like your friends are in trouble." Black's cold and mocking laughter cut through the noise and Kim's misplaced attention on her colleagues. "What's it going to be, Otto? Save them, or stop me?"

Kim's eyes narrowed, a newfound determination settling over her features. "Who says I can't do both?"

Kim launched toward Black. Bodies collided with bone-jarring force, and as they grappled, Lee came around a corner and sprinted toward them.

Kim shouted while narrowly avoiding a vicious blow from Black. "Get to Smithers!"

Lee hesitated. "I can't just leave you here."

Kim's voice strained as she continued to struggle with Black. "That failsafe bomb is the priority. Otherwise, we're all dead. Go."

Lee hesitated a couple of beats before she turned and sprinted toward Smithers, disappearing into the shadows as she reported her status into the comms.

Kim returned her full attention back to Black.

"It's just you and me now," she said with her gaze locked on her opponent.

Black's eyes glinted dangerously in the starlight. Her predatory smile spread across her face. "Wouldn't have it any other way. You're done here."

The fate of countless lives hung in the balance. Failure was not an option. Every second Kim kept Black occupied was another second Smithers could use to stop the detonation of the bomb.

"Come on then," Kim challenged. "Show me what you've got."

Black replied, "Oh, I intend to."

CHAPTER 58

Thursday, July 4
Independence Day
Rural North Carolina

IN HER COMMS, KIM heard Lee racing through the maze of corridors toward Smithers. Lee's footsteps synchronized with the blood pounding in Kim's ears. She could hear the echoes of gunfire growing louder, guiding Lee toward Smithers's position.

"Smithers!" Lee called out.

"About time," Kim heard Smithers say when Lee arrived to join him. "Molina's got me pinned down here. The bomb's active. We're running out of time."

Time was ticking away, lives were on the line, and they were all in danger.

"Hold on, Smithers," Kim muttered distractedly.

Her attention returned to the present and her vision cleared just in time to see Black's fist hurtling toward her face.

Kim twisted away from Black's fist. The blow grazed her cheek instead of landing squarely, which was why she was still standing. The pain sharpened her focus, bringing with it a surge of flashbacks.

Grueling training sessions flashed through her mind. Endless drills, bruises, and sweat. Her instructors' voices rang in her ears. Over and over, they'd said, *"When everything else fails, trust your gut."*

What would Reacher do? The question flashed through her head and the answer came instantly. *When someone hurts me, move toward the threat, not away.*

Kim centered herself, balancing her weight, prepared to rush the enemy.

Black, sensing her change in demeanor, hesitated for a split second.

Which was all Kim needed.

She feinted left, then struck right. Her fist connected solidly with Black's solar plexus, bending her in half. She stumbled back, surprise etched on her face.

Kim pressed her advantage, unleashing a flurry of strikes that drove Black further off balance.

"You're slipping," Kim taunted, echoing Black's earlier arrogance. "All that planning, and you still can't beat one agent half your size?"

The taunt hit home. Rage contorted Black's features. She charged forward, abandoning technique for brute force.

Kim was ready.

She sidestepped at the last possible moment, allowing Black's momentum to send her crashing into a nearby pump.

The impact of Black's head with the heavy machinery was sickeningly loud and gratifyingly effective.

Black slumped to the ground. Blood streamed from a long gash on her forehead. She struggled to rise, but her movements were sluggish.

Kim approached cautiously, all too aware that even wounded, Black was highly dangerous.

"It's over," Kim said, her voice firm. "Surrender now."

"It's never over," Black's laugh was more of a wheeze. She pulled a small detonator from her pocket.

Time seemed to slow.

Kim saw Black's thumb move toward the trigger on the detonator, making her intentions clear.

In that instant, Kim raised her weapon, aimed, and fired.

The gunshot echoed across the fracking site.

Black's body jerked once, then fell heavily to the ground. She lay still. The detonator dropped from her lifeless fingers.

Kim lowered her weapon, a maelstrom of emotions washing over her.

Mostly, she felt relief and the satisfaction of surviving.

Kim allowed herself a moment to regroup and then turned her focus to Smithers and Lee. There would be time for reflection later.

She hustled toward the basement. When she rounded the final corner, she saw Smithers was out of time.

Molina was holding off Smithers at gunpoint.

CHAPTER 59

Thursday, July 4
Independence Day
Rural North Carolina

MOLINA WAS LOADED, PREPPED, and ready. His head seemed to swivel in all directions.

"Face it, Smithers," Molina called out while reloading. "You're out of your depth. Why don't you make it easy on yourself and give up?"

Smithers's gaze darted around the room, searching for anything he could use. Kim saw him staring at a rack of chemicals near the bomb. He inclined his head in that direction as a signal to Lee who ducked her head around the corner.

"You know what, Molina?" Smithers shouted back loudly enough to reach both Kim and Lee through the comms. "I think you're right. I'm coming out."

Molina's surprised chuckle was infused with satisfaction. "Well, well. The old dog knows when he's beat."

Smithers sprinted from his cover position. Molina's gun tracked him, but instead of surrendering, Smithers dove for the chemical rack.

He crashed the containers to the floor. The containers broke open. Contents mixed to form a toxic cloud.

Molina cursed, momentarily blinded and choking.

Smithers held his breath and used the confusion to close the distance.

He tackled Molina, sending them both sprawling. They grappled on the floor, each fighting for control of Molina's weapon.

Smithers barely managed to wrench the gun away. There was a moment of stillness as their eyes met.

"Not bad, old man," Molina wheezed as he stared at the gun in Smithers's hand.

Smithers stood slowly, his body no doubt aching from the fight. He looked down at Molina, holding him on the ground with the threat of death.

Kim saw the bomb's timer showed less than five minutes remaining.

Molina crouched and leapt across the divide toward Smithers, knocking Smithers to the ground.

They wrestled for the gun, but this time, Molina had the upper hand.

Kim looked for an opening and couldn't find one. Her angle was impossible. She held her fire, scanning the area for a better answer.

"Molina!" Theresa Lee's voice yelled to capture his attention.

Briefly, he glanced in her direction.

Which was when she aimed true and shot him in the face.

Molina collapsed on top of Smithers, dead weight, sending them both to the floor.

Kim approached quickly, shoving Molina aside. "He's dead. Can you disarm that bomb?"

Smithers dusted himself off. "It's been a minute since I've defused live explosives."

"Well, you've had more training than I have," Lee said, coming up to join them while also defending against WRATH members possibly waiting in the wings. "So is it experienced you or amateur me?"

Smithers grinned. "Flip you for it?"

Lee shook her head. "No thanks."

"When you two are done socializing," Kim said, tilting her head toward the clearly visible bomb twenty feet away.

"I figured," Smithers said as he crept through a maze of pipes and control panels while Kim and Lee were prepared to provide cover.

The basement level was a warren of industrial equipment, corridors, and cubby holes.

The air was thick with the smell of oil and ozone, and the constant hum of machinery made it difficult to hear any approaching danger.

The bomb was a monstrous thing, a Frankenstein's creation of wires and explosives that looked capable of leveling half the state.

"It's big, nasty, and definitely not something you'd want at a Fourth of July barbecue," Smithers said into his comms in a quiet voice, as if he could detonate the bomb with a loud sneeze.

"Can you disarm it?" Kim asked, her voice strained even in her own ears.

"Definitely not," Smithers replied. "It's well beyond my expertise."

"Cannon knew all about bombs. So did Molina," Lee said quietly. "When is it set to explode?"

"Fifteen minutes," Smithers replied.

Kim listened to the exchange and made the decision. "Only one choice. Let's get the hell out of here before that thing blows."

"What about everyone who lives in this area?" Lee asked. "The casualties will be horrific."

"Get out. Now. I'll call for backup. But get everyone you can take with you as far away as possible."

Smithers was the first to put some distance between himself and the bomb. As he trotted past, he said, "Let's go. We don't have much time. And you'll get a better signal outside, anyway."

Kim gestured for Lee to follow Smithers, while she fished her satellite phone from her pocket and placed a call to Gaspar. Finlay or Cooper had more resources at their disposal but bringing them up to speed would take precious minutes she didn't have.

The sat phone had trouble connecting through the underground warren, but once she burst from the bunker into the open sky, the call connected.

"Zorro," she said as soon as he picked up. "We found a sophisticated bomb in the WRATH bunker. Anybody in the immediate area we can call on to defuse it?"

"How much time do we have?" Gaspar replied, already clacking his keyboard looking for assets he could deploy.

"Not long," she said breathlessly as she jogged along behind Lee and Smithers. "Not long at all."

Before she got the words out, a monstrous explosion sounded from the bowels of WRATH's bunker. A fireball the size of the entire entrance blasted through the door and outside where it rushed upward, almost like a nuclear mushroom cloud.

The force of the blast caused the bunker to implode. The ground shook like a powerful earthquake. It knocked Kim flat on her belly and forced her breath away.

She crawled beneath a stand of trees and ducked her head to shield herself from falling debris while hoping Smithers and Lee had found sufficient cover.

The dry forest caught fire. Balls of flame bounced across the tops of the trees, lighting them up like birthday candles.

Kim kept her head down and yelled into her comms as she ran, "Get out! While you can! Get Out!"

They ran through the forest, heading toward the road. Before they reached the pavement, a helo hovered overhead and landed. Four men climbed out carrying equipment. Kim guessed it was medical kits, unless they were expecting more bombs.

Kim jogged to the helo and stepped inside. Lee and Smithers followed.

The pilot was a man she recognized.

"Thanks for the ride, Russell," Kim said as she settled into the copilot's seat and fastened her four-point harness.

"Happy to be of service, Agent Otto," Russell replied. "Gaspar was quite insistent."

Kim grinned. "Yeah, he can be that way."

Smithers and Lee reached the helo and climbed aboard.

Russell lifted off before they had a chance to buckle up.

CHAPTER 60

Eighteen hours later
Washington, DC

AFTER DINNER, KIM AND Smithers walked along the bustling Washington, DC sidewalk, weaving through crowds of tourists and locals alike. The setting sun cast long shadows across the city, but the shade did little to alleviate the oppressive July heat.

They were headed back to their hotel when Kim's phone rang.

She glanced at the screen, then answered curtly. "Otto."

Finlay's voice came through the earpiece. "I've sent a car. It will pick you up there in five minutes."

Before Kim could respond, the line went dead. "Finlay says he needs to see us."

Smithers raised an eyebrow. "Now? Did he say why?"

Kim shook her head.

They scanned the street for potential threats, which was a habit acquired through years of experience. Thick humidity and the scent of street food from nearby vendors combined to form a cloying cocoon.

Tourists passed in herds, chatting excitedly about the upcoming fireworks display, oblivious to the undercurrents of tension caused by every gathering crowd in Washington, DC since terrorists attacked the Pentagon and the White House on 9/11.

Kim remembered the city fondly when she was a law student at Georgetown, more focused on her own life than anything else.

But even then, the locals said DC had been changed forever when the Twin Towers came down in New York. Bin Laden proved the US was vulnerable to attacks from terrorists around the world and within US borders. The knowledge had changed DC and the entire country forever.

Precisely five minutes after Finlay's call, a black stretch Escalade SUV pulled up to the curb. The rear door opened.

"Please get in," Russell said from its depths.

Kim and Smithers exchanged a quick glance before stepping into the backseat. Smithers closed the door, and the driver merged the Escalade smoothly into traffic.

When they were seated, Kim noticed a young woman in the shadows. She didn't introduce herself. Maybe thirty years old, slender, blond hair gathered at the nape of her neck with a wide barrette.

Kim gave her a nod and nothing more. She'd learn whatever she needed to know about the woman soon enough.

"Russell," Smithers said, breaking the silence. "Any idea what this is about?"

Russell offered a frank gaze in reply. "That's not for me to say."

Smithers was wasting his time questioning Russell. He would reveal what Finlay allowed him to reveal. No more and no less.

Kim studied the passing scenery. What was so urgent that Finlay had summoned them? Could have been simply convenient timing. But probably not.

The car pulled up to the Waldorf's Townhouse Suite and stopped discreetly at the private side entrance. When they stepped out of the Escalade, Russell sent the driver on his way and led them inside and to the private elevator. As always, his movements were economical and purposeful.

The young woman followed along behind.

In the elevator, Smithers spoke again. "Russell, that extraction earlier was something else. We owe you."

Russell's face remained impassive. "Someday, I'll collect the debt."

The elevator doors opened to reveal the Townhouse Suite's sprawling luxury spread across two palatial floors. Kim had been here before, but she followed Russell as he guided all three of them upstairs to the private living room.

Senator Sansom and Finlay sat in leather chairs, one on either side of the sofa.

Finlay stood as they entered. "Kim. Smithers. Excellent work with WRATH."

"Indeed. You've done your country a great service." Sansom remained seated, but his sharp gaze betrayed keen interest. "Someday, there might even be a commendation for you."

"All in a day's work," Kim replied with a nod. Her instincts were on high alert. She'd dealt with enough politicians and bureaucrats to know when something was off. "What's this about?"

Sansom leaned forward like a big cat about to pounce. "We have a proposition for you."

Before Sansom could continue, Finlay interjected casually. "But first, Agent Otto, we need to discuss the USB drive Lee left for you in that fire tower. Where is it?"

Kim's face remained impassive.

"I don't have it," Kim replied steadily.

Sansom leaned forward, frowning. "You lost it?"

"No," Kim said, meeting his gaze. "It was stolen."

Finlay and Sansom exchanged a look that Kim couldn't quite decipher.

"Stolen?" Finlay pressed. "By whom?"

Kim shook her head. "If I knew that, I'd be pursuing them right now instead of sitting here."

The tension in the room ratcheted up a notch. Kim could almost see the wheels turning in their heads, recalculating whatever plans they'd made before hearing this new information.

What followed was an hour of carefully crafted half-truths and veiled implications. Sansom praised Kim's work effusively, while Finlay dropped hints about future collaborations.

Throughout, the young woman stood to one side and said nothing.

Neither man fully revealed his plan and Kim found herself growing increasingly annoyed with the dance.

As the meeting seemed to be winding down, Kim could wait no longer. "Where's Theresa Lee?"

A ghost of a smile touched Finlay's lips as he flashed a quick look at the young woman still standing out of Kim's natural sight line. "My guess? She's with Reacher."

Kim cocked her head and Smithers let out a low whistle.

Before either of them could press for more information, a series of muffled booms echoed through the room.

Kim glanced through the large windows on the second floor toward the Potomac River.

Tonight's fireworks display had begun.

Finlay glanced at the clock and then stood. "We can continue this discussion another time. I'm sure you both have reports to file."

It was a clear dismissal. Kim and Smithers found themselves back on the sidewalk moments later, watching as red, white, and blue starbursts reflected off passing cars.

"What do you make of all that?" Smithers asked, his voice low.

Kim shook her head. "I'm not sure, but something doesn't add up. Why bring us here just to dance around the issue? And what's going on between Lee and Reacher?"

"Yeah, and who is the blond cutie and why is she standing in the shadows?" Smithers piled on.

Kim's phone rang again. She checked the display. "It's Cooper."

She answered, her voice clipped and professional. "This is Otto."

Cooper's response was hard, demanding. "You've been tracking Reacher. How's he mixed up with WRATH, Black, and Molina?"

Kim watched golden chrysanthemum fireworks burst against the night sky, buying herself a moment to think. "It'll all be in my report, when I have a chance to write it."

"Damned right it will," Cooper snapped. "Meanwhile, after the Hawkins situation, we deployed every available agent. Multi-agency."

"I heard," Kim said. "And what did you discover?"

"WRATH had ten separate targets. All set to blow during tonight's fireworks shows at ten locations around the country. All thwarted." He sounded quite proud of himself. Then he seemed to remember who he was talking to. "Thanks in part to you both, and inter agency cooperation, we stopped all ten."

He rattled off the list of targets in a rapid-fire fashion. Two nuclear power plants in two different states. Two dams. A chemical facility in Texas. A nuclear reactor in Illinois. An oil refinery in California. Two major bridges.

And the fracking operation in North Carolina.

"We've rounded up most of WRATH, but there's more to do. The Bureau's task force is working overtime," Cooper said. "We've uncovered more WRATH ecoterrorist cells in six countries so far."

"Sounds like we mounted a successful counteroffensive."

A quick frisson rose up Kim's spine when she realized someone was following close behind. She heard rhythmic footsteps coming up quickly.

Cooper's voice grew even harder. "What about the USB drive Lee left for you? The one with supposed evidence about a massive conspiracy?"

Kim's grip on the phone tightened. "The zip drive was stolen."

A beat of silence.

Then, "Stolen? When? By whom?"

"I'm still working on it," Kim replied, her frustration evident.

She stopped at the street corner to wait for the traffic light. Which was when she took the chance to look behind her. A small group had gathered. Was one of those folks following them?

Kim shrugged when the light turned green and stepped into the crosswalk with the rest of the group.

Cooper's sigh crackled through the line and then his annoyance returned. "Find that USB fast and protect it with your life. If the drive contains real, serious intel, it absolutely cannot fall into the wrong hands."

A massive silver starburst illuminated the street. Kim squinted against the glare as she tried to process the situation.

How did Cooper know about the USB? Why did he care about it? What was making him so nervous?

Who the hell was following her and why?

Cooper continued, brooking no excuses or arguments. "I've got new intel to pass along. Both of you in my office at 0800 tomorrow. Don't be late."

The line went dead. Kim turned to Smithers, now bathed in the glow of a green and gold sparkler cascade.

"Looks like our day isn't over yet," she said as she dropped her cell phone into her pocket.

Smithers nodded with a grin. "I'm always amused by people complaining about the forty-hour work week. They should try a few years in the FBI trenches, eh? A five-day work week would be a constant vacation."

They stood for a moment, watching the sky ignite. The air exploded with electricity and gunpowder, a fitting backdrop to the tension Kim felt building in her gut.

A group of revelers stumbled past, waving tiny American flags. One of them bumped into her.

"Sorry," the young man slurred, raising his beer in a mock salute. "Happy Fourth!"

Kim watched them stumble away, oblivious to the dangerous world they lived in.

How many people would have died if WRATH had succeeded today? How would these kids react if they knew how fragile the world actually was?

Smithers touched her arm. "We should go. We need sleep. Big day tomorrow."

Kim nodded, wondering what Cooper had in mind.

The Escalade was waiting at the next corner, the same driver once again at the wheel. They climbed inside. The driver didn't pull away from the curb immediately.

"Reacher wanted me to thank you," the blond woman said from the deep shadows.

"Who are you?" Smithers asked.

"Where is Reacher?" Kim said almost simultaneously.

"Zoe Seltzer," she said in response to Smithers. Then, to Kim, "Hard to say where he is right at the moment. Maybe you'll get more intel from Theresa Lee, once she resurfaces."

"Why was Reacher involving himself in the Daisy Hawkins situation?" Kim asked, thinking the topic might actually produce real answers.

"You know about the old New York City subway suicide. Reacher felt guilty. He tried to fix it, back then. But he didn't know why Peter Molina's mother killed herself. He also didn't know Molina's father or that Marcus Molina was Peter's half-brother," Zoe explained. "When he heard about Docherty, Reacher decided to get involved again. The more he learned about WRATH, the more determined he became."

The driver knocked on the window glass. Three short raps.

"Sorry. I've got to go." Zoe Seltzer opened the door and stepped outside. "Nice meeting you both."

"You gave the USB drive to Theresa Lee, didn't you?" Kim asked.

"Good guess. Reacher's right. You have solid instincts." Before she closed the door, she said, "He knows who you are. He knows that you're trying to find him. He gave me a message for you."

"Which was what?" Kim asked.

"He's not your enemy. Just the opposite," Zoe replied with a smile before she closed the door and slapped the roof of the Escalade with the flat of her hand to signal the driver.

As they pulled away from the curb, a massive batch of fireworks exploded overhead, bathing the street in red, white, blue, and green. The show was spectacular.

"What was that all about?" Smithers asked.

Kim shrugged. "Dunno."

"What do you think Cooper's new intel is?" Smithers asked, breaking into her thoughts.

"I don't know that, either." Kim's gaze remained fixed on the technicolor sky through the moon roof. "But it will have something to do with Reacher."

The Escalade merged into traffic, weaving between revelers and stopped vehicles. All around them, the nation celebrated, seemingly unaware of the dangers always lurking beneath the surface.

Kim tried to connect the dots. Reacher. WRATH. The ten targets. Theresa Lee. Zoe Seltzer. The USB drive.

How were they entwined?

What were Sansom and Finlay really after?

And how did it all tie back to finding Reacher, which was her original mission?

As they turned onto Pennsylvania Avenue, the Washington Monument loomed ahead, a silhouette in the pyrotechnics' foreground.

Smithers voiced what Kim was thinking. "We're missing something big here, aren't we?"

Kim nodded, her jaw set. "Yeah. But we'll figure it out."

The Escalade moved on through the fire-lit night, carrying them toward more questions. Kim wondered what role Reacher would play in all of this. Was he working with the conspiracy or against them? And did Theresa Lee fit into the picture? What about Zoe Seltzer, if that was actually her name?

Kim leaned back in her seat. The pieces were there, tantalizingly close. Cooper. Reacher. WRATH. Sansom. Finlay. Lee. Seltzer. The USB drive.

Tomorrow, they'd start fitting the pieces together.

The truth was there, too. Hidden beneath layers of bureaucracy and misdirection, sure. But it was there. And, with Gaspar and Smithers on her team, she would find it.

As the Escalade approached the hotel, Kim's attention returned to the USB drive.

Too many people knew about the USB and were curious about its contents. Why were Finlay, Sansom, and Cooper so interested?

"Meet for breakfast in the morning before we head over to face the lion?" Smithers asked as they stepped out of the car.

"Yeah. Knock on my door when you're ready to head down," Kim replied.

They walked into the hotel, leaving the fireworks and celebrations behind.

Inside her room, she locked the door and swept for surveillance devices. Finding none, she started a bubble bath in the tub, which was the only bit of luxury in the place. The hotel was cheap and clean, which was about the best that could be said for it.

She considered a quick call to Gaspar, but there would be time to catch him up tomorrow. She was bone weary. Sleep beckoned and she was powerless to resist.

While the tub filled, she opened a bottle of red wine from the minibar and poured it into a cheap wine glass. At least the glass wasn't plastic.

She grabbed a terry robe from the closet and tossed it on the bed as she undressed. She started by unzipping her boots. When she pulled the left boot from her foot, she flipped the boot over.

The stacked heel was still in good shape, despite hard use these past few days.

She pressed the hidden release lever on the flat of the heel while she swiveled the rubber sole to the outside of the boot at the same time.

The maneuver revealed the hidden compartment in her boot's clunky heel.

Inside the open, waterproof space, the USB zip drive she'd retrieved from the fire tower nestled snuggly.

She inspected the drive. It had not been damaged.

Kim was too tired to fully explore the drive's contents tonight. But she needed at least a cursory look.

She rummaged through her laptop bag until she found the portable USB drive she'd become forced to carry now that her newest laptop was no longer equipped with one.

She clicked a few keys and then plugged the external drive into the laptop. She pushed the USB into the drive's slot and waited for the contents to come up on the screen.

After a few seconds, the USB opened and displayed its contents on the laptop.

Or it would have, if there had been any files or images or other data available to display.

Which was simply not there.

She searched thoroughly, just in case she'd missed something.

She had not.

Her eyes were dry and scratchy, and she was bone weary. She'd try again tomorrow, but she already knew the result would be the same.

For now, she returned the USB to its secure location inside the heel of her boot.

Then she turned off the running water and sank into the tub full of bubbles for a good, long soak.

Slowly, her weary body relaxed, one sinew at a time.

Tomorrow would bring new challenges, new dangers, and hopefully, some answers.

But for now, Kim allowed herself to feel satisfaction.

She had won a major victory today.

Would she be as lucky tomorrow?

FROM LEE CHILD
THE REACHER REPORT:
March 2nd, 2012

The other big news is Diane Capri—a friend of mine—wrote a book revisiting the events of KILLING FLOOR in Margrave, Georgia. She imagines an FBI team tasked to trace Reacher's current-day whereabouts. They begin by interviewing people who knew him—starting out with Roscoe and Finlay. Check out this review: "Oh heck yes! I am in love with this book. I'm a huge Jack Reacher fan. If you don't know Jack (pun intended!) then get thee to the bookstore/wherever you buy your fix and pick up one of the many Jack Reacher books by Lee Child. Heck, pick up all of them. In particular, read Killing Floor. Then come back and read Don't Know Jack. This story picks up the other from the point of view of Kim and Gaspar, FBI agents assigned to build a file on Jack Reacher. The problem is, as anyone who knows Reacher can attest, he lives completely off the grid. No cell phone, no house, no car…he's not tied down. A pretty daunting task, then, wouldn't you say?

First lines: "Just the facts. And not many of them, either. Jack Reacher's file was too stale and too thin to be credible. No human could be as invisible as Reacher appeared to be, whether he was currently above the ground or under it. Either the file had been sanitized, or Reacher was the most off-the-grid paranoid Kim Otto had ever heard of." Right away, I'm sensing who Kim Otto is and I'm delighted that I know something she doesn't. You see, I DO know Jack. And I know he's not paranoid. Not really. I know why he lives as he does, and I know what kind of man he is. I loved having that over Kim and Gaspar. If you haven't read any Reacher novels, then this will feel like a good, solid story in its own right. If you have…oh if you have, then you, too, will feel like you have a one-up on the FBI. It's a fun feeling!

"Kim and Gaspar are sent to Margrave by a mysterious boss who reminds me of Charlie, in Charlie's Angels. You never see him…you hear him. He never gives them all the facts. So they are left with a big pile of nothing. They end up embroiled in a murder case that seems connected to Reacher somehow, but they can't see how. Suffice to say the efforts to find the murderer and Reacher, and not lose their own heads in the process, makes for an entertaining read.

"I love the way the author handled the entire story. The pacing is dead on (okay another pun intended), the story is full of twists and turns like a Reacher novel would be, but it's another viewpoint of a Reacher story. It's an outside-in approach to Reacher.

"You might be asking, do they find him? Do they finally meet the infamous Jack Reacher?

"Go…read…now…find out!"

Sounds great, right? Check out "Don't Know Jack," and let me know what you think.

So that's it for now…again, thanks for reading THE AFFAIR, and I hope you'll like A WANTED MAN just as much in September.

Lee Child

ABOUT THE AUTHOR

Diane Capri is an award-winning *New York Times*, *USA Today*, and worldwide bestselling author. She's a recovering lawyer and snowbird who divides her time between Florida and Michigan. An active member of Mystery Writers of America, Author's Guild, International Thriller Writers, Alliance of Independent Authors, Novelists, Inc., and Sisters in Crime, she loves to hear from readers. She is hard at work on her next novel.

Please connect with her online:
http://www.DianeCapri.com
Twitter: http://twitter.com/@DianeCapri
Facebook: http://www.facebook.com/Diane.Capri1
http://www.facebook.com/DianeCapriBooks

Made in the USA
Las Vegas, NV
24 November 2024

12492655R00239